ALFIE'S GUARANTEE

If you don't shudder with every twist and sudden thrust of these 16 terror tales . . .

if you are able to turn off your bedside lamp after closing this volume and drift off to a deep, dreamless sleep . . .

if you can drink your morning coffee without thinking there just might be a peculiarly bitter taste to it, or turn your back on your spouse or best friend without feeling a funny itching between your shoulder blades . . .

then that lovable old master of menace, Alfred Hitchcock, apologizes and personally guarantees you your full payment in horror. All you have to do is meet him in the cemetery under the next murderer's moon. . . .

ALFRED HITCHCOCK PRESENTS: 16 SKELETONS FROM MY CLOSET

ALFRED HITCHCOCK PRESENTS

16 SKELETONS FROM MY CLOSET

A DELL BOOK

Published by DELL PUBLISHING CO., INC.
1 Dag Hammarskjold Plaza, New York, New York 10017
© *Copyright 1963 by Dell Publishing Co., Inc.*
Dell ® *TM 681510, Dell Publishing Co., Inc.*
All rights reserved
First Dell printing—March, 1963
Second Dell printing—March, 1964
Third Dell printing—February, 1973
Printed in U.S.A.

ACKNOWLEDGMENTS

GHOST STORY *by Henry Kane*—© *1960 by H. S. D. Publications, Inc. Reprinted by permission of the author and the author's agents, Scott Meredith Literary Agency, Inc.*

WHERE IS THY STING *by James Holding*—© *1961 by H. S. D. Publications, Inc. Reprinted by permission of the author and the author's agents, Scott Meredith Literary Agency, Inc.*

THE BUTLER WHO DIDN'T DO IT *by Craig Rice*—© *1960 by H. S. D. Publications, Inc. Reprinted by permission of the author's agents, Scott Meredith Literary Agency, Inc.*

CHRISTMAS GIFT *by Robert Turner*—*Copyright 1956 by H. S. D. Publications, Inc. Reprinted by permission of the author and the author's agents, Scott Meredith Literary Agency, Inc.*

THE MAN AT THE TABLE *by C. B. Gilford*—© *1961 by H. S. D. Publications, Inc. Reprinted by permission of the author and the author's agents, Scott Meredith Literary Agency, Inc.*

DEATH OF ANOTHER SALESMAN *by Donald Honig*—© *1960 by H. S. D. Publications, Inc. Reprinted by permission of Theron Raines.*

MAN WITH A HOBBY *by Robert Bloch*—*Copyright 1957 by H. S. D. Publications, Inc. Reprinted by permission of Harry Altshuler.*

SAID JACK THE RIPPER *by Robert Arthur*—*Copyright 1957 by H. S. D. Publications, Inc. Reprinted by permission of the author and the author's agents, Scott Meredith Literary Agency, Inc.*

A GUN WITH A HEART *by William Logan*—*Copyright 1957 by H. S. D. Publications, Inc. Reprinted by permission of the author and the author's agents, Scott Meredith Literary Agency, Inc.*

ASSASSINATION *by Dion Henderson*—*Copyright 1957 by H. S. D. Publications, Inc. Reprinted by permission of Larry Sternig Agency.*

A LITTLE SORORICIDE *by Richard Deming*—*Copyright 1957 by H. S. D. Publications, Inc. Reprinted by permission of the author and the author's agents, Scott Meredith Literary Agency, Inc.*

THE MAN WHO GOT AWAY WITH IT *by Lawrence Treat*—*Copyright 1957 by H. S. D. Publications, Inc. Reprinted by Samuel French, Inc.*

SECRET RECIPE *by Charles Mergendahl*—*Copyright 1957 by H. S. D. Publications, Inc. Reprinted by permission of Harold Matson Company.*

DADDY-O *by David Alexander*—*Copyright 1958 by H. S. D. Publications, Inc. Reprinted by permission of the author and the author's agents, Scott Meredith Literary Agency, Inc.*

THE CRIME MACHINE *by Jack Ritchie*—© *1960 by H. S. D. Publications, Inc. Reprinted by permission of Larry Sternig Agency.*

HOMICIDE AND GENTLEMEN *by Fletcher Flora*—© *1961 by H. S. D. Publications, Inc. Reprinted by permission of the author and the author's agents, Scott Meredith Literary Agency, Inc.*

CONTENTS

INTRODUCTION

Shortly after the completion of shooting on my most recent motion picture, I remember reading about a murder which had occurred the day previous in the city of Chicago. Now, I can hardly think of a better place for the scene of a murder. Chicago has always seemed a *perfect* locale for such a crime: the cold wind coming in off Lake Michigan, long black cars speeding along major thoroughfares, the sudden, deadly sound of machine-gun fire. The perfect locale indeed.

However, the murder of which I speak was horribly disappointing. A matron of middle years, supposedly happily married for quite some time, went shopping in the afternoon and purchased a hat. The price for this headpiece was $39.98 "on sale." A fine buy, obviously. She brought it home proudly, and showed it to her spouse, just returned from a most difficult and trying day at the office. He, unfortunately, did not like the hat. Very calmly, then, the woman went to a desk drawer in the living-room, took from it a loaded thirty-eight caliber pistol, and shot her husband dead.

How dull. One shot and *poof*. How much better if she had emptied the pistol into the man in hysterical rage— but no, a single shot.

It seems to me that when our century was newer the crime would not have happened in so pedestrian a manner. I very much doubt a pistol would have been used, since a pistol is decidedly not a woman's weapon, as so many mystery writers have been quick to point out for so many satisfying years. Perhaps a rolling-pin, a jungle knife brought back from the Amazon country years ago by the original owner who had traveled with Theodore Roosevelt, a dose of poison in the soup, a thin but strong cord across the top of the staircase . . .

Such was the grandeur of yesteryear, when murder was done with flair and imagination.

Of course, we all recall the story of Miss Lizzie Borden, who took an ax and gave her parents forty whacks.

And then there was the gentleman on December 31, 1913, who stabbed his wife to death, dissected her body, and sent the pieces to friends and relatives with best wishes for a most enjoyable New Year.

The press would be much enlivened by a good garroting or a woman tied and left on a railroad track (of course, one would have to be sure the trains are still running).

I cannot promise such excitement in the future, but I can promise you a shudderingly good time in the pages to come.

ALFRED HITCHCOCK

Detectives should not be required to apprehend ghosts. It simply takes too much time. Moreover, though clothes may make the man, there's far more to a ghost than his bed sheet.

GHOST STORY
BY HENRY KANE

I do not believe in ghosts. Perhaps I do not believe in ghosts because I refuse to believe in ghosts and my mind rejects the possibility and seeks other explanation. In the Troy affair such explanation, for me, involved death-wish, hallucination, guilt complex, retribution, self-punishment and dual personality, but there again I am out of my ken: I am not a psychiatrist, I am a private detective. There are those who disagree with my conclusions, and you may be one of those. So be it, then. All I can do is render the events just as they occurred, beginning with that bright-white afternoon in January when my secretary ushered Miss Sylvia Troy into my office.

"Miss Sylvia Troy," said my secretary and departed.

"I'm Peter Chambers," I said. "Won't you sit down?"

She was small, quite good-looking, very feminine, about thirty. Close-cut wavy russet-red hair was capped about a smooth round face in which enormous dark-brown eyes would have been beautiful except for a flaw in expression almost impossible to put into words. There is only one word—haunted!—and that word, of course, is susceptible to so many different interpretations. Her eyes were far away, gone, out of her, not part of her, remote and lost. She remained standing while I, still seated behind my desk, squirmed uneasily.

"Please sit down," I said in as cordial a tone as I could muster within the embarrassment of trying to avoid those peculiarly-luminous, strangely-isolated, frightened eyes.

"Thank you very much," she said and sat in the chair at the side of my desk. She had a soft lovely voice, almost a trained voice as a professional singer's voice may be termed trained: it was round-voweled, resonant, beautifully-pitched, very feminine, melodious. She was wearing a red wool coat with a little black fur collar and she was carrying a black patent-leather handbag. She opened the handbag, extracted three hundred dollars, snapped shut the bag, and placed the money on my desk. I looked at it, but did not touch it.

"Not enough?" she said.

"I beg your pardon?" I said.

"The way you're looking at it."

"Looking at what?" I said.

"The money. Your fee. I'm sorry, but I can't afford any more."

"I'm not looking at it in any special way, Miss Troy. I'm just looking at it. Three hundred dollars may be enough or not enough—depending upon what you want of me."

"I want you to lay a ghost."

"What?"

"Please, sir, Mr. Chambers," she said, "I'm deadly serious."

"A ghost—"

"A ghost who has already killed one person and threatens to kill two others."

I directed my squirming to seeking in my pockets and finding a cigarette. I lit it and I said, "Miss Troy, the laying of ghosts is not quite my department. If this so-called ghost of yours has killed anyone, then you've come to the wrong place. There are constituted authorities, the police—"

"I cannot go to the police."

"Why not?"

"Because if I tell my story to the police I would be incriminating myself and my two brothers in . . ." She stopped.

"In what?"

"Murder."

There was a pause. She sat, limply; and I smoked, nervously.

Then I said, "Do you intend to tell me this story?"

"I do."

"Won't that be just as incriminating—"

"No, no, not at all," she said. "I *must* tell you because something must be done, because somebody—you, I hope—must help. But if you repeat what I tell you to the police, I will simply deny it. Since there is no proof, and since I would deny what you might repeat, nobody would be incriminated."

It was coming around to my department. People in trouble are my department. Had there been no mention of a ghost, it would have been completely and familiarly in my department. But it was sufficiently in my department for me to tap out my cigarette in an ashtray, pull the money over to my side of the desk, and say, "All right, Miss Troy, let's have it."

"It begins about a year ago. November, a year ago."

"Yes," I said.

"There are—or were—four of us in the family."

"Four in the family," I said.

"Three brothers and myself. Adam was the oldest. Adam Troy was fifty when he died."

"And the others?"

"Joseph was thirty-six. Simon is thirty-two. I am twenty-nine."

"You say Joseph *was* thirty-six?"

"My brother Joseph killed himself—supposedly killed himself—three weeks ago."

"Sorry," I said.

"And now if I may—just a little background."

"Please," I said.

"Adam, so much older than any of us, was sort of father to all of us. Adam was a bachelor, rich and successful—he always had a knack for making money—while the rest of us"—she shrugged—"when it came to earning money, we were no shining lights. Joseph was a shoe-salesman, Simon is a drug clerk, and I'm a nightclub performer and, I must confess, a pretty bad one at that."

"Nightclub performer. Interesting."

"I do voices, you know? I used to be a ventriloquist. Now I'm a mimic; imitations, that sort of thing. Nothing great. I get by."

"And Adam?" I said. "What did Adam do?"

"He was a real-estate broker, and a shrewd investor in the stock market. He was a stodgy stingy man—which is probably why he never got married. He *was* like a father to us but, actually, he never helped us with money unless it was an emergency. But advice—plenty. And criticism—plenty. I can't say he was *bad* to us, but he wasn't really *good* to us. I hope I'm making myself clear."

"Yes. Very clear, Miss Troy."

"Now about the wills."

"Wills?" I said.

"Last wills and testaments. We all have like it's called reciprocal wills. If one dies, whatever he leaves is divided amongst the rest of us. I'm sure you know about reciprocal wills."

"Yes, of course."

"All right. Now last year, Adam made a real big win in the stock market and he suggested that we take a vacation together, a winter vacation, and that he would pay for all of it. A couple of weeks of skiing, fun, out-of-doors, up in Vermont. Two weeks in a winter wonderland, you know?"

I nodded.

"We, the rest of us, Joseph, Simon, and I—we arranged for those two weeks—the two middle weeks in November

—and we all went up to a lodge at Mt. Killington in the Green Mountains of Vermont." She shuddered and was silent. Then she said, "I don't know how it began. Maybe we all had it in our minds, maybe that guilt was like a poison in all of us, but it was Joseph who said it first."

"Said what, please?"

"Said to get rid of Adam. Adam was upstairs sleeping and the three of us were sitting around downstairs in front of a big roaring fireplace, drinking, maybe getting a little drunk, when Joseph put out the suggestion and we were with him so fast it was like all of us said it together. I don't want to blame anyone. I say all three of us have the blame together. None of us ever had any money, real money, and all of a sudden it came to us, that we could have just that, real money, while we were still young enough to enjoy it." She shuddered again and put her hands over her face. She spoke through her hands. "From here I'd like to go real quick. Please?"

"Okay," I said.

Her hands dropped to her lap. "Next day, dressed warmly in ski suits, we went out on an exploring adventure, up into the mountains. Way up, high, Adam was standing near a crevice, a ravine, about a two thousand foot drop, with a little narrow river running on bottom. Joseph came up behind him, shoved, and Adam fell. That's all. He fell. All the way. There were like echoes coming back, and then —nothing. When we returned, we reported it. We said he had slipped and fallen. The police went up to investigate, there was an inquest, and that was it."

"What was it?"

"The coroner's verdict was death by accident."

I came up out of my chair. I walked my office. I walked in front of her, in back of her, and around her. She did not move. She sat with her hands clasped in her lap. I said, "All right. So much for the incriminating matter. Now, if you please, what ghost killed whom?"

13

She was motionless. Only her lips moved. "The ghost of Adam killed Joseph."

"My dear Miss Troy," I said. "Only a few minutes ago you told me that Joseph committed suicide."

"I'm sorry, Mr. Chambers, I did *not* tell you that."

"But you—"

"I said *supposedly* killed himself."

Grudgingly, I admitted my error. "True, you said that. But how can one possibly tell the difference? I mean—"

"May I tell it my own way?"

"Please do." I went back to my chair, sat, watched her as she spoke, but my eyes did not meet hers. Somehow, on this bright-white normal afternoon in January, in the accustomed confines of my very own office, I could not bring myself to look full upon this woman's eyes.

"I live at One-thirty-three West Thirty-third Street," she said.

"Uh huh," I said and happily business-like, I jotted it down, delighted for something prosaic to do.

"It's a one-room apartment on the fourth floor. 4 C."

"Yeah, yeah," I murmured, jotting assiduously.

"Two months ago, on November fifteenth, exactly one year from the time of his death, Adam came to visit me."

"Adam came to visit," I murmured as I jotted—and then I flung the pencil away. "Now just a minute, Miss Troy!"

Quite mildly she said, "Yes, Mr. Chambers?"

"Adam is the guy who's dead, or isn't he? Adam is the guy whom, allegedly, you people murdered, or isn't he?"

"Yes, he is."

"And he came to visit you?"

"Precisely."

I sighed. "Where?"

"On the afternoon of November fifteenth, I had gone out to the supermarket for a bit of shopping. When I came home, he was there, sitting quietly in a chair, waiting for me."

I recovered my pencil and pretended to make notes. "Are you sure it was Adam?"

"The ghost of Adam. Adam is dead."

"Yes, naturally, ghost of Adam. How did he look?"

"Exactly as he had looked on the day he died. He was even wearing the same clothes—the high-laced boots, the green ski suit, the green ski cap."

"He talked to you?"

"Yes."

"How did he sound?"

"As always. Adam had a deep booming voice. He sounded sad, aggrieved, but not, actually, angry."

"And what did he say?"

"He said that he had returned to visit retribution on us; those were the exact words—visit retribution. He said he was going to kill Joseph first, then Simon, and then me. Then he stood up, opened the door, and walked out."

"And you?"

"I called my brothers, they came to my apartment, and I told them just what happened. Of course, they didn't believe me. They told me it was my imagination, that I had been highly nervous of late. They suggested that I go see a doctor. All in all, somehow, they talked me out of it. I did nothing about it—not even when Joseph was killed."

"Suicide, even supposed suicide—"

"Joseph slashed his wrists and died. *But there was no weapon*. No weapon was found near the body; there was no weapon with blood anywhere in his apartment."

I lit a new cigarette. The flame of the match trembled. I blew it out quickly and deposited it in the tray. I inhaled deeply. I said, "Miss Troy, you did nothing about it then—why are you doing something about it now?"

"Because Adam came to visit me again last night. When I returned from work, he was seated in the same chair, dressed exactly as the other time. He said that he had accomplished his purpose with Joseph—and that Simon was next. Then he got up, opened the door, and went out."

"And you?"

"I fainted. When I came to, I became hysterical. That passed, and then I put on a fresh make-up, and went directly to my brother Simon. It was late at night, but I didn't care. Simon lives on West Fourth Street, quite near to where I work. I rang his bell until he woke up and let me in. I told him what had happened and again he just didn't believe me. He told me that he insisted that I go to a doctor and that he was going to make arrangements for just that. Today I decided I *had* to do something about it. I'd heard about you—and I'm here. Please, Mr. Chambers, will you help me? Please. Please."

"I'll do whatever I can," I said. I inquired and made notes about names, addresses and phone numbers, where she worked, where her brothers worked, all of that. Then I printed my home phone number on one of my business cards and gave it to her. "You may call me here or at home whenever you please," I said.

"Thank you." She smiled her first smile, gratefully.

I placed her three hundred dollars into a drawer of my desk and said, "All right. Let's go."

"Go? Where?"

"I'd like to see your apartment. May I?"

"Yes, of course." She stood up. "You're very thorough, aren't you?"

"That's the way I work," I said.

It was on the fourth floor, walk-up, of a six-story, new-fashioned, re-modeled house. It was a tiny one-room apartment: small living room with one tiny closet, a tiny bathroom, and a tiny kitchenette. There was no window in the kitchenette, one window in the bathroom, and two windows in the living room—each window with a secure inside turn-bolt.

"Excellent," I said. "Did you have these bolts put on?"

"No. The former tenant."

16

"They're good bolts in fine working order." I nodded approvingly, continued my inspection. "I see there's no fire-escape."

"No need," she said. "They were eyesores that were removed when the house was re-modeled because they made it fire-proof."

But the lock on the door was utterly deficient. Simple and ancient, it did not require an expert to solve it, and the door itself carried no secondary protection: no bolt.

"This'll never do," I mumbled.

"Beg pardon?" she said.

"Look, I don't know who's been visiting you, ghost or no ghost, but anyone can get in here with any old key, and a picklock can make this doorlock do somersaults. This has got to go."

"Go?" she inquired. "Go?"

"Where's your Classified Directory?"

She brought it to me and I checked a few locksmiths and called a few locksmiths and found one who was free and told him what I wanted. He promised to come within the next half hour and Miss Troy made coffee and sandwiches, and we munched and chatted but avoided any mention of ghosts, and she grew more animated and smiled more frequently, and I discovered that I was having a very pleasant afternoon.

"Why don't you come see me at the club this evening?" she said. "I told you where it is when you were making all those notes in your office. Cafe Bella on West Third in the Village."

"What time do you go on?"

"The show starts at nine, and it's sort of continuous. There are six acts—nobody's real great and they don't pay us much—but we don't work too hard and everybody has his own dressing room which is something. The show runs from nine to two, sometimes later, depending upon business. In between, I just sit around in my dressing room. I

17

don't like to mix with the customers and the owners don't demand that we do. I do wish you'd drop in and catch my act."

"I might," I said.

The locksmith came and he did as I requested. He installed a strong modern lock and he installed a sturdy steel slide-bolt. I paid him out of my pocket-money and I refused reimbursement from Miss Troy.

"Part of the fee," I said, "and it may do the trick. You may never be bothered again."

"I hope so, I hope so," she said. "God bless you. I'm beginning to feel better already. It's like when you go to a good doctor, you know, and he reassures you. Just your presence and your attitude—all these crazy things seem to be like a dream, a nightmare, and all of a sudden it's morning and it was all dreadful but silly, you know?"

"Yes, I do, and I'm glad. Just keep right on thinking like that. Good-by now, and thank you for the lovely lunch."

"Oh, don't mention it. Will you come see me tonight?"

"I'll try," I said.

Simon Troy worked in a drug store at 74th Street and Columbus Avenue. It was small, cluttered, and old-fashioned, and it did not have a soda fountain. It smelled of herbs and pharmaceuticals and germicidals and there was dust on the shelves and the dust in the air made you want to sneeze. Simon Troy, working alone, was a blond wispy little man with puppy-sad brown eyes, a beige-leather complexion, and small yellow teeth. His smile, as he greeted me, was perfunctory: a drug clerk greeting a customer. I told him who I was and why I was there and an expression of anxiety wizened his face as his smile receded.

"If you please," he said, "let us go in the back where we can talk."

The rear, partitioned by thick plate-glass from the front, was a narrow area dominated by a drawer-pocked wooden counter for the making of prescriptions. There were a couple of wire-backed, rickety, armless chairs, and he motioned me to one of them. Before I sat, I said, "You *are* Simon Troy?"

Impatiently he said, "Yes, yes, of course."

I produced cigarettes, offered one to him, and he grabbed at it with thin, bony, tobacco-stained fingers. He lit my cigarette, lit his, and puffed at it rapidly, shallowly, and noisily. I talked and he listened. I told him everything that Sylvia Troy had told me and I told him of the fee that she had paid me. When I was finished, he was finished with the cigarette, and he lit one of his own from the stub of the one I had donated. "Mr. Chambers," he said, "I assume you must realize how terribly worried I am about my sister."

I nodded, I said nothing.

"She's sick, Mr. Chambers. I'm certain it was apparent to you."

I nodded again. I said, "Would you tell me what happened up at Mt. Killington?"

"You mean about Adam?"

"If you please."

He told me. "We weren't even near him. He had gone over for a peek at that precipitous edge. We were quite far away, many yards from him, the three of us together. He must have had a seizure, a dizzy spell. We heard the scream as he slipped, toppled—and then he was gone. The Vermont police examined the site after we reported it. It had begun to snow and they could not make out any footprints on the edge. But from the points of the jagged crags below, which they could reach, they recovered bits of bone, bits of flesh, and bits of the ski suit he had been wearing. The body, of course, was never recovered." He put the tip of his right index finger between his teeth and bit upon the fingernail, audibly.

"Mr. Troy," I said. "Do you have any idea as to why your sister has come up with this wild story of hers?"

"I'm afraid there's only one explanation. I believe her to be in the throes of a severe nervous breakdown."

"But is there any basis for it? Any past history? Any reason?"

"She mentioned our reciprocal wills to you, didn't she?"

"Yes," I said.

"Well, Adam's estate, after taxes, was divided into approximately 'fifty thousand dollars for each of us. My brother Joseph, a childless widower, was a rather conservative man, as am I. We put that money away and continued in the even tenor of our ways—but not so Sylvia. She quit her nightclub work, went off to Europe, and within a year, she had squandered her inheritance in toto. I think this did something to her, disturbed her, that within a year she was back to where she had started. She was compelled to return to work for a living, and right then, right from the beginning, she began to act peculiarly. Then she began to prattle about a plot, our plot, to murder Adam. And now this terrible business about Adam's ghost."

"And what about Joseph?" I said. "His suicide. Would you tell me?"

"Precious little to tell. Joseph was a sweet, simple, meticulous man. He was quite a hypochondriac although he had a dread of doctors. About six months ago he developed stomach pains, nausea, vomiting. He refused to go to a doctor, but I finally dragged him. X-rays disclosed a mass in his stomach. The doctors believed it to be benign, but Joseph believed otherwise. We had arranged for an operation but, before the time for it arrived, he killed himself."

"Yes, I know, he slashed his wrists," I said. "But what about this business of no weapon?"

He smiled, yellow-fanged, sadly. "The police are satisfied with the explanation. Joseph committed suicide in his bathroom. He cut open his wrists and bled to death. Knowing Joseph, I know exactly what he did, once he made up his mind to do it. There was an open razor found nearby, without a blade. He took the blade from the razor, cut his wrists, dropped the blade into the toilet bowl, flushed the toilet, and bled to death. There was a good deal of blood, all over that bathroom, but no actual weapon. Joseph was meticulous, a creature of habit. He flushed the weapon away into the toilet bowl. The police agreed completely with my thinking in the matter. After all, I was his brother; I knew him."

I stood up, saying, "Thank you."

"Mr. Chambers, please." He fidgeted, hesitant, obviously embarrassed.

"Yes?" I said.

"Mr. Chambers," he blurted. "I believe you should return that fee to my sister."

"Why?"

"She doesn't need a private detective. She needs a doctor."

"I'm inclined to agree."

He smiled, seeming relieved that I understood and acquiesced. "I've already made inquiries," he said, "and I've selected a physician, nerve-specialist, psychiatrist, whatever the devil they call them these days. By some pretext or other, I'm going to get her to him."

"Good enough," I said. "As for the fee, I agree. It belongs with a doctor, rather than with me."

"You're extremely considerate. I thank you."

"I don't believe I should give it to her, though," I said. "No sense disturbing her any further. I'll bring it to you. I don't have it with me, but I'll deliver it later on to your apartment."

"Please keep fifty dollars of it, Mr. Chambers. You've certainly earned that."

"Thank you. Then I'll see you later."

"You know where?"

"Miss Troy gave me your address on Fourth Street."

"It's apartment 3 A. And, oh!"

"Yes?"

"Actually, I'm a night man here. I work from two in the afternoon and I close at ten. Then I go home, eat, shower, relax. So I'm not home until quite late."

"I'm somewhat of a night man, myself," I said. "Suppose I come around midnight. Is that all right?"

"Fine, fine. You've been very kind, Mr. Chambers."

He shook hands with me and I left.

At ten o'clock that evening, with two hundred and fifty dollars of her fee in my pocket, I sat at a back table of Cafe Bella and watched her act. Cafe Bella was dim and unpretentious, the service was poor, the liquor was bad, and so was Sylvia Troy's act. She came out in black trousers and a black blouse and she did imitations of celebrities, male and female. Her range of voice was marvelous—from deep male baritone to male tenor to male alto to female contralto to mezzo-soprano to the high squiggly soprano of elderly women—but her imitations were rank, her material wretched, her timing deplorable, and her woeful little jokes were delivered without a spark of talent. I left in the middle of her performance.

I had a late supper, I wandered in and out of some of the Village clubs, I had a few drinks, I watched a few dancing girls, and then at midnight I went to 149 West 4th Street which was Simon Troy's address. A self-service elevator took me up to the third floor and there I pushed the button of 3 A. There was no answer. I pushed again. No answer. I tried the knob. The door was open and I entered.

Simon Troy was seated, staring straight ahead, his elbows resting on the edge of a table for two. On the table in front of him was a large cocktail glass empty except for a cherry at its base. He was staring at a vacant chair opposite. On that side of the table, in front of the vacant chair, stood a similar cocktail glass brimming-full and untouched. I went quickly to Simon Troy, examined him, and then went to the telephone and called the police to report his death.

The man in charge was my friend Detective-Lieutenant Louis Parker of Homicide. His experts quickly ascertained the cause of death as cyanide poisoning. The cherry in the drained cocktail glass was thoroughly imbued with it. Simon Troy's fingerprints were on the stem of the glass. The other glass was free of poison. There were no fingerprints on its stem. Inspection revealed no vial or other container for poison in the apartment. After the body and the evidence were removed and Lieutenant Parker and I were alone, he said, "Well, what goes? What's the story on this? What are you doing here?"

"Do you believe in ghosts, Lieutenant?"

Cryptically he said, "Sometimes. Why? Are you going to tell me a ghost story?"

"I might at that," I said. I told him the entire story and I told him what I was doing in Simon Troy's apartment.

"Wow," he said. "Let's go talk to the little lady."

She was in her dressing room. She maintained that she had been in her dressing room, or out on the floor performing, all night. Her dressing room opened upon a corridor which led to a back exit directly on the street. Parker questioned all the employees in the place. None could disprove what Sylvia Troy had said. Then Parker took her to the station house and I accompanied them. There he questioned and cross-questioned her for hours, but she stoutly maintained that she had not left her dressing room except to go out on the floor and do her act. Policemen came and went and the questioning was frequently interrupted by whispered conferences. At length Parker threw his hands up. "Get out," he said to her. "Go home. And you better stay there so we know where we can reach you."

"Yes, sir," she said meekly and departed.

We were silent. Parker lit a cigar and I lit a cigarette. Finally I said, "Well, what do you think?"

"I think that little chick is pulling the con-game to end all con-games and we don't have a thing on which to hold her."

"How so, my friend?" I said.

"You know about those reciprocal wills, don't you?"

"Yes."

"The first one—Joseph's—is still in Probate. Now the second one goes into Probate. With these two brothers dead, that little dame stands to come into upwards of a hundred thousand dollars."

"So?"

"So we've got Joseph listed as suicide, but since no weapon was found, it could have been murder. Now this Simon could be suicide too, can't he?—except no vial, no container." He waved a hand. "Spirited away."

"The ghost?" I said mildly.

"The dame," he said. "She killed the two of them and concocted this ghost story as the craziest smoke-screen ever. And we don't have one iota of proof against her. But we're going to keep at it, baby; that I can assure you." Then he smiled, wearily. "Go home, boy. You look tired."

"How about you?" I said.

"Not me. I stay right here and work."

I got home at four o'clock, and as I opened my door, my phone was ringing. I ran to it and lifted the receiver. It was Sylvia Troy.

"Mr. Chambers!" she said. "Please! Mr. Chambers!" The terror in her voice put needles on my skin.

"What is it?" I said. "What's the matter?"

"He called me."

"Who?"

"Adam!"

"When?"

"Just now, just now. He said he was coming . . . for me." The voice drifted off.

"Miss Troy!" I called. "Miss Troy!"

"Yes?" The voice was feeble.

"Can you hear me?"

"Yes."

"I want you to close all your windows and bolt them."

"I've already done that," she said in that peculiar child-like sing-song.

"And lock your door and bolt it."

"I've done that too."

"Now don't open your door to anyone except me. I'll ring and talk to you through the closed door so you'll know who it is. You'll recognize my voice?"

"Yes, Mr. Chambers. Yes, I will."

"Good. Now just stay put. I'll be there right away."

I hung up and I called Parker and I told him. "This is it," I said, "whatever it is. Bring plenty of men and plenty of artillery. We figure to shake loose a murderer. I'll meet you downstairs. You know the address?"

"Of course."

I hung up and ran.

Aside from Parker, there were three detectives and three uniformed policemen—one of whom was carrying a carbine. As we entered the hallway, the detectives and the two remaining policemen took their pistols from their holsters. At the door to 4 C, Parker motioned to me and I rang the bell.

A deep booming masculine voice responded.

"Yes? Who is it?"

"Peter Chambers. I want to talk with Miss Troy."

"She's not here," boomed the voice.

"That's a lie. I know she's in there."

"She doesn't want to talk to you."

"Who are you?"

"None of your business," boomed the voice. "Go away."

25

"Sorry. I'm not going, mister."

The deep voice took on a rasp of irritation. "Look, I've got a gun in my hand. If you don't get away, I'm going to shoot right through the door."

Parker pulled me aside and called through the door: "Open up! Police!"

"I don't care who you say you are," boomed the voice. "I'm warning you for the last time. Either you people get away or I shoot."

"And I'm warning you," called Parker. "Either you open the door or *we* shoot. I'm going to count to three. Unless you open up, we're going to shoot our way in. One!"

No answer.

"Two!"

Deep booming derisive laughter.

"Three!"

No sound.

Parker motioned to the policemen carrying the carbine and he ranged up. Parker raised his right hand, index finger pointed upward.

"Open up! Last call!"

No sound.

Parker pointed the finger at the policeman and nodded. A stream of bullets ripped through the door. There was a piercing scream, a thud, and silence. Parker made a sign to two of the detectives, burly men. They knew what to do. They hurled themselves at the door, shoulder to shoulder, in unison, time and again. The door creaked, creaked, gave, and then burst from its fastenings.

Sylvia Troy lay on the floor dead of the bullets from the carbine. There was no one else in the apartment. The door had been locked and bolted. The windows were closed and bolted from the inside. Inspection was quick, expert, and unequivocal, but, aside from the corpse of Sylvia Troy— and now, ourselves—there was no one else in the apartment.

Detective-Lieutenant Louis Parker came to me, his

26

eyes belligerent but bewildered, his face angrily glistening beneath a veil of perspiration. His men, tall, thick-armed, strong-muscled, powerful, gathered like silent children, in a group about him. "What the hell?" said the Detective-Lieutenant, the words issuing in a curious hoarse whisper. "What do you think, Pete?"

I had to swallow before I could speak, but I clung to my premise. "I do not believe in ghosts," I said.

Perhaps I do not believe in ghosts because I refuse to believe in ghosts and my mind rejects the possibility and seeks other explanation. In the Troy affair such explanation, for me, involved death-wish, hallucination, guilt complex, retribution, self-punishment, and dual personality.

There are those who disagree with my conclusions.

You may be one of them.

Phobia has become an accepted term in this day of parlor-psychiatry. Yet, defined as an irrational fear, is it acceptable as a cause of death? On a death certificate, for example, would "Apiphobia" be acceptable to the coroner?

WHERE IS THY STING?
BY JAMES HOLDING

To say I was flabbergasted when I found out about Doris and that bachelor writer across the hall is putting it mildly.

Doris and I had been married four and a half years then, and I still couldn't believe my luck. She was medium tall, with high color in her face and jet black hair that had a shine to it, and a lovely soft mouth that smiled easily and often. Her eyes were electric blue, and with that black hair of hers, they really looked terrific. And her figure was for happy dreams . . . other guys' dreams. I had the girl herself. My wife, Doris.

So you can understand I was quite upset when I learned about her and Wilkins. If you really love your wife, as I do, and trust her, as I did, and she's just about the living end in beauty of face and figure, and you're sure she thinks the sun rises and sets on you, it's a definite kick in the teeth when you suddenly discover that while you're out of town covering your sales territory two weeks out of each month, your wife is playing house with the detective-story writer whose apartment is across the hall from yours. Especially, when he's a nothing-type guy like Wilkins was—tall, skinny, no visible means of support except a battered typewriter, and even beginning to lose his hair, for God's sake!

I'm no Adonis, understand, but on the worst day I ever lived, I'm a better man than Wilkins was. Believe me. That's why I was so burned when I found out that Doris whiled away her time during my absence with this Wilkins clown.

I made excuses for Doris, of course. I still loved her, despite her expeditions to the other side of the hall where the grass looked greener. A girl as beautiful as Doris, I told myself, as full of life and crazy for fun, naturally becomes a target for the wolfishness of every predatory male within a six-mile radius. And she's understandably lonesome while I'm away. Poor Doris.

I could make allowances for her. But not for that rejection-slip Casanova across the hall. No, sir. Him I was going to fix, and fix right.

But not in hot blood, Jim, I warned myself. Wait until you're calmer. Wait till you can cream him without any chance of being tagged for the job. Otherwise, what will it get you? Nothing but an overcharge of electricity from the state. I'd be dead, and Wilkins would be dead, and Doris would be left all by her lonesome.

So I didn't let on to Doris that I knew a thing about her and Wilkins. I behaved just as usual, and so did she, the clever little actress. And when I ran across Wilkins at the mailboxes in the apartment house lobby, or in the elevator, or dumping trash into the communal incinerator at the end of our third floor corridor, I nodded and smiled in neighborly fashion and he doubtless thought me a very pleasant fellow, as well as a blind fool.

That was all right with me; I just kept my own counsel and watched Wilkins at every opportunity. I was confident that if I had patience enough, and was smart enough, I'd find the proper way to fix his wagon and still appear as innocent of fixing anything as the average garage mechanic.

This went on for several months. And sure enough, early in August, when the weather was pure hot hell outdoors and I was coming home from the public golf course one Saturday after a morning round, I found the handle I was looking for.

I pulled up to park before our apartment house, and when I'd got my car nuzzled into the curb the way I wanted it, I looked through the windshield and there was Wilkins, getting out of his secondhand jalopy three cars ahead of me, with a big paper sack of groceries in his arms.

He nudged his car door shut with an elbow and started up the drive to the apartment entrance, carrying the bag. As he approached the bed of zinnias and snapdragons that bordered the drive on his left, he suddenly shied like a startled horse and stopped in his tracks. After a momentary hesitation, he began to make a wide circle to his right around the bed of flowers to get to the apartment entrance, clutching the groceries tightly and looking with terrified eyes toward the flowers. And just then, a bee that had been prowling around the flowerbed left his work and buzzed toward Wilkins to investigate him. I could see the bee's wings winking in the sunlight. And that's when Wilkins really flipped.

He'd been watching that bee all along, I guess. And when he saw it coming over to say hello to him as he went by, he came all apart at the seams in one shattering instant. You'd have thought all the fiends in creation were after him, instead of a harmless little honeybee. He yelled something in a strangled voice, dropped his paper sack of groceries on the concrete drive with a grand splash of breaking milk-bottles, and took to his heels like an hysterical woman frightened by a mad dog.

He swung his arms around him desperately in shooing motions as he ran; he rolled his eyes over his shoulder at the bee to gauge its flight; he fled up the drive in a galvanic tangle of arms and lanky legs and didn't pause until he shot through the apartment entrance and slammed the door shut behind him.

I sat in my car and watched the whole bit. What a jerk,

was my first thought, what a colossal, all-American jerk for my wife to fall for—a grown man that's scared of honeybees! And then my second thought came along and slapped me and I knew that this was it, this was what I needed to know about Wilkins.

For no sane adult is as scared of bees as Wilkins seemed to be—not without good and sufficient reasons. It just didn't figure.

I've mentioned that I'm a traveling salesman. But did I tell you what I sell? I guess not. Pharmaceuticals. I travel for one of the big midwestern pharmaceutical houses. And although I'm no M.D., I knew enough medical jazz to dope out Wilkins so he *did* figure.

And I had a nice warm feeling of satisfaction, right away.

I was leaving for my regular August swing around the territory the next day. I'd be gone two weeks, as usual. I looked deep into Doris' wonderful sapphire-colored eyes when I kissed her good-by, and I held her close with more than my usual affection when I left her.

I tended strictly to business for the next ten days, though it was a hard thing to do. I kept remembering that while I was away, that mouse of mine was probably playing like mad with that cat across the hall. But this is the last time, Jim, I told myself. Consolingly.

On the tenth day, I turned aside from my regular route and drove fifty miles out of my way to a little hick town in the northern part of the state. I wandered into the sleepy, half sporting goods, half hardware store there, and bought a dusty butterfly net from a clerk who was either on dope or mentally retarded, I couldn't tell which. I was pretty sure of one thing, though: he'd never remember me or what I bought from him.

I took the net and drove out of town on a country road for a few miles until I spotted a honeysuckle vine blooming on a stone wall that bordered the road in one place. I pulled up on the shoulder, put on an old pair of work

gloves I kept in the car's glove compartment, climbed out
and lifted the hood of my car as though I was having engine trouble. I waited until there wasn't another car in
sight in either direction on the road. Then, with the butterfly net in my hands, I jumped across the little ditch between the berm of the road and the wall. I made one pass
with the net over the honeysuckle vine. That's all I needed.
That one scoop netted me six lively honeybees.

Carefully, I shook them out of the net into an old one-
pound candy box I'd swiped from the dump in another
town, threw a handful of honeysuckle leaves and blossoms
in on top of them and clapped on the lid. I cut a few slits
in the box for air, wrapped it loosely in a piece of porous
brown wrapping paper, tied it with string and addressed
the package to Wilkins. I didn't put any return address on
it. The whole operation didn't take ten minutes.

I slapped enough stamps from my wallet on the light
package to carry it first class mail, and on my way back
through the village, I dropped it into the curbside mail
box outside the village post office. I didn't even have to get
out of my car. I just reached over and flicked the package
into the chute and was rolling again almost before I'd
stopped.

That was Wednesday. It was Friday afternoon when I
got home from my trip. I parked the Galaxie and climbed
out, stretching the kinks out of my muscles after my long
drive. I started for the entrance to the apartment house
and only then noticed that something unusual was happening.

A police ambulance stood in the driveway, motor running and back doors open. A cop was kicking moodily at a
rear tire. He was obviously the driver, waiting for his bud-
dies to bring him a passenger. I nodded to him and went
into the apartment and pushed the button for the automatic elevator.

Nothing happened for a minute, but when the elevator

finally dropped down to the lobby, the door was pushed open and a couple of cops came out carrying a stretcher. Somebody was lying on the stretcher, but I couldn't see who because a sheet covered him all up, even his face. A fussy little guy with a black bag got out of the elevator after the stretcher, a doctor I supposed. I stood back while they maneuvered the stretcher through the door and out to the ambulance. Then I took the elevator up to my floor.

Doris was waiting for me at the door of our apartment. Her eyes were big; she looked scared. But she looked so wonderful to me that I didn't think of anything else for a second except her.

"Hi, baby," I said, folding her into my arms before we even had the door shut.

"Hi, traveler," she said, kissing me. She called me traveler sometimes because of my job. "I'm glad you're home, dear."

"Me too." It was the understatement of the week. I sniffed. "Spare ribs?"

She nodded, thinking of something else.

"Good," I said, and threw my hat at the closet shelf. She kept her arm around my waist as we went toward the kitchen together. It was our routine. My first act when I got home from my trips was to mix a martini for us.

I said, "As I was coming in downstairs, they carried somebody out of here on a stretcher. Who's sick?"

She got down the gin and vermouth for me. "Not sick," she said in a shocked voice. "Dead, Jim. It was Mr. Wilkins, the fellow who lives—lived—across the hall from us."

"No!" I said. "What happened to him?"

"They don't know for sure." Doris passed me a tray of ice cubes. Her hand trembled. "He just died."

"What a lousy break. Nice, quiet neighbor, too." I started to measure out the gin into the pitcher. I looked up and caught her eyes on me, and she seemed pretty close to tears. "Why, baby!" I said, turning to put my arms

33

around her. "You're upset. You can't let a neighbor's death get to you like this. That's the way these things happen sometimes, that's all."

"B-but I'm the one who missed him," she explained haltingly. She shivered in my arms. "It j-just occurred to me this afternoon after lunch that I hadn't seen Mr. Wilkins in the hall or elevator the last day or-or two"—she cut her eyes at me to see how I took this explanation—"and when I went out on the landing, past his apartment door, I didn't hear his typewriter tapping, either. You know how the typewriter was always going. You could hear it through the door."

"Sure," I said.

"I went across the hall and rang his bell. Several t-times. When he didn't answer, I thought at first he was out. But then I remembered that he hardly ever went anywhere, especially in summer"—she didn't explain how she was so sure of a peculiar fact like that—"so I called the building superintendent and asked if Mr. Wilkins was away. He said not that he knew of. So I told him I was worried, and asked him if he didn't think he'd better investigate."

"I see. And the Super went in and found him."

"Yes. He used his passkey. I went in with him. And we found poor Mr. Wilkins lying on his sofa in the living room and not b-breathing at all!"

"Just like that, eh? Boy, that's the way to go. In your sleep."

"But he wasn't lying straight and flat, Jim. Not like sleep. More like he fell on the sofa when he was dying. His eyes were wide open and looked terrified, somehow." She hugged me tightly. "It was h-horrible!"

"Sure, baby. I wish you hadn't seen him like that. A man knows he's dying, he gets that scared look in his eyes. I saw it in the service. It's natural."

"The superintendent called the police emergency squad. And the police doctor came and they took Mr. Wilkins away just now."

"What'd the doctor say? Heart attack, I suppose."

"He didn't know," Doris said. "He couldn't tell for sure without one of those—you know—examinations after you're dead."

"Autopsy," I said. She nodded miserably. My heart was hammering with excitement. I was afraid she'd notice it. "I'm going to look at Wilkins' apartment, Doris. I guess I'm morbid. I want to see where you found him, poor fellow. Want to come?"

"I certainly don't!" Doris said. "I've had all I want of that dreadful place today!"

"Pour out the drinks," I said. "I'll be back in a minute."

I went across the hall to Wilkins' door. I intended fiddling with the lock, using the key to my own apartment. But I was pleasantly surprised to find the door open. I looked at the sofa where they'd found Wilkins' body. But my eyes didn't linger there a second. They went right on past to the end table beyond, where my candy box lay in the midst of its discarded wrappings, its lid fallen off the table onto the floor.

I grinned, picturing vividly what had happened when those imprisoned bees, innocently released by Wilkins as he opened his mail, had come boiling out of the box. It couldn't have taken long after he panicked and began shooing and striking at them as he almost surely did, because when you're allergic to bee-venom the way Wilkins was, one good dose of multiple bee-stings will collapse your circulatory system and stop your breathing so quick you wouldn't believe it.

I found them in the kitchen.

Wilkins had a row of African violets blooming in pots on the kitchen window sill, and the bees were buzzing drowsily against the screen over the open window behind the violets, anxious to get out into the warm August air again.

Nobody will ever figure this one out, I told myself. I allowed myself a wise smile as I opened the screen behind the violets and watched the little yellow murderers stream gladly through to freedom.

I went back to Doris and my martini. I took her into my lap as we drank. I thought how nice it would be to have her all to myself again. What a doll! I looked at her fondly. So maybe she was inclined to take up with other men when I was away. Out of sheer boredom only. Just to dilute her loneliness. Nothing else.

Suddenly it occurred to me that there was one good way to put a stop to that: quit this crummy selling routine that kept me on the road half the time.

I put down my empty martini glass and turned her face to me and kissed her. I kissed her good. I said, "Baby, I've decided to quit my job."

"You what?" She was thunderstruck.

"Yeah. I want to be home more, Doris. With you. I get so lonesome on the road."

"I get lonesome, too, Jim," she murmured contritely into my shoulder.

"Sure you do, honey. And you know what? I've thought of a job that would let me stay right here with you all the time."

She raised her head. "What?"

"Writing detective stories. Like poor old Wilkins across the hall. I think I'd like to try my hand at that." I kissed her again. "I have an idea I might be pretty good at murder."

Her arms tightened around me. "Darling, I'd love having you home with me," she said, "but you've never written a story in your life!"

"You've got to start sometime," I said.

So this is the first one.

Did you like it?

*There's more to being a butler than the ability to stand
stiffly erect. One must also be able to look down one's nose,
while keeping one's ears open and one's mouth shut. Understandably, butlers are a vanishing race.*

THE BUTLER WHO DIDN'T DO IT
BY CRAIG RICE

"Please, Malone," the beautiful brunette said,
in a passionate tone. "You've got to help me!"

John J. Malone flicked his cigar inaccurately toward
the ashtray on his desk and closed his eyes. When he
opened them again the woman was still there, seated across
the desk. He sighed. "What do you want me to help you
do?" he said. The choice of words, he reflected, was just a
little unfortunate, but it really didn't matter. He knew he
would have to take the job, whatever it was. So long as it
wasn't anything definitely illegal. And he wasn't sure that
would stop him, either, he reflected. The bank balance
was at its lowest ebb in years. Mentally, Malone ticked off
a list of people he owed money to: the telephone company,
the electric company, Maggie, Joe the Angel, Ken, Judge
Touralchuck (an unfortunate poker game) . . .

It seemed endless.

"It's my husband," the woman said. "The police think I
murdered him."

Malone sighed again. "Why?" he said. "For that matter,
who's your husband? And who are you?" He thought of
adding: "And why did you have to pick me, of all people?"
but decided against it. He needed the money, he reminded
himself. And the woman was beautiful.

Malone felt a resurgence of gallantry in his breast. He flicked cigar ash off his vest and waited quietly .

"Oh," the woman said. There was a little silence. "I'm Marjorie Dohr," she said.

Malone blinked, and said nothing at all.

The woman spelled her last name. "My husband's James Dohr. I mean . . . he *was* James Dohr. Before he—" Her lips tightened. Then she put her head down on Malone's desk and began to sob.

"Please," Malone said, patting the head ineffectually. "Please. Stop. I—"

After a few seconds she looked up, dabbed at her eyes with a handkerchief and murmured: "I'm sorry. But it was all so sudden . . . James was—dead, and then there were the police, and I—"

"Ah," Malone said. "Tell me about the police."

Mrs. Dohr dabbed at her eyes again. "You—will help me?" she asked.

"I'll try," Malone said. "Did you kill your husband?"

Mrs. Dohr stared. "Of course not," she said. "I told you—"

"I just wanted to make sure," Malone said defensively. "But the police think you did."

She nodded. "That's right," she said. "You see, James didn't feel well, so he stayed home. I went to the movies. And when I got back, he was—he was lying there, right in the living room, with that knife in his back, and I—I was going to call the police."

"But you didn't?" Malone asked gently.

"No," she said. "They came in—just a few seconds after I got home. And they accused me of murdering James. For his—money."

"Money?" Malone said hopefully.

"That's right," Mrs. Dohr said. "When old Gerald Deane died, he left James five thousand dollars. And the police thought I killed James for that."

"Very silly of them," Malone murmured. "Your husband was related to Gerald Deane?" He remembered the aircraft magnate. Five thousand dollars seemed a small sum to leave to a relative, even a distant one, if your estate was the size of Deane's, but people did funny things.

"Oh, no," Mrs. Dohr said. "They weren't related at all, not at all."

"Ah," Malone said. "Just good friends."

Mrs. Dohr shook her head. "Not exactly," she said. "You see—maybe I should have explained before. My husband is—was—a butler. He worked for old Mr. Deane, and then he worked for his son Ronald. He was working for Ronald until he—until he died."

"A butler," Malone said.

"That's right," she said. "Malone—you will help me, won't you? You don't think I killed my husband, do you? Please say you'll help me!"

Malone sighed. "I'll help you," he said obediently. "And I don't think you killed your husband. As a matter of fact, I'm sure you didn't," he added in a burst of confidence.

"You mean—you can prove I didn't kill James?" Mrs. Dohr said. "Then who did?"

Malone coughed gently and took a puff on his cigar. "Before we answer that," he said, in what he hoped was a confident tone, "we'll have to have a few more facts."

An hour later, armed with facts about James Dohr, Gerald Deane, his surviving wife Phyllis and his son and daughter-in-law, Ronald and Wendy, Malone set off for Joe the Angel's Bar. It would be, he told himself, a nice place to collect his thoughts and make up his mind on his first move.

But the atmosphere wasn't quite as friendly as he remembered it from other days. Joe was brooding about Malone's bar bill, and he made it fairly obvious. Malone had a few drinks for old times' sake, but his heart wasn't really in it. And, beyond deciding that his first place of inquiry would be the Deane household, he did no thinking worth mentioning.

The Deanes were, he told himself, his prime suspects, almost entirely because they were his only suspects. James Dohr seemed to have been a saint on earth, Malone reflected; according to his tearful widow, he had had absolutely no enemies. Even his friends had liked him. And this narrowed the field of suspicion considerably.

Mrs. Dohr had a motive for murder, Malone knew. And her story of the movies was pretty vague, and could be shot full of holes by a six-year-old child. Not only that, he told himself, but hers was the only motive around.

Nevertheless, he believed her story. She had been tearful and beautiful, and she had sounded sincere. Besides, Malone thought, she was his client.

That meant finding somebody else who had a motive. And who else was there?

Well, Malone considered, a butler is in a position to discover all kinds of things about the household he works for. That was a point worth considering. It pointed the first finger of suspicion squarely at a dead man, Gerald Deane, but there was always his widow, and the rest of his family. Possibly there was even another butler.

Malone drained his glass and got up. With a friendly wave to Joe, a wave that was meant to impart great confidence about the paying of Malone's bar bill, the little lawyer went to the door, pushed it open, and started looking for a cab.

The Deane estate was a large house set in the middle of a larger area of grounds. Malone drove up the winding drive to the front door of the marble palace, got out, tipped the cabbie and walked up the steps.

The door was solid mahogany. Malone took hold of the knocker and used it. The door swung open.

A tall red-headed man grinned at him. "Now who are

you?" he said. "You can't possibly be the new butler. You don't look like a butler. You look like a—like a—" He posed thoughtfully in the doorway for a few moments. "Like a bootlegger," he said at last. "An old-fashioned, slightly under-the-weather bootlegger." He stepped aside and called into an entranceway at the left of the door: "Aren't I right, Wendy?"

A woman's voice floated back: "Certainly you're right. If you say so, you're right. How far would I get if I argued with you? You're always right."

Malone sighed. "Excuse me," he said.

"Ah," the red-haired man said. He looked scarcely old enough to remember Prohibition, Malone thought. "I'm afraid you're out of date," the red-haired one said. "We haven't taken any bathtub hooch in this house for years."

Malone said: "But—"

"I know," the red-haired man said. "I know. It's just off the boat. Even so, I'm afraid—"

"I'm a lawyer," Malone said, feeling desperate. "I'm here about the death of James Dohr."

"Well," the red-haired man said, "of course if you— What?"

"James Dohr," Malone said.

There was a little silence. At last the red-haired man said: "Of course." His voice had become sober and, Malone thought, about eight years older. He now seemed to be forty-five or so. "Sorry for my little by-play. Can't resist having fun; that's my trouble. You said you were a lawyer?"

"That's right," Malone said. "John J. Malone." He began to fish for a card.

"Never mind all that," the red-haired man said. "Just formality—come in, instead. I'll introduce you around and you can take care of your business. Anything we can do, of course. James worked here over forty years, though of course you know that—"

"Yes," Malone said. He stepped inside and the great

door swung shut behind him. The red-haired man made a motion, and Malone followed him through the entrance arch at the left into a large, well-lit room. There were three people in the room.

One of them was a maid, Malone saw, in full regalia. The other two were an old, old woman in a straight-backed armchair, and a younger edition. Mrs. Deane, Malone thought, and Mrs. Deane. The red-haired man, by elimination, was Ronald. Fun-loving Ronald, he corrected himself bitterly.

Ronald said: "Mother—Wendy—this is Mr. Malone. He's come here to ask us some questions about the death of James Dohr."

The younger Mrs. Deane blinked and said: "Ask us some questions? What do we know about it, Ronald?"

Ronald shrugged. His mother stirred slightly, leaned forward and pinned Malone with a look. "Young man," she said, in a voice that sounded even older than she looked, "do you wish to question *me?*"

There was nothing, Malone thought, that he would rather avoid doing. But he nodded very slowly. "That's right," he said.

"Very well," the old, old woman said. She looked around at the others. "Leave us," she said simply.

The room emptied itself. The old, old woman patted a chair next to the one she sat in. "Come over here, young man," she said. "Talk to me."

Feeling just a little like Snow White, Malone went over to the chair and sat down. There was a second of silence. Malone wiped a tiny bead of sweat off his forehead.

"Well?" the ancient voice said.

Malone tried to think of a logical first question. "How well did you know James Dohr?" he said at last.

The old woman chuckled. "Well?" she said. "Very well indeed. He worked here for a long time, and I don't doubt he knew a lot about us, too. Whoever shot him probably did this family a service."

"A what?" Malone said, feeling shocked.

The woman smiled gently. "I'm old enough," she said, "to be realistic about things like this. And I tell you that James had secrets locked away in that brain of his—secrets that will never be told now."

Malone drew a deep breath. "He was trying to blackmail you?" he said.

Laughter. "Blackmail?" the old woman said at last. "Young man, you have been reading too many thrillers. I only say that he had the secrets—as anyone who worked here for so long would have them—and now the secrets have been buried with him, and better so. Why, Gerald's hush-money was barely necessary, after all."

Malone blinked. "Hush-money?" he said.

"That's what the will called it," the old woman said. "You have heard about the bequest which Gerald left to him? The five thousand dollars?"

"That was hush-money?" Malone said.

"Of course," the old woman said, as if it were the most natural thing in the world. "And now that his wife has—"

"She didn't do it," Malone said instantly.

"Ah?" the old woman said. "Indeed. Then you suspect one of us."

"I—"

The old woman lifted a hand. "Please," she said. "There is no need to apologize. If his wife did not kill James Dohr, then perhaps one of us did. I understand that James had few friends."

"That's right," Malone said weakly.

"Well, then," the old woman said in a triumphant tone, "certainly you don't mean to suggest that James was murdered by an utter stranger?"

Malone took a deep breath. "Funnier things," he offered at last, "have happened."

"Indeed they have," she said. "But since you suspect one of us, you must have questions to ask, Mr. Malone. Ask them."

Malone tried to think of a question. But there was, after all, only one. "Did you kill him?" he said.

"Why, no," the old woman said pleasantly. "As a matter of fact, I didn't. I was fond of James. He had secrets, you see."

Malone tried to tell himself that everything was perfectly normal. "You liked him because he had secrets?" he said after a second.

"That's right," the old woman said. "Perhaps I'd better explain."

"It might," Malone said cautiously, "be a good idea."

"Gerald hated the idea of those secrets," the old woman said. "Gerald was disturbed whenever he thought of them; and yet there was nothing he could do except put that hush-money clause into his will. As long as James Dohr was in this house, Gerald was unhappy. And that pleased me."

Malone opened his mouth, shut it again, and finally said: "Oh."

"So you see," the old woman said, "that I had some motive, perhaps, for harming Gerald—a motive which I cheerfully admit, since I did not kill him. But I had no such motive for doing away with James Dohr."

"Well," Malone said, and wondered what other words could possibly follow that. At last he said: "I suppose I ought to talk to your son next."

"You ought to talk to everyone," the old woman said. "You must gather all the facts, Mr. Malone, and satisfy your mind." She clapped her hands together sharply, and the maid appeared suddenly in the doorway. "Please send Ronald to us," the old woman said.

A few minutes later Ronald came in. His mother smiled at him. "Mr. Malone wants to ask you some questions," she said casually. "I shall remain while he does so." Malone opened his mouth to object, thought better of it and kept quiet. "It should be very interesting," the old woman said.

"Fascinating," Ronald said, "I don't doubt. Am I supposed to have knifed James, in some back-alley brawl?"

"I'm sure I don't know," the old woman said smoothly. 'Mr. Malone, you have some questions to ask?"

Malone wiped some more sweat from his forehead. "I uppose so," he said.

Ronald was, he discovered, the helpful type. He cheerully admitted that he knew nothing, but that didn't stop aim from having all sorts of ideas, theories and suggestions. Iis mother watched the interview for a time with her oright, beady eyes, but she seemed to get bored after a while, and devoted herself to what was, Malone thought, . kind of half-sleep. She sat with her eyes closed, shifting osition now and again, as far away from the interview as f she had been in Kamchatka.

"What about enemies?" Malone said at last, feeling little desperate.

"Enemies?" Ronald said. "James didn't have any enmies. Except us, of course."

"You?"

"Well—Gerald," Ronald said. "You know about that, 'on't you?"

Malone nodded.

"And when I was little I used to tease James. You know ow kids are. I really don't think he ever entirely liked me."

"How about Gerald Deane?" Malone said.

"You mean how did James feel about Gerald?" Ronald aid. "I really don't know. He was always a good butler. 'here just didn't seem to be much else to bother about."

"Well, then," Malone said. He was coming to the final uestion, and he dreaded it. But there was nothing else to o. "Did you kill James Dohr?" he said.

"Who?" Ronald said with a surprised look. "Me?"

Malone had the horrible feeling that he was forging head into a complete vacuum, but he tried to ignore it. t was obvious, he told himself sternly, that Mrs. Dohr was mocent. And, as far as he could see, that meant that one

45

of the Deanes was the guilty one. One of them had killed James Dohr.

The only trouble was that he didn't know which one and he didn't know how he was going to find out.

Well, he thought, there was still one more Deane to cross-examine.

He asked for her.

Wendy, Ronald's wife, came into the room slowly, looking confused. Old Mrs. Deane was asleep in her chair. Ronald had left for another part of the house. Malone took a deep breath, but Wendy spoke before he had a chance.

"I don't see why you have to ask us about this terrible thing," she told him at once. "Whoever killed James had nothing to do with us. How could he have?"

Malone sighed. "I just thought you might know something," he said slowly. "For instance, suppose James had some information about the family. That could be important. If he knew something nobody wanted to talk about—"

"Oh, that," Wendy said, in a discouraged tone. "My goodness, yes. Only it's no good asking me what information he had. I wouldn't know, and the will was drawn up long before I even met Ronald or anybody."

"Ah," Malone said intelligently. "But you do know about it?"

"Oh, naturally," Wendy said. "Ronald's mother made sure everybody knew about it; she loved it, she loved to talk about it. It made old Mr. Deane so uncomfortable."

"I take it," Malone said, "that you didn't like her talking about the hush-money all the time?"

Wendy shrugged. "It got boring," she said. "Especially when you didn't know what the secrets could possibly be or anything."

Boring, Malone told himself, was not the word. Confusing was more like it. He certainly had a lead—or, anyhow, he thought he had. Only it was a lead that didn't lead to anything, if that made sense. It didn't go anywhere.

Or did it?

Malone decided, with great suddenness, that it did.

He knew exactly who the murderer was.

And Wendy Deane had told him.

"But what I don't see," Mrs. Dohr said, later that afternoon, "is how you managed to figure out what the secret was. I mean the secret Gerald was paying hush-money for."

"Simple," Malone said. "The secret had to involve Gerald, his wife or Ronald. It couldn't have anything to do with Wendy; she wasn't even around when the will was drawn up. She said so herself, and it's easy enough to check."

"That still leaves three people," Mrs. Dohr objected.

"Not for long it doesn't," Malone said. "If the secret was something to do with Gerald, then there was no reason for James to be killed. Gerald's dead already."

"And that," Maggie said, "leaves old Mrs. Deane and Ronald. Why Ronald?"

"Because Mrs. Deane liked the secret, and liked the whole idea of James' having it. She said so—and so did Wendy. She wouldn't have liked it so much if she'd been the object of that secret. Right?"

"I suppose so," Mrs. Dohr said.

"So it couldn't have been Mrs. Deane," Malone said. "It had to be Ronald. Simple elimination."

Mrs. Dohr frowned slightly. "But, Malone," she said. "What was this secret? What did James know?"

Malone took out a fresh cigar and lit it with a casual air. "Frankly," he said, "I don't have the faintest idea. Ronald knows, but he won't tell. And James Dohr, of course, was a good butler. He kept his mouth shut."

"So we still don't know why my husband was killed," Maggie said.

"That's right," Malone said. "We don't know why. But,

47

somehow, it doesn't seem to matter now. After all, the killer's safely behind bars."

Mrs. Dohr looked worshipful. "Malone," she said, "you're wonderful."

Malone took a slow, relaxed puff on his cigar. "That," he said with becoming shyness, "is a hell of an understatement."

You might like this Christmas story very much. You might not like it at all. But of this I feel sure: you will remember it for many months to come.

CHRISTMAS GIFT
BY ROBERT TURNER

There was no snow and the temperature was a mild sixty-eight degrees and in some of the yards nearby the shrubbery was green, along with the palm trees, but still you knew it was Christmas Eve. Doors on the houses along the street held wreaths, some of them lighted. A lot of windows were lighted with red, green and blue lights. Through some of them you could see the lighted glitter of Christmas trees. Then, of course there was the music, which you could hear coming from some of the houses, the old familiar songs, *White Christmas, Ave Maria, Silent Night.*

All of that should have been fine, because Christmas in a Florida city is like Christmas any place else, a good time, a tender time. Even if you're a cop. Even if you pulled duty Christmas Eve and can't be home with your own wife and kid. But not necessarily if you're a cop on duty with four others and you're going to have to grab an escaped con and send him back, or more probably have to kill him because he was a lifer and just won't *go* back.

In the car with me was McKee, a Third-Grade, only away from a beat a few months. Young, clear-eyed, rosy-cheeked. All-American boy type and very, very serious about his work. Which was fine; which was the way you should be. We were parked about four houses down from

49

the rented house where Mrs. Bogen and her three children were living.

At the same distance the other side of the house was a sedan in which sat Lieutenant Mortell and Detective First-Grade Thrasher. Mortell was a bitter-mouthed, needle-thin man, middle-aged and with very little human expression left in his eyes. He was in charge. Thrasher was a plumpish, ordinary guy, an ordinary cop.

On the street in back of the Bogen house, was another precinct car, with two other Firsts in it, a couple of guys named Dodey and Fischman. They were back there in case Earl Bogen got away from us and took off through some yards to that other block. I didn't much think he'd get to do that.

After a while McKee said: "I wonder if it's snowing up north. I'll bet the hell it is." He shifted his position. "It don't really seem like Christmas, no snow. Christmas with palm trees, what a deal!"

"That's the way it was with the first one," I reminded him.

He thought about that. Then he said: "Yeah. Yeah. That's right. But I still don't like it."

I started to ask him why he stayed down here, then I remembered about his mother. She needed the climate; it was all that kept her alive.

"Y'know," McKee said then. "Sarge, I been thinking; this guy Bogen must be nuts."

"You mean because he's human? Because he wants to see his wife and kids on Christmas?"

"Well, he must know there's a *chance* he'll be caught. If he is, it'll be worse for his wife and kids, won't it? Why the hell couldn't he just have *sent* them presents or something and then called them on the phone? Huh?"

"You're not married, are you, McKee?"

"No."

"And you don't have kids of your own. So I can't answer that question for you."

"I still think he's nuts."

I didn't answer. I was thinking how I could hound the stinking stoolie who had tipped us about Earl Bogen's visit home for Christmas, all next year, without getting into trouble. There was a real rat in my book, a guy who would stool on something like that. I was going to give him a bad time if it broke me.

Then I thought about what Lieutenant Mortell had told me an hour ago. "Tim," he said. "I'm afraid you're not a very good cop. You're too sentimental. You ought to know by now a cop can't be sentimental. Was Bogen sentimental when he crippled for life that manager of the finance company he stuck up on his last hit? Did he worry about *that* guy's wife and kids? Stop being a damned fool, will you, Tim?"

That was the answer I got to my suggestion that we let Earl Bogen get in and see his family and have his Christmas and catch him on the way out. What was there to lose, I'd said. Give the guy a break, I'd said. I'd known, of course, that Mortell wouldn't have any part of that, but I'd had to try anyhow. Even though I knew the lieutenant would think of the same thing I had—that when it came time to go, Bogen might be twice as hard to take.

McKee's bored young voice cut into my thoughts: "You think he'll really be armed? Bogen, I mean."

"I think so."

"I'm glad Mortell told us not to take any chances with him, that if he even makes a move that looks like he's going for a piece, we give it to him. He's a smart old cop, Mortell."

"That's what they say. But did you ever look at his eyes?"

"What's the matter with his eyes?" McKee said.

"Skip it," I said. "A bus has stopped."

We knew Earl Bogen had no car; we doubted he'd rent one or take a cab. He was supposed to be short of dough. A city bus from town stopped up at the corner. When he came he'd be on that, most likely. But he wasn't on this one. A lone woman got off and turned up the Avenue. I let out a slight sigh and looked at the radium dial of my watch. Ten-fifty. Another hour and ten minutes and we'd be relieved; it wouldn't happen on our tour. I hoped that was the way it would be. It was possible. The stoolie could have been wrong about the whole thing. Or something could have happened to change Bogen's plans, or at least to postpone his visit to the next day. I settled back to wait for the next bus.

McKee said: "Have you ever killed a guy, Sarge?"

"No," I said. "I never had to. But I've been there when someone else did."

"Yeah? What's it like?" McKee's voice took on an edge of excitement. "I mean for the guy who did the shooting? How'd he feel about it?"

"I don't know. I didn't ask him. But I'll tell you how he looked. He looked as though he was going to be sick to his stomach, as though he should've been but couldn't be."

"Oh," McKee said. He sounded disappointed.

"How about the guy that was shot? What'd he do? I've never seen a guy shot."

"Him?" I said. "Oh, he screamed."

"Screamed?"

"Yeah. Did you ever hear a child scream when it's had a door slammed on its fingers? That's how he screamed. He got shot in the groin."

"Oh, I see," McKee said, but he didn't sound as though he really did. I thought that McKee was going to be what they called a good cop—a nice, sane, completely insensitive type guy. For the millionth time I told myself that I ought to get out. Not after tonight's tour, not next month, next week, tomorrow, but right now. It would be the best Christmas present in the world I could give myself and my family. And at the same time I knew I never would do that. I didn't know exactly why. Fear of not being able to make a living outside; fear of winding up a burden to everybody in my old age the way my father was—those were some reasons but not the whole thing. If I talk about how after being a cop so long it gets in your blood no matter how you hate it, that sounds phony. And it would sound even worse if I said one reason I stuck was in hopes that I could make up for some of the others, that I could do some good sometimes.

"If I get to shoot Bogen," McKee said, "he won't scream."

"Why not?"

"You know how I shoot. At close range like that, I'll put one right through his eye."

"Sure, you will," I told him. "Except that you won't have the chance. We'll get him, quietly. We don't want any shooting in a neighborhood like this on Christmas Eve."

Then we saw the lights of the next bus stop up at the corner. A man and a woman got off. The woman turned up the Avenue. The man, medium height but very thin, and his arms loaded with packages, started up the street.

"Here he comes," I said. "Get out of the car, McKee."

We both got out, one on each side. The man walking toward us from the corner couldn't see us. The street was heavily shaded by strings of Australian pine planted along the walk.

"McKee," I said. "You know what the orders are. When we get up to him, Thrasher will reach him first and shove his gun into Bogen's back. Then you grab his hands and get the cuffs on him fast. I'll be back a few steps covering you. Mortell'll be behind Thrasher, covering him. You got it?"

"Right," McKee said.

We kept walking, first hurrying a little, then slowing down some, so that we'd come up to Bogen, who was walking toward us, just right, before he reached the house where his family was but not before he'd passed Mortell and Thrasher's car.

When we were only a few yards from Bogen, he passed through an open space, where the thin slice of moon filtered down through tree branches. Bogen wore no hat, just a sport jacket and shirt and slacks. He was carrying about six packages, none of them very large but all of them wrapped with gaudily colored paper, foil and ribbon. Bogen's hair was crew cut, instead of long the way it was in police pictures and he'd grown a mustache; but none of that was much of a disguise.

Just then he saw us and hesitated in his stride. Then he stopped. Thrasher, right behind him, almost bumped into him. I heard Thrasher's bull-froggy voice say: "Drop those packages and put your hands up, Bogen. Right now!"

He dropped the packages. They tumbled about his feet on the sidewalk and two of them split open. A toy racing car was in one of them. It must have been still slightly wound up because when it broke out of the package, the little motor whirred and the tiny toy car spurted across the sidewalk two or three feet. From the other package, a small doll fell and lay on its back on the sidewalk, its big, painted eyes staring upward. It was what they call a picture doll, I think; anyhow, it was dressed like a bride. From one of the other packages a liquid began to trickle out onto the sidewalk and I figured that had been a bottle of Christmas wine for Bogen and his wife.

But when Bogen dropped the packages, he didn't raise his hands. He spun around and the sound of his elbow hitting Thrasher's face was a sickening one. Then I heard Thrasher's gun go off as he squeezed the trigger in a reflex action, but the flash from his gun was pointed at the sky.

I raised my own gun just as Bogen reached inside his jacket but I never got to use it. McKee used his. Bogen's head went back as though somebody had jolted him under the chin with the heel of a hand. He staggered backward, twisted and fell.

I went up to Bogen with my flash. The bullet from Mc-Kee's gun had entered Bogen's right eye and there was nothing there now but a horrible hole. I moved the flash beam just for a moment, I couldn't resist it, to McKee's face. The kid looked very white but his eyes were bright with excitement and he didn't look sick at all. He kept licking his lips, nervously. He kept saying: "He's dead. You don't have to be worrying about him, now. He's dead."

Front door lights began to go on then in nearby houses and people began coming out of them. Mortell shouted to them: "Go on back inside. There's nothing to see. Police business. Go on back inside."

Of course, most of them didn't do that. They came and looked, although we didn't let them get near the body. Thrasher radioed back to Headquarters. Mortell told me: "Tim, go tell his wife. And tell her she'll have to come down and make final identification for us."

"Me?" I said. "Why don't you send McKee? He's not the sensitive type. Or why don't you go? This whole cute little bit was your idea, anyhow, Lieutenant, remember?"

"Are you disobeying an order?"

Then I thought of something. "No," I told him. "It's all right. I'll go."

I left them and went to the house where Bogen's wife and kids lived. When she opened the door, I could see past her into the cheaply, plainly-furnished living room that somehow didn't look that way now, in the glow from the decorated tree. I could see the presents placed neatly around the tree. And peering around a corner of a bedroom, I saw the eyes, big with awe, of a little girl about six and a boy about two years older.

Mrs. Bogen saw me standing there and looked a little frightened. "Yes?" she said. "What is it?"

I thought about the newspapers, then. I thought: "What's the use? It'll be in the newspapers tomorrow, anyhow." Then I remembered that it would be Christmas day; there wouldn't *be* any newspapers published tomorrow, and few people would bother about turning on radios or television sets.

"Don't be alarmed," I told her, then. "I'm just letting the people in the neighborhood know what happened. We surprised a burglar at work, ma'am, and he ran down this street. We caught up with him here and had to shoot him. But it's all over now. We don't want anyone coming out, creating any more disturbance, so just go back to bed, will you please?"

Her mouth and eyes opened very wide. "Who—who was it?" she said in a small, hollow voice.

"Nobody important," I said. "Some young hood."

"Oh," she said then and I could see the relief come over her face and I knew then that my hunch had been right and Bogen hadn't let her know he was coming; he'd wanted to surprise her. Otherwise she would have put two and two together.

I told her goodnight and turned away and heard her shut the door softly behind me.

When I went back to Mortell I said: "Poor Bogen. He walked into the trap for nothing. His folks aren't even home. I asked one of the neighbors and she said they'd gone to Mrs. Bogen's mother's and wouldn't be back until day after Christmas."

"Well, I'll be damned," Mortell said, watching the men from the morgue wagon loading Bogen onto a basket.

"Yes," I said. I wondered what Mortell would do to me when he learned what I'd done and he undoubtedly would, eventually. Right then I didn't much care. The big thing was that Mrs. Bogen and those kids were going to have their Christmas as scheduled. Even when I came back and told her what had happened, the day after tomorrow, it wouldn't take away the other.

Maybe it wasn't very much that I'd given them but it was something and I felt a little better. Not much, but a little.

He who keeps his head may also keep his seat, at the poker table. Which only goes to prove that win, lose or draw, the prime requisite in the cutthroat game of poker is cool courage.

THE MAN AT THE TABLE
BY C. B. GILFORD

Byron Duquay sat alone at the octagonal, green-topped table. At his right side was a small stand on which were stacked poker chips, red and white and blue. At his left side was a tea cart loaded with Scotch, Bourbon, a siphon bottle, a dozen clean glasses, and a large container full of ice cubes.

As he sat there alone, Byron Duquay toyed with a deck of cards. His slim, well-manicured fingers riffled the deck, cut it, then played through a little game that seemed to be a weird combination of solitaire and fortune-telling. Duquay's handsome, lean, ascetic face did not change expression as the cards turned up. There was no other sound in the room, or for that matter in the whole vast apartment, except the flick-flick of the cards as they passed through Duquay's hands.

No sound, that is, until the small metallic one of the door's opening. The door was around the corner, out of Duquay's vision, so he called out in a friendly voice, "Come on in, whoever it is."

He was expecting a fellow cardplayer. But the man who came into Duquay's view in half a minute had obviously not come there to play cards. He was a small man, several inches under six feet, and extremely thin. He wore

57

stained gray trousers, a rumpled white shirt with rolled up sleeves and open at the neck, and his hair, rather long and sand-colored, was tangled and awry. His small, narrow face was twisted, and there was desperation in his pale eyes. In his right hand was a sizeable knife.

Byron Duquay didn't try to get up from the table. But he stopped his little card game. "What do you want?" he asked.

The stranger didn't answer the question. Instead, after glancing suspiciously about the room, he asked one of his own. "Are we alone here?"

Perhaps unwisely, Duquay nodded.

"Okay," the strange young man said. "Don't give me any trouble, and you won't get hurt."

"What do you want?" Duquay asked again. But this time his voice was slightly steadier, calmer, and the question less automatic.

But still the young man didn't answer. He looked around the room again, perhaps trying to decide if there was anything here that he did want. On this inspection of the room he saw the bottles at Duquay's elbow, and his eyes lighted. "I could use a drink," he said.

"Sit down," Duquay said, "and I'll pour you one."

But he waited till his visitor was seated. The young man, possibly for caution's sake, chose the place exactly opposite Duquay and thus also the farthest away from him. He kept his right hand on top of the table. The blade, perhaps six inches long, gleamed against the green baize surface like a diamond against a background of black velvet.

"What do you drink, Bourbon or Scotch?"

Almost taken aback by the fact there was a choice, the young man hesitated. "Bourbon," he said finally. "A big one, with ice cubes."

There was another silence while Duquay served up the drink as requested. Then he pushed it across the table. The young man accepted it with his free left hand, took a long sip, made a slight grimace.

"I want some money," he said afterwards, "and your car keys, and I want to know where your car is parked. I also want some clothes."

Duquay made no immediate movement to supply any of these. "This doesn't sound like an ordinary stick-up," he said.

"So it ain't an ordinary stick-up." The young man took another long taste of the whiskey. "Come on, you heard what I said."

But Duquay changed the subject. "Who are you, by the way?"

"None of your damn . . ."

"You must be Rick Masden."

The faintest of proud smiles flickered over the young man's face. "I guess you listen to the news on radio and television," he said.

"Occasionally," Duquay nodded.

"Okay, I'm Rick Masden. I cut up two people in a bar last week. My girl and her new boy friend. A couple of days later they caught me, but yesterday morning I got away from 'em." He grinned. "Because I found me another knife."

"Do you mind if I have a drink with you?" Duquay asked, reaching for one of the decanters.

But Masden's left hand, leaving his own unfinished drink, banged suddenly and hard on the table. "Never mind the drink!" he almost shouted. "I told you what I wanted, and I want 'em now."

Duquay desisted from the preparation of his drink, but he made no other movement. "Let's talk this over, Masden," he began.

Masden's right hand came off the table a couple of inches, and the knife twisted restlessly in his fingers. "Look, mister," he said slowly, "you either do like I say, or I'll cut you up just like I did the others."

But Duquay didn't flinch. "Sit still, Masden," he said quickly, and his voice had the edge of command in it, so that for the moment at least Masden obeyed. "Before you decide to try to cut me up, you'd better listen to what I have to say."

Masden seemed to sense the danger, the challenge. He sat quite still. Even the knife became immobile. "I'm listening," he said finally.

"Good. Now let's analyze our situation, Mr. Masden. We're sitting on opposite sides of this table, about six feet apart. You have a knife, and I at the moment have no weapon. But it has been running through my mind, Mr. Masden, what I might do if you were to decide to become violent. I certainly would try to defend myself. Do you know how I would go about attempting that? I'll do just this. If you made the slightest motion toward getting up from your chair, I'd up-end this table on you. I'm quite sure I could do it too. You may be a little younger than I am, Masden, but if you'll notice, I'm approximately twice your size. So there we'd have the first phase of our little battle. You'd be on the floor with the table on top of you, or if I weren't so lucky, you'd at least be back against the opposite wall, with the table between us. Do you follow me?"

Fascinated, despite his suspicion and his fury, the young man nodded. "Yeah, I get you," he said.

"Then let's proceed to Step Two. Observe the desk behind me and to my left, Masden. I think you can see what I'm referring to from where you're sitting. I use it for a letter opener, but actually it's a jeweled Turkish dagger. Now it's pretty obvious from here on, isn't it, Masden? The instant I succeeded in upsetting the table on you, I would grab that dagger. Then we'd be approximately even, wouldn't we, Masden?"

The young man stared, then when Duquay paused for a moment, he blinked his eyes several times and licked his lips. But he didn't say anything.

"So much for Step Two," Duquay continued, now with even greater precision of speech. "We might call the completion of Step Two the end of the preparation for battle. Step Three would be the beginning of the battle itself. Now how would we stand there, Masden?"

Again there were the blinking and the licking of the lips, but again also, no comment.

"Let's consider the weapons, Masden. What kind of knife is yours?"

"A sharpened kitchen knife," Masden answered almost unwillingly. "A guy slipped it to me in the jail."

"If you don't mind my saying so," Duquay said with a slight smile, "I think I'd have a slight advantage over you in the matter of weapons. At least I certainly wouldn't trade my Turkish dagger for your kitchen knife."

"Look, Mister . . ."

But Duquay pressed on. "More important than the weapons, however, are the men involved in this battle. How do you think we compare, Masden? How old are you, by the way?"

"Nineteen."

"I'm thirty-one. Perhaps you have a slight edge there. How much do you weigh?"

"A hundred and twenty."

"I'm sixty pounds heavier, Masden. Score that for me then. Now how well can we handle ourselves? I'll offer my qualifications first. All-Conference quarterback at State ten years ago. Almost as good as a basketball forward. Far above average at tennis, swimming, et cetera. Furthermore, I keep in shape with at least one hour's exercise every day. Haven't gained an ounce since I left college. That ought to prove something, don't you think? Now, how athletic are you, Masden?"

The young man across the table had grown paler and tenser. He licked his lips again. It seemed as if he wanted to answer, but no words came.

"Let me analyze you then as I see you, Masden. You're a case of chronic malnutrition, I would guess. Not because you ever actually starved, but rather because you grew up unsupervised, and so you never ate the right things. You're abnormally thin, you know. Now add to that a few bad habits. You probably started smoking when you were about nine or ten. I've noted the excessively heavy nicotine stains on your fingers. Lord only knows what you smoke now, maybe something stronger than tobacco. And you also drink, I see. I'd bet anything that you drink more than I do. Look at me, Masden, and look at yourself. Tell me who you think is the better physical specimen."

The young man was frowning now. His rather thick eyebrows were drawn almost together, and his eyes stared very hard at his host.

"But we haven't discussed the most important factor of all," Duquay said. "I'm speaking of courage, the willingness to do battle, to take the necessary risks. You were very brave, of course, when you first came into this room. You were brave because you had a knife, and you presumed I was unarmed. But how brave are you now? Not quite as brave as a few minutes ago, I would guess. You could swagger in here and make those threats about cutting me up, but now that there seems to be a good chance of your own flesh being cut up a little, it doesn't sound quite as inviting, does it?"

"You're bluffing!" Rick Masden had finally found his tongue, and the two words came out in a small explosion.

Duquay smiled a bit wider. "You think so?" he asked. "All you have to do to find out is to make one move to leave your chair, Masden."

There was another silence, heavier this time, fuller of hostility and hatred. Masden didn't move.

"One last matter, of course," Duquay continued after a moment, "that I shouldn't overlook. It's the matter of motivation. Though you may not be the bravest man in the world, you do have a good reason to put up a fight. If you kill me, no harm's done, and you get my money, my car, and whatever else you decide to take. On the other hand, if you get killed, you're no worse off than you were before you escaped."

Something resembling hope now lighted in the thin young man's pale eyes. "What have you got to win by fighting me, mister?" he wanted to know. His voice sounded cunning.

"That's a good question," Duquay admitted. "I suppose I could just let you have whatever you wanted, and make the job for the police just a little harder, put off your capture for another day or two, or week or two. And I could hope that having gotten what you wanted you'd leave here peacefully, doing nothing worse than tying me up perhaps. But as it happens, I don't trust you to that extent. You're a vicious punk, and you enjoy doing violence, causing pain, hurting people. You might be satisfied to kick me around a little, but on the other hand—with murder already on your record, I don't imagine you'd hesitate to kill me."

The young man's brows had lowered. His frown darkened. Pure malice was reflected in his eyes.

"And besides, Masden, I just happen to dislike you very much. You're scum, nothing but scum. I wouldn't mind taking the risk of getting hurt, or even of getting killed, for the privilege of being able to take a crack at·you."

Rick Masden, although he really didn't make a movement, nevertheless squirmed in his chair, and his right hand seemed to twitch. "So you and I are going to have a knife fight, huh, mister?" he asked.

"We certainly are if you get up from that chair."

Masden took a long drink from his glass, draining it finally, and grimacing at the burn of the liquor. He scowled at Duquay, then blustered:

"Okay, you start it, dad. Go ahead, start something."

"I didn't say I was going to start anything," Duquay answered. "I've only been telling you what I intended to do if you started anything."

Now the silence was deep and lengthy. The two men faced each other, each with both hands visible on the table. In Masden's right hand was the kitchen knife. Both of Duquay's hands were empty. But Masden's gaze flicked over to the desk, saw the dagger there, came quickly back again. Seconds and minutes ticked away.

Then Masden said, "Why don't you give me what I want? A few bucks, a suit of clothes, and your car keys. You got insurance. Then neither one of us gets hurt. Why don't you?"

"Certainly not."

Masden chewed his lips now, thoughtfully. "Then what happens, dad? We just sit here? You said if I make a move you're going to upset the table and grab that knife. Then the fight starts. We either fight or sit here, huh? I gotta get moving . . ."

Quite suddenly then a new light flashed in the fugitive's gray eyes. He started to stand up, then changed his mind, but his body quivered now under the restraint of the other's threat.

"I get it, I get it now," Masden said between clenched teeth. "You're expecting some guys here to play cards, and you're trying to keep me here till they come."

Duquay remained calm. "I'm doing a pretty good job of it, don't you think, Masden?" he asked. "Yes, I'm expecting them in a few minutes."

"But you're not going to get away with it."

"You can still make a choice. You leave your chair, I upset the table and go for my dagger. You can still try your luck that way."

"I'd be nuts to just wait here . . ." The thin body trembled irresolutely.

"There's one more alternative, of course, Masden."

"What do you mean?" Hope was in the fugitive's voice now.

"Well, if we fight, I'll be taking a risk too. I'm not anxious to take that risk just for its own sake. So I might be willing to make a trade. My safety for your escape. Your empty-handed escape, I might add."

Rick Masden wasn't as confident or as truculent as he had been previously. "I'm listening to you, dad," he said.

"Well, it's like this. I feel in danger as long as you're holding that knife. You jump up suddenly, how do I know whether you intend to attack me or run away. So whatever you intend, if you do jump up, I have to defend myself. Then the battle's joined, whether we intended it that way or not. See what I mean?"

Masden nodded. "I think so."

"The key to the whole situation then is in your knife. You want to escape from here. I don't want to have to fight you if I don't have to help you and co-operate with you. But as long as you have that knife in your hand, you can't move in any direction without starting a fight. So the only way out I can see is for you to toss your knife to the center of the table."

"What!"

"That's right. Then neither of us will be armed."

"Then what happens to me? You're a football player. I suppose you . . ."

"The table is between us. You have that much of a head start. You ought to be able to get out of here before I can catch you."

"But you'll telephone the cops."

Duquay smiled. "You're a smart boy, Masden. I hadn't thought about it, but as a public-spirited citizen, I probably would have. All right, I'll make a deal with you. My phone for your knife."

"How do you mean?"

"My phone's right here within arm's reach on my desk. If you'll allow me, I'll reach around and rip it out of its connection. I'll go first, of course. I'll rip out the phone first, and then you throw your knife to the center of the table and start running. What do you say?"

The young man's brows contracted. He was thinking

furiously. Now and then he looked at Duquay, measuring his man, his width of shoulder, his tenacity of purpose.

"Okay," he said after a moment. "You jerk out the phone. But first. I'll keep my knife while you do. And if you go for that dagger of yours instead of the phone . . ."

"You just keep an eye on me, Masden."

Slowly, not making any sudden movements, and managing to keep his eyes on his adversary all the while, Duquay half turned in his chair, extended his left arm to the side and behind him, reached the phone, got a good grip on it. Then he pulled firmly and steadily. Finally there was a snapping sound, and the cord dangled loose.

"Satisfied that it's out?" Duquay asked. He dropped the phone and it landed on the thick rug with a soft thud. "Now your knife, please. In the center of the table where neither of us can reach it too easily."

They eyed each other again, neither still quite believing in the other's word, still not trusting each other. There was a long pause while neither moved.

"Come on, Masden. As long as you're holding the knife, you can't leave that chair."

Silently, with obvious reluctance and regret, the young man conceded the point. With a flick of his wrist, he sent the shiny object spinning toward the center of the table. It pirouetted through two revolutions, then lay still.

"Now keep your seat, dad," Masden said, "because I'm taking off."

"I'm sorry I can't wish you good luck, Masden," Duquay replied.

They said their farewells silently. And then both the farewells and the silence were interrupted by a small noise. Both men at the table heard it.

Masden didn't hesitate in reacting to it. His chair flew back behind him as he left the table on the run. Duquay didn't move, but instead gripped both arms of his chair and shouted at the top of his voice, "Sam, stop that man, he's a criminal!"

There was yelling and scuffling and cursing out in the other room. Byron Duquay didn't go to join it or watch it. He sat where he was, content with listening. The scuffling sounds reached a crescendo, till finally one tremendous single sound ended it all—the solid crash of fist on bone.

Duquay sat back and relaxed. The bright light over the card table revealed sweat on his upturned face . . .

. . . Captain Sam Williams put in his second appearance at Byron Duquay's poker game about two hours later. It had taken about that long to dispose of Rick Masden, to put him back behind bars, and to fill out a complete report giving all details of the capture.

"Byron," he said, shaking his grizzled head, "I don't know whether I dare sit down at a poker table with you any more. Man, I never realized you had such a capacity for bluffing."

"You flatter me, Sam," Duquay said. "I was lucky, that's all. Before Virginia left this evening, I insisted she help me out of the wheelchair and put me here. Sometimes I prefer receiving you gentlemen in a regular chair, you see. Makes me feel less like an invalid. If I'd been in my wheelchair, I could never have bluffed Masden, not for one single moment."

Sam nodded in agreement. His gaze wandered through the open bedroom door, to where a pair of silvery wheels gleamed in the semi-darkness. Rick Masden had missed seeing those. Or if he had seen them, he just hadn't connected them with the man at the table.

*In addition to what they're selling, salesmen, as you know,
must sell themselves. Their smile must be turned on wide.
And the shine on their shoes must be impressively blind-
ing. Such perfect individuals, naturally, make perfect victims.*

DEATH OF ANOTHER SALESMAN
BY DONALD HONIG

There was no view from his tenth-floor hotel
window, only the blank wall of the building next door. He
didn't mind though. He had decided not to check into the
best hotel, as the other salesmen always did (and as he had
always done before, before he had begun to lose his accounts and feel the insecurity of lukewarm handshakes),
nor did he ask for the best room in this one. He knew he
was going to have to improve his work and create a better
impression on the home office and he felt that cutting expenses would be one way.

He had been sitting reading all evening. Then he had
dozed off, he didn't know for how long. It was quite late
when his sleep was broken by sounds coming from an adjoining room. At first he thought it was a fragment from
a vanishing dream, but then realized he was awake. He sat
up with the stunned, puzzled fascination of one abruptly
awakened, his eyes squinting, trying to become accustomed
both to wakefulness and to the alien noises.

He heard voices, a man's and a woman's. They were
conducting a harsh, bitter argument behind the thin wall.
They brought him fully and alertly awake. He came for-

ward in his chair, then pushed to his feet. He stole to the wall and tilted his head, his eyes wide-staring.

"You can't pull this on me," the man's voice said.

The woman's voice retorted, her words indistinguishable, but their quality was unmistakably coarse.

Then the man's again: "You will, will you? Well, maybe you won't!"

The woman's shrill and its words clear this time: "You can't stop me. All I have to do is walk out that door. Then try and explain it."

"And I'm telling you right now that you'd better not try!" the man's voice snarled.

"Well, let's see you try and—" The woman's voice, her threat, was broken off abruptly. There was a sharp cry of surprise and something fell to the floor. A sound of scuffling followed. It sounded as though the woman were trying to scream, but each effort was stifled.

With cold fascination, and with fear too now, the salesman listened, his ear flat against the muffling wall, entranced by the struggle. It sounded now like people were crawling on the floor, a soft prowling punctuated by abortive cries and frequent thuds. And then the sounds stopped. It became utterly silent. He remained at the wall, hungering for another sound, but none came. An eerie, unanswering stillness filled the other room. It came through the wall and gripped him.

He waited for a long while. Then, quietly, he drew away from the wall, feeling the uneasy guilt now of an interloper along with his fear. Backing away, he stared at the wall as though trying to see through it, expecting the scene on the other side to materialize for his benefit. The stark blank wall offered him nothing more than a melancholy emptiness.

He sat down, on the edge of the chair this time, his fingers pinching his underlip, great nervous concern in his face. There was an almost overwhelming desire to mind his own business, the natural human impulse to turn from and ignore trouble. But underlying it was a persistent concern for the woman, a quiet, unappeasable nagging. Had the man merely silenced her with a blow or had he actually murdered her—as it had sounded (and as his aroused imagination kept insisting)?

After five minutes of intense pondering indecision, he got up and went to the wall again and leaned his head hopefully to it—hoping to hear the soft laughter of lovers reunited. But the silence remained. It almost made him angry. Why didn't they start talking to each other again? They were probably sitting there in silent brooding, glaring at each other, with no consideration whatever for his predicament.

The silence was unsatisfactory. He decided he could not ignore what had happened. How would it be for him to wake up in the morning and hear that the woman had been murdered and the murderer had escaped into the night? Already he felt guilt massing. Perhaps something could still be done, if not to save the woman's life at least to apprehend her murderer while the crime was still warm on his hands.

Quietly he sat down and put on his shoes. Stealthily, as though he himself were committing something reprehensible, he opened his door and stepped out into the hall. It was empty. He realized the lateness of the hour. Everyone else was probably asleep, hence he had been the only one to hear the disturbance. He stood and wrung his hands for a moment, gripped by a maddening indecision. Then resolution became assertive and he strode to the self-service elevator and pressed the button. As he waited, he stared at the door of the room in which the conflict had taken place. Even the door itself seemed to suggest something desperate, some silent, uncanny, urgent message.

The elevator arrived with a grunt, the door sliding aside. The little box-like room awaited his entrance. Quickly he stepped inside, pressed the first-floor button and watched the door slide across. He stood nervous and perspiring as—with a slow, funereal sinking, like a coffin being lowered—the elevator descended, the passing floors clicking off in solemn cadence.

The door slid open upon a drowsy, empty lobby, the lobby typical of a second-class hotel, hopelessly dreary in the long night hours. The clerk was behind the desk reading a newspaper. As the salesman walked toward the desk he was wondering what he ought to say, and how, whether or not to be serious about it or to perhaps treat it light-heartedly. He did not want to be an alarmist. Perhaps a disturbance from that room was not an unusual thing and the clerk would laugh and acknowledge it. Perhaps that was why no one else had come down to report it. He began to feel foolish. He would have kept going and have contrived a purchase at the cigarette machine had the clerk not looked up and put down his paper.

"Yes, Mr. Warren?" the clerk asked.

Mr. Warren stopped at the desk, looking down at the clerk. The clerk stood up, smiling a thin, competent, professional smile.

"It seems," Mr. Warren said, "it seems there was a rather heated argument in the room adjoining mine."

"Really?"

Encouraged, Mr. Warren went on. "Yes. A man and woman were arguing . . . about something. It was rather a bitter argument. The man struck her . . . I believe. It sounded like a terrible struggle. And then it stopped. On what note I don't know. But I heard nothing further. I felt that I ought to . . . report it, just to be safe."

The clerk was looking at the register.

"Which room?" his bent head asked.

"The one to my right."

"Let's see. You're 10 C. That would be 10 E."

"Yes," Mr. Warren said, hugely gratified by the clerk's interest. "10 E is the one."

"Well, there's a Mr. Malcolm registered there. Alone."

71

"Alone?"

The clerk looked up at Mr. Warren with pale, unsympathetic eyes. "Yes," he said.

"But that's impossible. I mean . . . I heard . . ."

"Perhaps you heard someone's radio playing," the clerk said.

"No, it was not a radio," Mr. Warren said with indignation. "I had been dozing and I heard quite distinctly . . ."

"Dozing?" the clerk said suggestively.

"I was not dreaming. I was fully awake when I heard it."

"I see," the clerk said. He turned over his wrist and glanced at his watch. "Well, it's quite late. I would hate to call anyone now, unless you insisted."

He had put it squarely up to Mr. Warren, clamped the responsibility upon his shoulders. It was a challenge. He could insist or he could back down and walk back across the lobby with the clerk staring condescendingly at him. He felt his resolution being drained, depleted. It made him angry. He leaned both hands on the desk.

"Yes," he said, his voice suddenly firm. "I think we ought to check into it."

Without a further word the clerk lifted the house phone and dialed a number. There was a rather long wait before the ringing—Mr. Warren could hear it—was broken. A man's voice, terse, annoyed, answered.

"Mr. Malcolm?" the clerk asked. "This is the desk. Sorry to disturb you at this hour. Your neighbor, Mr. Warren, has come downstairs to report a disturbance in your room. Has there been any trouble?"

Mr. Warren could not distinguish the exact words, but there was an indignant disclaiming in the man's voice. The clerk nodded, eyeing Mr. Warren with cool, superior satisfaction. Mr. Warren flushed.

"I see. Thank you, Mr. Malcolm. So sorry to have bothered you." The clerk put the phone down and stared at Mr. Warren. "He's been asleep since ten o'clock," the clerk said, a gratuitous innuendo in both his manner and voice.

"That's impossible," Mr. Warren said. "I . . ." He was going to describe how intently he had been listening, but felt that such an admission would be embarrassing. "All right," he said quietly. "Perhaps I was mistaken. Sorry to have troubled you. Good night." He turned and walked away, feeling the clerk's eyes on his back as he moved to the self-service elevator.

He went back to his room and sat down again. Could he have been mistaken. They had been telling him at the office that he was getting old, slowing down. They had wanted to take him off his route and give it to a younger man. Despite a decrease in his volume of sales, he had insisted he was as good a man as he ever was. But he was getting old, tiring easily. He knew that as you got older, your senses began playing tricks on you. Had he been hearing things? The idea made him dizzy, gave him a headache. But then he told himself, sternly, to stop that kind of thinking. It was ridiculous. He was only fifty-seven. Was that so old?

That whole mode of thinking angered him. He could have been ninety-nine, he told himself, and doddering and senile, but still he had heard those voices and the sound of that scuffle and there was no sense in trying to deny it to himself. Mr. Malcolm had lied. And if he had lied then he had a damn good reason for lying.

He would call the police. Mr. Warren decided that, closing his fist. The police would not be as easily put off as the clerk. They would not take Mr. Malcolm's word, but would go up to the room and have a look for themselves. Buoyed by this new idea he went to the phone. But then he hesitated. The phone suddenly turned lethal. Yes, if he insisted, the police would come. They would knock on Mr. Malcolm's door and search the room, on the complaint of Mr. Warren. And what if they found nothing? Then it would not pass so easily. Mr. Malcolm could raise a con-

73

siderable protest if he chose, and probably would. People in hotels, Mr. Warren knew from wide experience, were unusually touchy. Irritation bubbled close to the surface. The hotel could be sued and the police would have to make a report. And in the center of it all would be Fred Warren. A report would surely be sent to the home office and what would they think then? It would serve to further affirm their suspicions. Fred Warren was beginning to hear murders in the middle of the night.

Wearily, dejectedly, he sat down again, staring at the floor.

He was sitting like that when he heard a soft tapping at his door. Coming alert, suspicious, he rose and went to the door, pondering it gravely for a moment before he spoke.

"Yes?" he asked.

A man's voice whispered, "Mr. Warren?"

"Yes."

"May I speak to you? It's quite important."

The man's tense whispering bespoke of some urgency. Intrigued, Mr. Warren opened the door. Standing before him was a rather tall, youngish man, wearing a light blue bathrobe over pajamas. An urgent note was in his face.

"May I come in?" he asked.

"Why?"

"It's about . . ." and the man finished the sentence with a surreptitious nod toward the next room.

Now Mr. Warren welcomed him in and closed the door quietly. The visitor fidgeted, clasping and unclasping his hands.

"This is most irregular," he said. "I'm awfully sorry to bother you at this hour. But I was wondering if you had heard what went on next door. I assumed you did, being so close—the way you are."

"Indeed I did," Mr. Warren said. He offered his hand. "Fred Warren," he said.

Timidly, the man accepted. "John Burke," he said.

74

"Well, I called the clerk and he told me in effect to go back to sleep, that I had had a nightmare, that there was only a single person in that room and that I couldn't possibly have . . ."

"Told me the same thing," Mr. Warren eagerly told his new ally. "I went down there and made him call up. *He* said," Mr. Warren indicated the next room contemptuously with his thumb, "that I was crazy."

"Well, we can't both be crazy," Mr. Burke said stoutly.

"Of course not. How about the others?"

"Others?"

"Aren't there other people on the floor who might have heard? Maybe they're too afraid to . . ."

"Most of the other rooms are unoccupied. There's an old lady at the other end of the hall and she's near deaf. I met her in the elevator this morning and she can't hear a nickel's worth."

"I see," Mr. Warren said. "What do you propose we do?"

"Well, that was what I had come to ask you."

"I . . ." Mr. Warren said and stopped. The other was leaving the decision to him. He was the captain—the older, wiser man. He felt suddenly the terrific responsibility and became determined not to shirk it. "Well, we've got to do something," he said firmly, taking the helm. "We can't just stand by and let . . . and let whatever went on in there be ignored."

"I agree," Mr. Burke said.

"I was going to call the police, but I thought twice on that. There's always the chance, the very, very small chance, that we could have been mistaken. Then it would be very embarrassing."

"I quite agree," Mr. Burke said.

"Not that I think we are mistaken, mind you. But I think we might be able to handle it without calling the police."

"Good."

"Did you try the keyhole?" Mr. Warren asked. It sounded foolish. But it was a suggestion.

"No."

"Let's give it a try then."

Quietly, they stepped out into the hall. There, while Mr. Burke, in bathrobe and pajamas and overlarge bedroom slippers, stood guard, Mr. Warren, with weary cracking bones, got down on one knee and squinted into the keyhole. He got up. He took Mr. Burke's arm and guided him back into the room, closing the door.

"Well?" Mr. Burke asked anxiously.

"It's pitch dark," Mr. Warren said.

"Oh," Mr. Burke said with disappointment.

Mr. Warren looked at him. "But we can't just ignore it," he said. "We have a certain duty."

"I agree."

"Maybe we can insist the clerk open the door for us. Why should we just take that man's word? After all—"

"It could lead to a libel suit," Mr. Burke said.

"Yes," Mr. Warren said thoughtfully, rubbing his chin. And that would get back to the home office too. Mr. Burke watched him, waiting for some leadership.

"If only we could have a look into that room," he said.

"There's no way," Mr. Warren said.

"There is a way," Mr. Burke said in a small, timorous contradiction.

"How?"

"From the ledge."

"The ledge?"

"There's a ledge that runs around the building."

"How wide is it?"

"It's wide enough. The window cleaners use it."

"But they have belts," Mr. Warren said.

"No," Mr. Burke said. "Balance. It's dangerous, of course . . ."

"It would give us a peep into that room," Mr. Warren said.

"At least then we would know how to proceed. We'd know if there were one or two in there."

Mr. Warren went to the window and opened it. He looked out at the ledge. It seemed wide enough. He looked at the next window. It was about eight feet away. Then he looked down. It was too dark to see the courtyard. The dark was a mighty, bottomless shaft.

"Maybe you shouldn't," Mr. Burke said nervously. "You've certainly shown a lot of courage already."

Mr. Warren turned around and looked at him. A young man, but nervous and looking up to him. The home office could learn a lot from him.

"It's the only way," he said. "That man next door is too cocksure. We've got to see that he gets what he deserves. Why, you didn't hear that poor woman crying like I did."

Mr. Burke nodded dutifully.

"You stand by the door," Mr. Warren ordered, "and keep an ear cocked. I'll get out there and have a look."

"Will you be able to tell, in the dark?"

"I'll be able to tell," Mr. Warren said. "I've got extremely good night vision."

"And a lot of courage," Mr. Burke said.

That was the last word. Now lions couldn't keep Mr. Warren from leaping right out onto the ledge.

He pushed the window up as high as it would go and then, holding onto the window jamb, put one foot up on the sill, then the other, and in a shaky crouch stepped out onto the ledge. The night immediately surrounded him with a swarm of dark winds that whistled and swept and darted past him. He pressed his back against the cold brick wall and spread his arms for balance and began to edge along, keeping his head against the wall, his jaw jutting up as though trying to stay out of water.

Each small step was like an eternity. A terrific vanity excited him. He couldn't wait to get back into the room— not because he was afraid, but because he wanted to look back upon his achievement and talk of it to Mr. Burke.

The window, a few feet away, loomed like a wondrous prize. Suddenly he didn't even care if there were two people in there or not, whether a dead woman lay there or not. He breathed the wild dark winds and it exhilarated him.

And a moment later it made no difference who was in that room, because he didn't get to the window. From behind he heard Burke hissing. Slowly, carefully, he turned his head and saw his ally's face poking out the window, turned toward him, one hand up to his throat pinching shut his bathrobe, the other gesturing excitedly to him to return.

So he started back, moving the same way, except that his head was turned in the other direction now.

As he neared the little platform of light under his window, Burke looked up at him and said, "I think I've found what you're looking for."

At his window now, shakily trying to ascertain his footing, Mr. Warren had a quick glimpse in. He saw, lying across his bed, the body of a woman looking quite disheveled and dead. And it was only that quick glimpse that he had of the room's interior, because he immediately saw Burke's hands, palms upturned, rushing up at him from out of Burke's diabolically gleeful face, the hands landing with an astonishing thrust in his mid-section, and then the window and the light were performing a sharp loop, rushing from his vision into a swarm of plunging, depthless blackness . . .

"He said he'd heard noises from Mr. Malcolm's room," the desk clerk told the detective.

"Actually," Mr. Malcolm said, drawing his light blue bathrobe more tightly around himself, "the noises were coming from his room, but I didn't want to make an issue of it. I believe in minding my own business."

"I see," the detective said.

"He must have slipped the girl in without anyone knowing," the desk clerk said. "He probably figured he'd complain about a woman being next door, just to cover himself."

"I heard them in there all night," Mr. Malcolm said. "Then I dozed off. They started fighting again; then she screamed; then, a few minutes later, I heard him hit the courtyard." He looked toward the window where the curtains were fluttering. He almost laughed, remembering the look on Mr. Warren's face, the utter astonishment.

The detective looked at the sheet-covered body on the bed.

"The stories they tell about traveling salesmen," he said. "I guess they're true."

If you don't mind, I should like to suggest that this not be the last story you read before turning out the lights. Dreams, you know.

MAN WITH A HOBBY
BY ROBERT BLOCH

It must have been around ten o'clock when I got out of the hotel. The night was warm and I needed a drink.

There was no sense trying the hotel cocktail lounge because the place was a madhouse. The Bowling Convention had taken that over, too.

Walking down Euclid Avenue I got the impression that Cleveland was full of bowlers. And most of them seemed to be looking for a drink. Every tavern I passed was jammed with shirt-sleeved men, wearing their badges. Not that they needed extra identification; many of them carried the standard bowling-bag holding a ball.

When Washington Irving wrote about Rip Van Winkle and the dwarfs, he understood bowlers all right. Well, there were no dwarfs in this convention—just man-sized drinkers. And any sound of thunder from the distant mountain peaks would have been drowned out by the shouting and the laughter.

I wanted no part of it. So I turned off Euclid and kept wandering along, looking for a quiet spot. My own bowling-bag was getting heavy. Actually, I'd meant to take it right over to the depot and check it in a locker until train-time, but I needed that drink first.

Finally I found a place. It was dim, it was dingy, but it was also deserted. The bartender was all alone down at the far end of the bar, listening to the tail-end of a double-header on the radio.

I sat down close to the door and put the bag on the stool next to me. I signalled him for a beer. "Bring me a bottle," I said. "Then I won't have to interrupt you."

I was only trying to be polite but I could have spared myself the trouble. Before he had a chance to get back to follow the game, another customer came in.

"Double Scotch, never mind the wash."

I looked up.

The bowlers had taken over the city, all right. This one was a heavily-built man of about forty, with wrinkles extending well up toward the top of his bald head. He wore a coat, but carried the inevitable bowling-bag; black, bulging, and very similar to mine. As I stared at him, he set it down very carefully on the adjoining bar-stool and reached for his drink.

He threw back his head and gulped. I could see the pasty white skin ripple along his neck. Then he held out the empty glass. "Do it again," he told the bartender. "And turn down the radio, will you, Mac?" He pulled out a handful of bills.

For a moment the bartender's expression hovered midway between a scowl and a smile. Then he caught sight of the bills fluttering down on the bar and the smile won out. He shrugged and turned away, fiddling with the volume-control, reducing the announcer's voice to a distant drone. I knew what he was thinking: If it was beer I'd tell him to go take a jump, but this guy's buying Scotch.

The second Scotch went down almost as fast as the volume of the radio.

"Fill her up," said the heavy-set man.

The bartender came back, poured again, took his money, rang it up, then drifted away to the other end of the bar. He crouched over the radio, straining to catch the voice of the announcer.

I watched the third Scotch disappear. The stranger's neck was red now. Six ounces of Scotch in two minutes will do wonders for the complexion. It will loosen the tongue, too.

"Ball game," the stranger muttered. "I can't understand how anyone can listen to that stuff." He wiped his forehead and blinked at me. "Sometimes a guy gets the idea there's nothing in the world but baseball fans. Bunch of crazy fools yelling their heads off over nothing, all summer long. Then come fall and it's the football games. Same thing, only worse. And right after that's finished, it's basketball. Honest to God, what do they see in it?"

"Everybody needs some kind of hobby," I said.

"Yeah. But what kind of a hobby do you call that? I mean, who can get excited over a gang of apes fighting to grab some kind of a ball?" He scowled. "Don't kid me that they really care who wins or loses. Most guys go to a ball game for a different reason. You ever been out to see a game, Mac?"

"Once in a while."

"Then you know what I'm talking about. You've heard 'em out there. Heard 'em yelling. That's what they really go for—to holler their heads off. And what are they yelling most of the time? I'll tell you. *Kill the umpire!* Yeah, that's what they're screaming: *Kill the umpire!*"

I finished the last of my beer quickly and started to slide off the stool. He reached out and rapped on the bar. "Here, have another, Mac," he said. "On me."

I shook my head. "Sorry, got to catch a train out of here at midnight," I told him.

He glanced at the clock. "Plenty of time." I opened my mouth to protest but the bartender was already opening a bottle and pouring a Scotch for the stranger. And he was talking to me again.

"Football is worse," he said. "A guy can get hurt playing football, some of 'em get hurt bad. That's what the crowd likes to see. And boy, when they start yelling for blood it's enough to turn your stomach."

"I don't know," I said. "After all, it's a pretty harmless way of releasing pent-up aggression."

Maybe he understood me and maybe he didn't, but he nodded. "It releases something, like you say, but I ain't so sure it's harmless. Take boxing and wrestling, now. Call that a sport? Call that a hobby?"

"Well," I agreed, "people want to see somebody get clobbered."

"Sure, only they won't admit it." His face was quite red now; he was starting to sweat. "And what about hunting and fishing? When you come right down to it, it's the same thing. Only there you do the killing yourself. You take a gun and shoot some dumb animal. Or you cut up a live worm and stick it on a hook and that hook cuts into a fish's mouth, and you sort of get a thrill out of it, don't you? When the hook goes in and it cuts and tears—"

"Now wait a minute," I said. "Maybe that's good. What's a fish? If it keeps people from being sadists—"

"Never mind the two-dollar words," he cut in. He blinked at me. "You know it's true. Everybody gets the urge, sooner or later. Stuff like ball games and boxing don't really satisfy it, either. So we gotta have a war, every so often. Then there's an excuse to do real killing. Millions."

Nietzsche thought *he* was a gloomy philosopher. He should have known about double-Scotches. "What's your solution?" I tried hard to keep the sarcasm out of my voice. "Do you think there'd be less harm done if they repealed the laws against murder?"

"Maybe." The bald-headed man studied his empty glass. "Depends on who got killed. Suppose you just knocked off tramps and bums. Or a floozie, maybe. You

ROBERT BLOCH

know, somebody without a family or relatives or anything.
Somebody who wouldn't be missed. You could get away
with it easier, too."

I leaned forward, staring at him.

"Could you?" I asked.

He didn't look at me. He gazed down at his bowling-
bag for a moment before replying.

"Don't get me wrong, Mac," he said, forcing a grin. "I
ain't no murderer. But I was just thinking about a guy who
used to do it. Right here in town, too. This was maybe
twenty years ago."

"You knew him?"

"No, of course not. Nobody knew him, that's the whole
point. That's how he always got away with it. But everybody knew about him. All you had to do was read the papers." He drained his drink.

"They call him the Cleveland Torso Slayer. He did
thirteen murders in four years, out in Kingsbury and
around Jackall Hill. Cops went nuts trying to find the guy.
Figured he came into town on week ends, maybe. He'd
pick up some bum, lure the hobo down into a gully or the
dumps near the tracks. Promise to give him a bottle, or
something. Did the same thing with women. Then he
used his knife."

"You mean he wasn't playing games, trying to fool himself. He went for the real thing."

The man nodded. "That's right. Real thrills and a real
trophy at the end. You see, he liked to cut 'em up. He
liked to cut off their—"

I stood up and reached for my bag. The stranger
laughed.

"Don't be scared, Mac," he said. "This guy must of
blown town way back in 1938 or so. Maybe when the war
came along in Europe he joined up over there. Went into
some commando outfit and kept on doing the same thing—
only then he was a hero instead of a murderer. See what
I mean?"

84

"Easy now," I said. "I see what you mean. Don't go getting yourself excited. It's your theory, not mine."

He lowered his voice. "Theory? Maybe so, Mac. But I run into something tonight that'll really rock you. What you suppose I been tossing down all these drinks for?"

"All bowlers drink," I told him. "But if you actually feel the way you do about sports, how come you're a bowler?"

The bald-headed man leaned close to me. "A man's got to have some kind of hobby, Mac, or he'd blow his stack. Right?"

I opened my mouth to agree, but before I could answer him there was another noise. We both heard it at the same time—the sound of a siren down the street.

The bartender looked up. "Heading this way, sounds like, doesn't it?"

The bald-headed man was on his feet and moving towards the door.

I hurried after him. "Here, don't forget your bag."

He didn't look at me. "Thanks," he muttered. "Thanks, Mac."

And then he was gone. He didn't stay on the street, but slipped through an areaway between two adjoining buildings. In a moment he had disappeared. I stood in the doorway as the siren's wail choked the street. A squad car pulled up in front of the tavern, its motor racing. A uniformed sergeant had been running along the sidewalk, accompanying it, and he came puffing up. He glanced at the sidewalk, glanced at the tavern, glanced at me.

"See anything of a big, bald-headed guy carrying a bowling bag?" he panted.

I had to tell the truth. "Why, yes. Somebody went out of here only a minute ago—"

"Which way?"

I gestured between the buildings and he shouted orders at the men in the squad car. It rolled off; the sergeant stayed behind.

"Tell me about it," he said, pushing me back into the tavern.

"All right, but what's this all about?"

"Murder. Over at the Bowling Convention, in the hotel. About an hour ago. The bellboy saw him coming out of her room, figured maybe he was a grab artist because he used the stairs instead of the elevator."

"Grab artist?"

"Prowler—you know. They hang around conventions, sneak into rooms and pick up stuff. Anyway, this prowler leaves this room too fast. Bellboy got a good look at the guy and notified the house dick. The house dick found this dame right on the bed. She'd been carved, but good. But the guy had too much of a start."

I took a deep breath. "The man who was just in here," I said. "A big bald-headed guy. He kept talking about the Cleveland Torso Slayings. But I thought he was just drunk, or rib—"

"The bellboy's description checks with the one a newsie gave us just down the street from here. He saw him coming this way. Like you say, a big bald-headed guy."

He stared down at the bowling bag. "He took his with him, didn't he?"

I nodded.

He sighed. "That's what helped us trace him to this tavern. His bowling bag."

"Somebody saw it, described it?"

"No, they didn't have to describe it. It left a trail. Notice how I was running along the sidewalk out there? I was following the trail. And here—take a look at the floor under the stool."

I looked.

"You see, he wasn't carrying a bowling ball in that bag. Bowling balls don't leak."

I sat down on the stool and the room started to spin. I hadn't noticed the blood before.

Then I raised my head. A patrolman came into the

tavern. He'd been running, judging from the way he wheezed, but his face wasn't red. It was greenish-white.

"Get him?" snapped the sergeant.

"What's left of him." The patrolman looked away. "He wouldn't stop. We fired a shot over his head, maybe you heard it. He hopped the fence in back of the block here and ran onto the tracks. And smack into this freight train."

"Dead?"

The patrolman nodded. "Lieutenant's down there right now. And the meat-wagon. They're gonna have to scrape him off the tracks."

The sergeant swore softly under his breath. "Then we can't know for sure," he said. "Maybe he was just a sneak-thief after all."

"One way," the patrolman said. "Hanson's coming up with his bag. It rolled clear of the freight when it hit."

The other patrolman walked in, carrying the bowling bag. The sergeant took it out of Hanson's hands and set it up on the bar.

"Was this what he was carrying?" he asked me.

"Yes," I said. My voice stuck in my throat.

I turned away. I didn't want to watch the sergeant open the bag. I didn't even want to see their faces when they looked inside. But of course, I *heard* them. I think Hanson got sick.

I gave the sergeant an official statement, which he requested. He wanted a name and address and he got them too. Hanson took it all down and made me sign it.

I told him all about the conversation with the stranger, the whole theory of murder as a hobby, the idea of choosing the dregs of life as victims because they weren't likely to be missed.

"Sounds screwy when you talk about it, doesn't it?" I concluded. "All the while, I thought it was a gag."

The sergeant glanced at the bowling bag, then looked at me. "It's no gag," he said. "That's probably just how the killer's mind worked. I know all about him—everybody on

87

the force has studied those Torso Slaying cases inside and out for years. The story makes sense. The murderer left town twenty years ago, when things got too hot. Probably he did join up over in Europe, and maybe he stayed on in the Occupation countries when the war ended. Then he got the urge to come back and start all over again."

"Why?" I asked.

"Who knows? Maybe it *was* a hobby with him. A sort of a game he played. Maybe he liked to win trophies. But imagine what nerve he had, walking into a Bowling Convention and pulling off a stunt like that? Carrying a bowling bag so he could take the—"

I guess he saw the look on my face because he put his hand on my shoulder. "Sorry," he said. "I know how you feel. Had a pretty close shave yourself, just talking to him. Probably the cleverest psychopathic murderer who ever lived. Consider yourself lucky."

I nodded and headed for the door. I could still make that midnight train, now. And I agreed with the sergeant about the close shave, the cleverest psychopathic murderer in the world.

I agreed that I was lucky, too. I mean there at the last moment, when that stupid sneak-thief ran out of the tavern and I gave him the bowling bag that leaked. Lucky for me he never noticed I'd switched bags with him.

I wish to direct myself particularly to the realists among you. Dummies—the ones I know at any rate—can be quite vocal. May I ask that you never pooh-pooh the utterances made by them and other inanimate objects. If you, for example, should bark your shins on a chair that gets in your way, kick it, berate it, but, for heaven's sake, do not deny it its right to talk back.

. . . SAID JACK THE RIPPER
BY ROBERT ARTHUR

Two weeks before the annual opening, Atlantic Beach Park was a ghost town by night, wrapped in shadowed silence. A mist riding in from the ocean twined itself around the Ferris wheel, hid the deserted roller coaster, made the street lights into shimmering yellow blobs.

Inside the one big room of the rickety building that housed Pop Dillon's Chamber of Horrors—*The Waxworks Museum Supreme*—a dusty bulb on the end of a long drop cord gave a little light, but left the corners full of shadows that seemed to crouch as if about to spring. A lifetime in the carnival business had made Pop, a wizened little man, a night owl. Now he was getting his assortment of murderers, cutthroats, criminals and victims ready for the coming season—mostly a matter of brushing off the winter's dust or mending a few moth holes in the costumes.

Humming tunelessly, Pop adjusted the flowing necktie of Holmes, the Chicago murder king whose odd hobby had been to cut up pretty young women in his basement. Then he went on to John Dillinger.

89

"Row, row, row your boat, gently down the stream," Pop sang in a monotone to himself, "merrily, merrily, merrily, life is but a dream . . . Hello, Mr. Dillinger. You're looking fine. But what a condition to let your gun get into. Rusty!"

Dillinger didn't answer. Sometimes he did; sometimes he didn't. It depended on his mood. Pop was always willing to chat when one of his wax figures seemed in the mood, and he had had a number of interesting conversations with some of them, such as the ones he had with Jack the Ripper, who was naturally boastful. Others, though, never spoke a word—they were the silent types. Pop never tried to force them to talk—even a wax dummy had a right to privacy, he figured.

Pop was dusting Jack the Ripper, who with knife in hand kneeled over a female victim, a fiendish smile on his face, when he heard the front door open.

"Pop!" It was Hendryx, the beat cop, a friendly, burly young fellow who came forward into the circle of light as Pop turned. "Got something to tell you."

"Yeah," Pop said eagerly, curiously.

"Want to warn you. It happened just a couple hours ago."

"Yeah?"

"Your old pal Burke Morgan escaped. On the way to the Shore Beach Penitentiary—"

"Morgan escaped?" Pop's creased features registered dismay. "But he's going to the electric chair at midnight."

"Was going."

"You mean he's not?"

"He had the nerve to petition the Governor to postpone his execution. Said he wasn't well enough to be executed. Imagine that. He'd been in the prison hospital with something or other. What do you think of that for nerve?"

Pop could only shake his head.

"Of course the Governor said no. But the way it turned

out, that didn't make any difference, far as Burke's getting out. So I thought I'd better warn you."

"That's bad," Pop said. "His escaping."

"It was all set. Then things start happening. The Governor he orders Morgan transferred to Shore Beach Pen when they find the chair up at the state pen's not working."

"But you said he wasn't going to be electrocuted—"

"He got away. Four guards in the prison van, and he got away. A big truck comes along, smacks into the van and knocks it over."

"Oh, that's very bad."

"They had to cut Morgan out of that van with acetylene torches. And these two guys that done it had machine guns —that's the way I heard it."

"Oh, he must be caught," Pop moaned. "My whole summer'll be ruined if he isn't."

"I wanted to warn you. They think he's wounded. And that's not going to help his disposition none. Well, I got to be on my way. Just wanted to tell you so you'd be on the lookout."

"My whole summer," Pop said dolefully. "Look over here, Hendryx, at this new display. It'll be a great drawing card, but only if Morgan is electrocuted."

"Should be going," Hendryx said as he followed Pop to a realistic electric chair set on a platform in the middle of the room. Then he asked, "What's the pitch, Pop?"

"Why, down in the workroom I'm making a wax figure of Burke Morgan. It's going to sit in that electric chair. Nice one, isn't it? And you know I got it quite reasonable from that theatrical supply firm down on Race Street."

"That girl holding the tray. That's supposed to be Alice Johnson, isn't it?"

"And sitting at the table is Pretty Boy Thomas. It's the same table he was eating at when Morgan stepped up to the window of the Briny Spray Oyster House down by the

91

boardwalk and shot him because of their little argument."

"That sure looks like Pretty Boy, Pop. He sure looks alive —which of course he ain't."

"I'm going to call this exhibit, 'Burke Morgan, the Quiz Winner, Electrocuted as His Victims Watch.'"

"Good idea, Pop. But now I gotta get going. Just wanted to warn you. Case you hear anybody trying to get in, you'd better call us quick."

"That Burke Morgan's a vain one. Being on that quiz program just blew him up all the more. Always boasting how much he read on Crime and Criminals, so having that subject on the quiz was a natural for him. Just the same he did come to me to talk about my boarders."

"That's Morgan all right," Hendryx said.

"You know what he said to me? He said other criminals were illiterate and that's why they were always caught. And he tells me that he had killed twelve men—one whole dozen—and had never even been suspected."

"Okay, Pop. Just you be careful."

Hendryx left. For a moment Pop looked gloomy as he walked over to the carefully set table where a handsome, curly-haired figure sat as if eating. Pop began to dust the dishes and silver and rearrange them.

"That's life, Pretty Boy," he sighed. "Get a nice exhibit worked out and then Burke Morgan has to escape. But maybe I can save it yet—reenact the murder maybe, when Morgan shot you just as you were eating oysters. What was that quarrel about between you two, anyway?"

He waited, but Pretty Boy did not answer. Probably Pretty Boy felt upset over the escape, too. Naturally, he'd rather have been part of an exhibit showing Morgan electrocuted than of one that re-created his own violent death.

Pop turned to the wax figure of Alice Johnson, a slender girl with dark brown hair and rather wistful eyes, the girl who had witnessed the murder. He straightened Alice's apron, made sure the tray was firm. Then he fluffed up her hair. "There," he said, "you look pretty, Alice."

He thought he heard her say, "Thank you," but he couldn't be sure. Alice was still extremely shy and hardly ever talked above a whisper.

Alice looked so pretty that Pop could not restrain himself from saying, "If only you hadn't screamed, Alice, Morgan might not have noticed you and shot you. But there, don't look so upset, I shouldn't have brought it up. I know it's a painful memory, but you'll be happy here with us, Alice, really you will. This summer you'll get to see thousands of new people, and they'll all admire you, you'll see. And after all, it was because you screamed that Morgan got caught."

Pop tactfully left Alice to recover her composure and went on dusting his way toward the darkest corner of the room. There he stopped. The figure standing there was out of place.

"Now, Burke Morgan," he said reprovingly, "what are you doing in this corner?"

"All right, Pop," the figure said softly. "Take it easy, don't make me kill you."

Pop's expression became severe. His figures were allowed to talk, but they weren't permitted to threaten him.

"Don't talk like that, Morgan," he said, "or I'll put you in a dark closet for a week. Besides, you're not finished yet. So you just go right back down to the workshop."

The waxworks figure stepped forward, blue-steel glinting in its hand.

"This is me, Burke Morgan," the soft, curiously cultured voice said. "You don't really think one of your dummies is going to start talking to you?"

"Of course they do," Pop told him, realizing that this Burke Morgan was flesh and blood, not wax. Apparently, he had slipped into the Chamber of Horrors to hide. "Almost all of them talk to me. Jack the Ripper and Billy the Kid are especially good talkers. They're the boastful type. Only Jesse James never says a word. I think Jesse James is angry because folks don't pay him much attention any more."

"Break the connection, *you're* talking too much." Morgan stepped forward, patted Pop's pockets, then put away his own gun. "If you want to be around to open this nightmare factory next month, you'd better do just as I say."

"Oh, I will," Pop promised. "So will everybody here. We don't want to get hurt. Most everybody here except me has been killed once already, and that's enough."

"The cops have this place surrounded. And I have a flesh wound in my shoulder. I must get to the hiding place my friends have waiting for me. That's where you come in."

Pop shook his head doubtfully. "There just isn't any way. The police will spot that prison suit right away."

"But what is the one thing they won't notice tonight?" Burke Morgan almost purred. "Another cop. You have a half dozen dummies here wearing police uniforms. I want one of those uniforms."

"Why, that's very clever." Pop cocked his head and listened. "They all think it's very clever, Burke. Jack the Ripper says you're a very artful dodger."

"Never mind Jack the Ripper. A man has to have brains and imagination to stay on top in any business, Pop, and I have them. That's why I'm here now and not up in the state pen waiting to walk through that little green door. Now help me off with this— My shoulder! You'll have to cut this jacket off me."

"Oh, I don't want to do that! Why, if I can get that suit off without cutting it, I can still have an exhibit. I can show the very prison suit you escaped in, the night you were to be electrocuted."

"Pop, don't get me angry. The doc at the prison said getting angry was bad for me, so I'm being gentle with you. I don't care if twenty-five years of running this private morgue has scrambled your gears so you think your dummies talk to you, but just don't play games with *me*."

"Oh, they don't just talk to me," Pop explained. "They talk to each other too. You should have heard them talking the night you killed Pretty Boy and Alice Johnson, right over by the boardwalk. My, they were excited— Oh, I'm sorry. I'll cut that coat right off you and I won't say another word."

"Pop!" The word was like a pistol shot. "Someone's rattling the front door!"

"Probably Hendryx came back." Pop looked toward the door. "He's the only one it could be."

"Get rid of him!" The tall man with the strange light blue eyes slipped behind a group of figures at a card table. One of the figures was Jesse James, and behind him Howard, his slayer, was creeping up with a drawn revolver. At the card table Morgan froze into immobility, appeared to be a spectator.

"I'll stand here until he's gone," Morgan whispered. "Remember, I have you covered. The wrong word and you and the cop'll be exhibits in this three-dimensional cemetery."

"I'll be careful," Pop promised. "Everybody, you must promise not to make a sound. Especially you, Billy the Kid!" He raised his voice. "Is that you, Hendryx?"

The burly young cop came through the door.

"Just wanted to warn you again, Pop. Morgan was seen entering the amusement park an hour ago. We're going to search the whole place inch by inch. We got orders to shoot to kill."

"Oh, please don't shoot him! If you catch him alive, he'll still go to the electric chair and then I can use my new exhibit."

There was a tiny sound, a brief movement. Young Hendryx stared toward the group of dummies around the card table.

"Pop, one of those dummies moved!"

"Oh, they couldn't have! I made them promise not to."

But Hendryx already had his gun out, moving toward

the card table tableau. He had taken no more than two steps when the muzzle flare of a .38 flickered shadows over the wax faces of a score of dummy figures, making them seem to grimace in excitement and horror. Hendryx grunted as the bullet hit him, gave a long gurgling sound, and pitched forward on his face.

Pop stood very still.

"You'd better be leaving, Morgan," he said. "Even if the police outside didn't hear that shot, they'll be here soon, because they're searching the whole amusement park. They'll find Hendryx and they'll find you, because there isn't any place here to hide either of you."

"Oh, yes there is," Burke Morgan told him. "So I'm staying. First, lay two or three dummies in police uniforms on top of this flatfoot. If anybody asks, they're all going back to the workshop for repairs."

"That might work, yes indeed, it might," Pop agreed. "Dr. Crippen, the English poisoner, says he thinks it will work. But what about you?"

"Don't worry about me, Pop. You forget—I have imagination! So when the police get here, I'll be ready. And you won't give me away or you'll get what Hendryx got. Now get busy piling those dummies on him."

"Yes, Morgan, I will. And I'll not breathe a word to the police. That goes for all the rest of you." Pop raised his voice. "If the police come, not a word about this, do you hear?"

He waited, then nodded.

"They've promised, Morgan," he said. "Even Billy the Kid has promised. For my sake. They won't say a word."

"Keep your eyes open, Pop," the police inspector called back as he headed for the door. "Blow that whistle I gave you if you hear anything. We'll come running. Morgan's around some place."

"I will, Inspector," Pop Dillon answered, staying carefully in front of the seated figure in the electric chair—a figure with a black cloth over its face, with a metal plate clamped to its skull, with straps holding its wrists and ankles in place.

" 'Night now," Inspector Mansfield said and went out, following his men.

As the door closed, the figure in the electric chair stirred. Burke Morgan lifted the false bands that seemed to bind his arms and legs. He pushed back the metal bowl on his head and lifted the black cloth from his face. He winced as his stiffened shoulder protested.

"Seemed like they were here an hour," he said. "Good thing they were in a hurry, my shoulder was getting pretty bad. But, you see, they never gave me a second look."

"Oh, it was very smart," Pop agreed. "But now what can you do? If you go out even in a police uniform, they'll recognize you; there are so many of them."

"I don't think so. But anyhow I'm going to stay here for a couple of hours until they move to another part of the park. If anyone comes back, we'll work the same trick. I'm going to take it easy right here in this chair, and you can sit there, in your old rocker. We'll wait together, Pop."

Pop only nodded. It seemed to him he had heard Jack the Ripper ask, "And what does he plan to do about you when he leaves, Pop?" But he didn't feel he should pass the question on to Burke Morgan.

"Turn out that light," Morgan directed. "They know you're staying here and that you can't sleep with the light on."

Obediently, Pop pulled the cord. The tall, thin man swore.

"Pretty Boy Thomas and the girl!" he said. "Their faces are shining in the dark!"

"Phosphorus," Pop told him as he settled into his old rocker. "They're supposed to be ghosts, sort of, watching you die. You should hear the spiel I worked up. It's very dramatic."

97

"That's enough gab. I could get sore about that exhibit idea of yours, but I won't."

Pop leaned back comfortably. Many a night he had drowsed until daylight in his old rocker. He watched Morgan trying to relax in the rigidity of the prop electric chair, and knew that Morgan's shoulder must be getting worse now—a lot worse. Morgan began to twitch uneasily.

"The laddie is suffering for a drug. Morphine, I suspect." That was Dr. Crippen, whispering in his ear.

"He's got it bad." That was Dillinger, making the observation in a cool, professional manner. "They probably gave him a shot when they sprung him, and now he needs another. His nerves probably feel like copper angleworms inside his skin."

Pop agreed. He'd seen too many addicts in the carny business not to know the symptoms. Burke Morgan was suffering. But Pop couldn't do anything about that. He closed his eyes. His breathing became deep and regular. In a few minutes he was snoring a little.

The tall man in the chair on the little platform listened to the snores and scowled. The pain in his shoulder had settled down to a burning sensation interrupted by fleeting stabs of pain. He could feel the sweat standing out on his forehead. His hands twitched. He wanted to yell, curse, make a break for it, shoot his way through the police outside.

But he did nothing. That was how a man got himself killed—through acting impulsively. He'd killed Pretty Boy Thomas impulsively, and they had caught him. Now he settled himself in the chair, determined to be still, and he was. He pin-pointed his concentration on getting through the night.

He had been here, in Pop Dillon's waxworks museum, many times. Now, in the darkness broken only by the faintest of light coming from a street lamp outside the windows, he could feel the wax figures of cutthroats, footpads, killers and victims all around him. He could feel them almost on the point of moving, of speaking. No wonder Pop, after so many years, could hear the dummies talk. In the silence, Burke Morgan found himself waiting for a voice to break the quiet.

"Morgan . . ." He could almost swear that he had heard his name spoken. "Burke Morgan . . ." He had heard it! He looked toward Pop. By the faint light he saw Pop asleep in his chair, lips parted as he snored, chest rising and falling unevenly.

Burke Morgan licked his lips. It was the craving for the white stuff. He shouldn't have taken that first shot when they got him out of the prison van. But it had helped. Now he'd turn off his imagination. It took imagination to have the electric chair gimmicked by a bribed electrician, to figure on being transferred, to plan a getaway, to carry it out in spite of everything going wrong. But he mustn't let his imagination get away from him now. He could wait it out. He had before.

The silence stretched out and out, like a rubber band being pulled until it had to break, but wouldn't. He clamped his teeth together and gripped the arms of the chair to still the shaking of his hands.

"Burke Morgan . . ." He heard it plainly this time, but he knew it was a sound in his mind, not in his ears. The phosphorescent face of Pretty Boy Thomas seemed to be smiling at him. "How does it feel to be waiting for them to pull the switch at midnight? How does it feel to know you only have a couple of minutes left?"

He almost answered before he realized it. Then he clamped his lips shut. That was how you went mad, talking back to voices that weren't there. Again the silence stretched out to the breaking point.

"He doesn't know." It was a girl's gentle voice. He looked at Alice Johnson and could swear he saw her lips move. "Tell him he's just dreaming he's free and he'll understand."

"That's all this is, Burke." And this time he knew he

99

could hear Pretty Boy's voice. "You're dreaming of us. It's almost midnight and you need the white stuff bad and they've strapped you into the electric chair. You can't bear to die so you're dreaming that you've escaped, dreaming you're going to get away. But you aren't."

Burke Morgan closed his mouth and shut off the answer he had almost made. He'd heard about this business of imagining you were free just before they pulled the switch on you. The mind escaping from reality, they called it. But this was real. This was no dream.

He bit his lips until the blood came, and the faces of Pretty Boy Thomas and the girl ceased to be alive, became mere wax masks again.

Silence, stretching, stretching—

"Almost midnight," Alice Johnson said, and Morgan jumped.

"You'll be joining us in a minute," Pretty Boy said. "Listen, you can hear the big clock striking midnight now."

He did not have to listen. The first stroke of the big tower clock set the air to vibrating, and it was the sound of a knell tolling, tolling for him.

"It'll be over soon." Pretty Boy's voice was almost gentle. "On the sixth stroke they'll throw the switch and three thousand volts will crash into your body and burn your nerves and short circuit your brain. Listen, there's the fourth stroke—and the fifth—"

Burke Morgan seemed to hear a whole chorus of voices whispering the count together. *Four—five—six—*

He tried to shut them out, shut out the clanging clock, shut out everything. But he could not shut out the venomous hiss of electric current surging into the chair. He could not ignore the great shower of sparks that flamed around his head, his hands, his feet, the smell of burning . . .

Burke Morgan leaped up wildly. He gave a single scream, and it seemed to him a hundred throats echoed it. Then silence, darkness, nothingness.

Pop Dillon settled back into his old rocker. There would be photographers and reporters there early and he wanted to be on hand for them. There would be columns in the newspapers tomorrow about The Chamber of Horrors. Oh, it would be a fine summer. Now the police had finally gone, taking with them the bodies of Burke Morgan and poor Officer Hendryx, two for the morgue who would eventually be immortalized in wax in the Chamber of Horrors.

"Pop." It was Pretty Boy Thomas' voice—yes, it was. "That was clever, Pop. Even to me it sounded like my own voice."

"And mine did to me." That would be Alice Johnson speaking in her shy, soft voice.

"Well, after all, I was a pretty good caster," Pop answered modestly, but pleased by the praise. "I was one for all of ten years, in a carny show. You know what a caster is? A ventriloquist. Yeah. Carny people use that short name."

"You handled him well." It was Jack the Ripper this time. The voices were no louder than the rustling of mice in the woodwork, or the fluttering of curtains at the windows. To anyone but Pop, they would have seemed just that. "I was wondering if you were going to try that shower of sparks effect you worked out to give the crowds a thrill, taking them by surprise when you put your foot on a button beside the platform."

"Yes," Pop answered. "I thought it would startle him long enough for me to run to the door and call for help."

"Of course you didn't know it was his heart that had put him in the prison hospital," Dr. Crippen, the poisoner, said with professional detachment. "But the combination of a craving for drugs, tremendous tension, shock and a bad heart killed him. Right there in your electric chair."

"He got what was coming to him," Dillinger growled. "You should let me have real bullets in my gun and I'd a saved you the trouble."

101

"This way was better," Billy the Kid said. "We'll have a great summer. The crowds will be flocking in."

"They'll be flocking in to see *me,* not you old dusty, moth-eaten has-beens!" a new voice sneered, and a sudden, shocked silence filled the big room.

Pop Dillon's eyes opened wide in surprise, and looked at the figure of Burke Morgan, which he had brought up and seated in the electric chair for the benefit of the photographers.

"Is that any way to talk, Morgan?" Pop asked severely. "Hardly dead yet and boasting already?"

"It's true and you know it," Burke Morgan said. "They'll mob the place to see the electric chair I died in, right at midnight, just when my sentence said I was to die."

Pop was about to answer when Jack the Ripper spoke up.

"Let him talk all he wants," Jack said. "Just don't answer him and he'll get tired of being left out. There's no point in being concerned over who draws the crowds, because what's good for one of us is good for all of us. Why think what would happen if Pop ever had to go out of business. We'd be sold, melted down—*killed.*"

There was a little murmur all over the room, a stirring a rustle of anxiety, like the creak of old woodwork settling

"Oh, I'm good for a long time yet," Pop told them all "But I want you to be on your best behavior this summer and put on the finest show we ever had."

"We will . . . We will . . . We certainly will . . ." the whispers assured Pop. He closed his eyes with satisfaction. They were a good troupe to work with. It was going to be a fine summer.

As he drifted off to sleep, he could hear the rustle of tiny voices rise and fall in the darkness. All of them were now busily discussing the evening's events.

Even Jesse James.

I have found killers to be men who love their work. At the close of a day, as they wend their way homeward, they do indeed have a feeling of great accomplishment. Unlike the white collar man in his gray flannel suit, they see a whole job through to the end—the end of someone or other.

A GUN WITH A HEART
BY WILLIAM LOGAN

"I don't want to come back without him," George said. His wife sat down at the white kitchen table, a sock and darning egg in her hand. She put the egg in the sock and looked up. "Why don't you want to?" she said. "What difference would it make?"

"A difference to me, first of all," George said. "And, second, I'm known as a dependable man. I've got to stay dependable. It's a matter of reputation."

"Terry's not going to get rid of you because you come back without this one man," his wife said. "You can leave, and spend a couple of days looking—really looking. You know where he won't be, if you see what I mean. You can make it all look good, George. And then you can come back—and what's the harm?"

"I don't like it, that's the harm," George said. "I never did anything like that."

"You never had an assignment like this before, either," his wife said.

George went to the refrigerator and opened it. He studied the contents for a second, brought out an orange and began to peel it carefully, sitting at the other side of the white table. "That's not the question," he said. "The thing is, am I dependable or am I not dependable?"

"George—"

"I don't like it any better than you do. But Terry knew what he was doing when he asked me to take this one on. He must have figured I knew him better than anybody else, and so I was the man to look for him. He would figure like that."

George put a section of orange in his mouth. His wife watched him. "How can you sit there and eat, and talk about it?" she said. "You're so calm. It's like nothing at all to you."

"Don't say that," George told her, swallowing the section of orange. "We were close. We were very close at one time, like brothers. I can feel that. But what else can I do?"

"You can do what I told you," his wife said. "Put on a good act of looking. Didn't you ever not find somebody before?"

George nodded. He put another section of orange in his mouth, chewed and swallowed it. "Just once," he said. "It turned out later the man was dead, died of natural causes."

"No matter how it turned out," his wife said. "Did Terry want to get rid of you then?"

"Well, he wasn't happy about it," George said.

"You're still here," his wife said. She placed the sock and the darning egg on the table. "You're still around."

"Yeah," George said. "Sure. I'd better get going. I got a long drive."

"You think about what I said," his wife said. "You think about it, I mean really."

"Sure," George said.

He got up, swallowing the last of the orange. He put on his shoulder holster and shrugged a jacket over it. "Maybe I better take a raincoat," he said. "It might rain out there. You never can tell."

His wife sat without answering him. George went to the

hall closet, picked out his raincoat and folded it neatly over his arm. "I'll see you when I see you," he said.

"George, please—"

"Let's not fight about it," George said. "I'm leaving. I got to leave."

"I don't like it," his wife said.

"I'll think about what you said," George told her. "I honestly will."

"Can't you do what I want?" his wife said. "It's what you want too, or what you tell me you want."

"We've been over this," George said. He went to the front door. "Now I'm leaving," he said.

"Please, George," his wife said.

George shrugged. "I'll give you a call when I'm ready to come back," he said.

George drove carefully, and not too quickly, out of town and onto the turnpike. There was very little traffic; George allowed himself the luxury of a cigarette as he drove and thought about his next move.

Fred was his cousin, he thought, and maybe his wife was right; you had to pay some attention to that. It wasn't like going out after a stranger. And he and Fred had been closer than most cousins; they'd almost been like brothers for many years. George could remember secrets they had shared, expeditions they had gone on together; when Fred had finished with high school, George, a year older, was already a runner for the organization, and he had managed to get Fred his first job.

Now Fred had walked out. Fred had announced he was going straight, and he didn't want to have anything more to do with the organization. Of course, Terry had been right, too; you couldn't let a man get away with that; a man in a responsible position had to have his mouth shut for him if he ever decided to walk out. You could never trust a man once he was away from the organization. And if the man knew too many secrets, you had to get rid of him. Even aside from Terry's talk about teaching the rest of the crowd a lesson, there was that business of knowing too much, and George could see that Terry was right.

Fred hadn't been a small-time runner or even a single-owner when he left, not like some little man who runs a book or a numbers drop and knows very little about the higher-ups and the organization work. Fred had been part of the inner group, a rough-house boy who'd made good. Fred had never been a gun, of course; he just didn't have what it took to do that job and George, who knew he was one of the best guns in the organization, knew that, too, about his cousin. But Fred had been valuable in his own way, valuable and trusted. If a man in a responsible position gets away from the organization, George told himself, you have to shut his mouth for him; you can't trust him. George knew that was perfectly right, even if you'd put the man in the responsible position yourself, even if the man were close to you, as close as if you'd been brothers.

George had to do the job, then, and he knew that. But as he drove down the turnpike, getting closer and closer to New York, where Fred had gone and where he would be hiding, he began to feel strange.

She should have known better than to argue with me, George told himself. He felt nervous, without knowing why; he thought perhaps he felt conscience or compassion but he didn't know quite what they would be or what they might feel like; he put it down to nervousness alone. She should have kept quiet, George thought; she knows me and she knows I'll do the best thing. Now she has to start me thinking.

George was afraid it would affect his search, or the moment after the search was over. He was afraid he would do something wrong, and then where would he be? In spite of the brave talk, in spite of his wife's confidence, he had no idea what would happen if he reported failure to Terry. It was altogether possible Terry would decide George's usefulness was over, and then George would be

the hunted man. George would have to run for his life
. . . and finally face another gun, with the orders of the
organization behind him.

Fred should have known better, he told himself. It's not
my fault, what he did. He knows what's coming to him.

George kept telling that to himself, over and over. The
drive through the dark, lamp-lit night was long and lonely.
Fred had known what he was doing, George told himself.
I can't afford to get myself in bad, or get myself killed, just
because of Fred. If he wants to play it foolish, that doesn't
mean I can't go on playing it smart.

And the way I feel . . . This is my job. This is what I
do, and what I'm supposed to do. I can't just fool around
with my work, as if it didn't mean anything.

George reached the outskirts of the city, the first turnoff
into Queens, and slowed down. The drive was almost over;
the search was about to start. Stop this foolish thinking, he
told himself desperately. Stop it.

It was going to be simple finding Fred. George knew he
would be with a girl, and he knew the girl . . .

Fred hadn't taken the trouble to hide anything, he told
himself. For some reason that irritated him, and he had
no idea why; he tried not to think about it. There were so
many things about this job that made him feel strange; it
was almost like a different kind of thing altogether, not a
job like all the jobs he had grown used to doing.

At any rate, George knew the girl lived on Fifty-third
Street, East, and he knew Fred would be there sooner or
later. He drove his car through the massed New York
traffic, taking great care not to be involved in an accident
of any kind, and pulled to the curb three doors away from
the apartment house in which Fred's girl lived.

No sooner had he parked, than a cab drew up before
the apartment house and a girl got out. George wondered
if he should wait for Fred, and decided that since the girl
had come home, he would be better off waiting upstairs
with her, and not giving Fred any chance to get away.

There was the possibility, too, that Fred might already be inside. He was thinking mechanically now, not letting himself feel even the pleasure he remembered from other jobs well done, neatly planned and carefully executed; there could be no pleasure in this job. With any feeling at all, George knew, there was the danger that those strange sensations might come, the conscience or compassion or whatever they were; he could hardly afford that, at this final stage of things.

He followed the girl through the apartment house door and to the elevator. He looked at the mirror-walls of the lobby, at the front door behind him; he and the girl were strangers and neither talked nor gave any indication that they were aware of each other. After a few seconds, the elevator came. The girl stepped in and George was behind her.

She pressed the fourth-floor button. George stood waiting. When the elevator stopped, the girl opened the door and stepped out and George followed her. She went to her door without pausing, probably thinking, if she were thinking about him at all, that George was visiting some other apartment on the floor. But he kept close behind her until she had reached her own door. He took out his gun carefully, keeping it almost totally concealed under his jacket.

"Just open the door and go in ahead of me," he said suddenly, in a quiet voice, "and then there won't be any trouble."

The girl turned and faced him.

"No . . ." she said, finally.

"Just open the door," George said. "I don't want to hurt you."

"You're looking for . . . he's not here," the girl said. "I don't know what you want."

"You know just what I want," George said. "Let's not stand here talking. Come on. Let's go inside."

"You can't—"

George motioned with the gun.

"—they're waiting for you inside. They'll kill you."

George shook his head. "Now I'm tired of wasting time," he said. And he made an angry, jabbing gesture with the gun.

The girl turned without a word, opened the door and stepped inside. At the last second, she tried to close the door in George's face, but he threw himself forward and came through into the apartment.

He closed the door behind him and stood leaning against it for a minute. There was a long hallway in front of him, carpeted in dull red, the walls painted pearl-gray. At the end of the hall was a large room. Doorways opened off the hall to his left.

George took the gun from under his jacket. The girl's eyes widened.

"Don't try making any noise," he said. "Maybe somebody would get here, but they'd be too late as far as you go. And it wouldn't help your Fred, anyhow."

"Fred?" the girl said. "I don't know any Fred. Who're you talking about?"

"Don't kid around with me."

"Really . . ." the girl said. "Please. Please believe me, I don't know any Fred."

George moved away from the door, keeping himself between it and the girl. He backed the girl down the hallway into the large living room, and sat down on a red-upholstered couch. "Just sit down and listen," he said to her. "Could be we've got a long wait."

"I don't know any Fred," the girl said. "You must have the wrong place. Really . . . I—I don't know what you're talking about."

"Sure," George said. "Sure."

"You can go downstairs and ask," the girl said. "They'll tell you I live alone. So whoever you're looking for—"

"Sit down," George said. He pointed with the gun. The

109

girl dropped dazedly into a straight-backed chair. "You live alone," he said. "Sure you do. And Fred takes care of the rent. Now you can't kid me and there isn't any use trying to."

The girl was silent for a long moment. George figured she was trying to decide whether or not to go on with her bluff.

"You can't kill him," she said, gently, softly. "Fred doesn't want to do anybody any harm. All he wants is to be let alone."

"I got a job to do," George said.

"But Fred hasn't done anything. He won't do anything."

"That's a chance we can't take," George said.

He studied the girl, and admired Fred's taste. She was slim and about medium-height, with light-brown hair and a heart-shaped face. And her prettiness and pleasantness were somehow one thing.

Suddenly, George didn't know if he could go through with the job. He was frightened and tried to push away his feelings.

"Please," the girl said. "Please, I'll do anything." She was pleading now.

"That's no good," George said irritably, "and you know it." If he left now, Terry would only send someone else, and maybe find a third gun to send after him. It was crazy to even think about leaving the job undone . . .

"What are you doing to me?" he said. "Now I want you to just sit right where you are and not say anything. One word out of you and this gun goes off. It's silenced, so I'll still be able to wait here for Fred."

"Please . . ."

The girl was silent.

They sat without moving. The apartment was soundless; they were enclosed in a great blanket of cotton, George felt, and there was no way out, no way to escape, to go back to a simpler period in his life.

He held the gun in his hand like a weight, and sat still, waiting.

The doorbell rang, and George and the girl walked slowly out of the living room and into the hall. George walked behind her, and now the gun and his hand were in his jacket pocket. "Open it," he told the girl.

The doorbell rang again as she put her hand to the knob.

A voice outside said, "Cleaners."

She opened the door.

The boy standing outside had a dress on a hanger, poised on one hand. "Dollar-fifty," he said.

To George the boy looked a little like Fred. He had the same eyes, the same shape of jaw, thin, nervous; but George knew the boy had nothing to do with Fred. George felt the gun in his pocket and tried to move his hand away from it but his hand remained, touching the cold metal.

George thought the boy looked at him strangely, after he was paid and as the door closed.

Some day I might be after him, George thought. And then: Why would I think anything like that? What's wrong with me, anyhow?

"Maybe Fred won't be here today," the girl was saying. "Maybe—"

"If he doesn't show up today," George said, "I'll wait until he does. Just go on and sit down."

The girl sat on the straight-backed chair. George walked around the room nervously, stopped abruptly when the knob of the door rattled and they heard a key fitted into the outside lock.

The girl stood up, and George moved quickly to her side. "No sound," he whispered, and put the gun in her back.

Like her body, the girl's silence seemed tensed. The door swung slowly open.

Fred saw them both at once, but he stepped inside and shoved the door shut behind him. He grinned, let his face

111

go slack, stood pressed against the door, without saying anything.

"I've been waiting for you," George said.

Fred's face was thin; he was going bald. George also noticed that Fred was wearing a brown, plain suit, like one he had hanging in the closet at home. He thought of putting a bullet through the suit and felt strange, a blend of fright and distaste.

Fred said, "No . . ."

George stepped away from the girl, holding the gun in front of him and moving to a position from which he could watch both of them. Fred made a half-turn toward the door, and George pointed the gun directly at him.

"You wouldn't make it," he said. "Before you were half out the door you'd have had it."

Fred moved back into the room very slowly. "You wouldn't kill me," he said carefully. "Not you, George. You couldn't do it."

"I came here to do it," George said.

"I'm Fred," Fred said.

George coughed, cleared his throat. He asked himself: Why don't I shoot? Why don't I finish the job and get out . . .

The silence was long.

"Listen," Fred said. "What I want to say . . . she's all right. You can leave her alone."

"All right," George said.

"Listen, I wouldn't do anything either, George. I wouldn't go to the police. What do you think I am? You know me."

"Yeah," George said. "Yeah. You ran out."

The girl said, "Oh, God, please . . . listen, he's right. He wouldn't do anything. You can leave us alone . . ."

George stood silent, waiting, and he didn't know for what.

"A man has a chance to go straight, George," Fred said.

112

George nodded.

"I just felt I didn't have to stay with the organization . . . forever," Fred said.

"You don't have to do anything," George said, agreeing too readily. "That's right."

"Look, George, why're you acting like this? We were friends, we were better than friends . . ."

George stood holding the gun. "I can't listen to you," he said. "I can't do it." He heard the voice of his wife, Fred's voice, the girl's voice, his own voice, all moving and speaking in his mind, stirring there in noisy fragments.

"You've got to listen to me," Fred said. "You've got to, George."

The girl, standing near him, suddenly moved and George turned, but not soon enough. The girl was upon him, trying to swing him around, but George swung with his free hand effortlessly, hitting the girl and knocking her away.

Fred rushed forward, but stopped abruptly. George had backed away, the gun was up again and leveled.

"It's no good," George said.

Fred said, "God . . ." and George felt his fingers tighten on the trigger. There was the noise of the gun, and, with surprise, George saw Fred fall, in a world of silence, a pantomimed world of horror and conscience, the strange feeling he knew, now, and recognized, and would never be without.

The girl was kneeling at Fred's side. George watched the girl who was like a figure made of stone, like an idol towering over sacrifice.

"Why did you have to . . . ?" the girl said, staring down at Fred, her eyes brimming over with tears and pain.

George looked at the gun in his hand. There was nothing to do now, no decision to make. You had to live with the world the way it was, he thought; you had to be dependable, and take care of your responsibilities. You had a job to do and you had to do it, whether you liked it or not, whether you thought about it or not, no matter how you felt . . .

The girl was no danger, he knew.

The apartment, the apartment house was silent.

George told himself he had to leave quickly. He had a long drive back; the police would arrive soon; Terry would want to know what had happened. He stood in the room, holding the gun in his hand, and then he turned and walked to the door, very slowly in the silence, very carefully.

He felt as if he would never reach the door, or the empty, free corridor beyond it.

*In days gone by, a man could make a public speech with-
out really risking life or limb. The audience, as a matter
of fact, usually stood to suffer more than did the orator.
Now that we live in an age in which everything has been
improved upon, a no-good ruler, making a no-good speech
had better have a very good bodyguard.*

ASSASSINATION
BY DION HENDERSON

Inside the auditorium, the premier was making
the final speech of his goodwill visit. Outside in the restricted area behind the stage door were the police—the
city police and the county police and the state police and
the auditorium police and two of the premier's own security police standing by the luggage. All of them swung
ominously, like the turret piece of a complicated weapon,
when the taxi screeched perilously to a halt at the barricade that guarded the parade limousines.

A tall gray haired man wearing a double breasted blue
serge suit and carrying a black dispatch bag climbed hastily
out of the cab. A perspiring uniformed police sergeant
blocked his path.

"Sorry," he said. "Only cleared personnel here."

"Are you in charge?" the gray haired man asked.

"I'm in charge," the sergeant said unhappily. "I am because of a Secret Service guy who isn't here right now."

"I know," the gray haired man said apologetically.
"Awfully sorry I'm late. Ran off the road on the way and
bumped my driver a bit. I had to get a cab."

He took a worn leather folder from an inside coat pocket.

"Mr. Smith," the sergeant said thankfully, catching the name off the State Department identification card. "Boy, am I glad to see you."

The relief was visible. It communicated to the rest of the policemen. There was an audible sigh as they relaxed, all but the two security police from the premier's own country. They never relaxed. They had turned with the others when Smith arrived but they had remained tense, alert.

Smith and the sergeant walked past them, to the stage door. Inside, you could hear the premier's big voice speaking, then the comparative silence while the interpreter translated, and occasionally a polite spatter of applause.

The sergeant said, "I hope no one was hurt in the accident."

"No. Not really an accident," Smith said. He looked down the empty corridor that led to the stage. Two officers there. He turned and checked the restricted area—the lineup of the parade limousines, the posting of officers—all quickly and smoothly and professionally without really seeming to do it. "Actually, we only lost a tire and my driver ran off the side of the road. I pulled the car into a side road out of the way. Perhaps you could send a radio car after it when we get his nibs here safely off."

"Sure thing," the sergeant said. "Does everything look all right here?"

"Fine," Smith said. "You've done very well, scarcely need me at all. Although," he said, "don't you think it might be a good idea to post a man down there at the turn of the boulevard?"

"Where, sir?"

Smith grunted, found the dispatch case awkward and put it down by the rest of the luggage. He said, almost parenthetically to the two security police from the premier's country, "Keep an eye on it, will you?"

The security police looked at him, almost expressionless, arms folded. They did not say anything.

Smith turned back to the sergeant, pointing down the street.

"Lovely field of fire there, if one had had a mind. Of course no one does, but it would be an ugly incident."

"Yes sir," the sergeant said with conviction. "It wouldn't make me cry if someone blasted the guy, but they're not going to do it in my town."

"Just so," Smith said with his quiet smile. "And I have a little larger area to worry about. I can't allow it to be done in my country."

"Yeah," the sergeant said, nodding. He gave orders and a motorcycle roared.

Smith said, "Of course you've gone through this once, clearing the route to the airport and all."

"Yes sir," the sergeant said. "We made that dry run last week with one of your guys. The county guys are handling the airport, with the airlines police."

"I'm sure they'll do a fine job, too," Smith said. "But I wonder if perhaps we might run out there, a few minutes ahead of the official party. Just to look things over."

"Sure thing," the sergeant said. "And we'd better hurry. Sounds like they're winding things up in the auditorium."

"All right then," Smith said. "Let's go."

They took an unmarked squad car, with a patrolman driving. The parade route was as direct as possible. It would not be much of a parade. Previous parades the premier had made in other cities discouraged slow and extensive parades. It gave members of the premier's party too much time to read derisive slogans on curbside banners, and even to hear and understand some of the shouts from spectators. But this was his last parade and it would go very fast. There were few spectators waiting along the route. There was only one banner. It said, "Good-bye and Good Riddance."

117

Smith frowned. The sergeant said, "Think we ought to encourage the boys to take it down?"

"No," Smith said. "Free speech and all that. Besides, it's a good sign. When they're thinking up slogans they're not thinking up positions for a rifleman."

At the air terminal, they went on past the main gates and swung into a service drive guarded by two sheriff's deputies. The service drive made a long sweep over the flat approach skirts of the terminal, then came in between the two main wings of the terminal building. There were guards at the turn where they entered the terminal, and a barricade where they turned again to drive out on the apron of the aircraft loading area. Deputies lifted the barricade for them and the sergeant said to them out the window, "Another ten minutes."

They drove out on the apron, getting the sudden feeling of having the city disappear as they turned toward the vast expanse of signal-picketed landing area. The apron had been cleared of all aircraft but the premier's ship, which stood alone well out in the area, unfamiliar and ominous in the oncoming dusk.

They left the squad car in the angle of the buildings. Above them was the tower, its radar screens turning ceaselessly, and on either side the long wings of the terminal stretched out like peninsulas reaching out into a calm sea, the windows of the upper level behind the balconies growing brighter as twilight deepened.

Smith stood a moment, making the same quick inspection that he had at the auditorium, while the sergeant talked with the captain of deputies who was in charge of the county police detachment.

"Only one area we really need to go over," Smith said. He gestured. "The balcony up there, the part with the open view."

"Yes sir," the captain of deputies said. "The cars with the big guy and his people will swing right around there, and the balcony will look right up the gangplank."

"Well," Smith said smiling, "shall we take a walk up there?"

They went upstairs and walked along the promenade. There were not many people on it. At the end of the promenade, the three men stopped.

"Looks all right," the sergeant said.

"Yes," Smith said. "Except for the girl outside, you noticed her of course. I wonder," he said to the captain of deputies who obviously had not seen the girl at all, "if I might borrow a man for a few moments?"

The captain signaled and they met the new deputy when he came up the escalator. Then they walked the promenade again casually, and Smith went out on the balcony to lean on the railing close to the girl. She wore low heeled shoes, not quite shabby. You saw the shoes, and the golden earrings.

Smith did not look at her as he spoke, quietly.

"I beg your pardon, Miss. But we can't have any of that, you know. If you'd just step back of the glass now, and chat with that officer over there until the airplane leaves, there won't be any fuss about it."

She did not turn. The only sign that she had heard was the tightening of her hands on the big purse she carried.

"Come along now," Smith said, still quietly.

The girl began to weep, silently, but she went.

The sergeant said, "Maybe we'd just better have a look at that purse now."

"Please don't," Smith said.

"But," the sergeant objected, "she may have a weapon in there."

"I'm sure she has," Smith said, smiling. "And if we found it, we'd have to take her into custody. Then we'd have things in the newspapers, and a dreadful international uproar."

"Oh," the captain of deputies said, with sudden comprehension. He said to his officer, "Just stand close to her and look friendly. Don't let her get outside."

"Right," the deputy said. "It won't be bad duty."

It wasn't. She was very pretty, even with the tears. But she had not said anything and she did not say anything now. Below them, on the apron, the first of the official cars had gone by. It was the advance car, carrying the baggage. It pulled up close to the premier's airplane and crewmen opened the baggage hatch. They moved very smartly.

"Confound it," Smith said suddenly. "Those people have my dispatch case. I put it down with the other bags at the auditorium."

"Let's go down and retrieve it," the police sergeant said. "If we don't, those slobs will fly away with it."

"Right," the captain of deputies said.

The three of them went downstairs, walking on the down escalator. They didn't want to waste any time. Outside again, they walked rapidly toward the airplane and the crewmen reaching bags up from the car. Just as they reached the car a crewman took out the black dispatch case, looked at it, then reached up with it.

"Here, here," Smith said. "That's mine, you know."

Two of the premier's security police materialized from the dark area underneath the plane. They stood with their arms folded, almost expressionless.

Smith said to one of them, "Colonel, be good enough to have your boys hand back my bag."

The man he spoke to almost grinned sardonically, but not quite.

"I did not see any identification," he said. It was the first time any of the premier's security guards had spoken.

"Well, get it back," Smith said, annoyed. "I'll show you the identification."

"I'm extremely sorry," the premier's security colonel definitely was sneering now. "The premier's party is on a very close timetable. We do not have time to correct mistakes made by other people at this time."

"Don't be rude," Smith said mildly. "Just get me the case, like a good automaton."

The colonel did not understand the word. Enjoying himself, he said, "When we return to the capital and check out the baggage, if we find one that appears to have been the property of the so-great Department of State of your country, we will return it to your embassy."

"After photographing everything, including the hinges," Smith said.

The premier's security colonel stood with his arms folded, grinning. The captain of deputies whispered something in Smith's ear.

"No, mustn't do that," Smith said. "Not really important. If I hadn't made a point of it, I suppose these chaps would have hurled the thing out of their luggage in a rage."

He shrugged away his annoyance and smiled suddenly at the captain.

"Actually, you know, it means mostly that I'll have to buy a new razor and shaving things."

The captain and the police sergeant both grinned happily.

"Wait until they analyze my after-shave lotion," Smith said. "That'll give their biochemical boys a lovely time."

They had walked away from the airplane now. Sirens rose faintly in the distance. It was the premier's party itself. The sirens grew louder and louder, and in a few minutes the big, black cars drove up fast onto the apron, their sirens sinking to a growl as they stopped. Smith moved still farther away from the airplane and stood with his back to it, with his back to the official party, watching the balconies and the windows. In one, the girl stood with the deputy close beside her. They did not appear to be talking. Behind him, the official party was boarding the aircraft. A flash bulb popped and the premier's security colonel shouted angrily. There were no more flashes. In a very few minutes, there were the final sounds of the hatches closing, and then the engines started.

Smith turned then, looking at his watch.

"Another minute," he said to the captain of deputies and the police sergeant. "Then you're through."

"I'm glad to see them go," the captain said with conviction. "And I'm glad you got here."

"You people had the whole thing beautifully organized," Smith said. "All I could do was walk around a bit. That's always the way, you know. We're spread so thin."

"But we'd have missed the girl," the sergeant said. "Standing up there, she could have pulled out a heater and boom, maybe we're in a war or something."

"Oh, not that bad," Smith said. "Range was much too long for her to do much good. But it would have been a nasty mess."

"What shall we do with her?" the sergeant said. "Take her in now?"

"No," Smith said. "Even if you took her in for something inconsequential like walking on the grass, she might talk to a reporter. If it's all right with both of you, I'll take her along with me and perhaps chat a bit."

"Yes, sir, perfectly all right," the captain of deputies said gratefully. "That will leave everything in the clear, officially."

The sergeant said, "Would you like to take a prowl car back, sir?"

"No thanks," Smith said. "Have to go downtown and make a report and then scurry right back to central division. Probably have another job for me by this time. Now don't you forget my car, parked down there by the roadside. Driver's probably lonesome."

"It's been a real pleasure," the sergeant said. "Come back when you have a few days. The fishing's pretty good around here."

"That would be fine," Smith said, smiling. The deputy was bringing the girl down now. They shook hands all around, the girl standing calmly at one side. Out in the darkness the engines of the premier's plane roared, the roar standing still for a moment, then moving, gathering speed and then quite suddenly going fast and fading, out and up over the city, over the miles of countryside dotted with other bright cities and then the ocean and another world, the premier's world.

Smith and the girl walked through the terminal lobby, his hand politely on her arm, then outside again and into a cab.

Once in it, she said in a soft, bitterly disappointed voice, "Why didn't you let me do it? The world would really be better without him."

"Possibly," Smith said, soothingly. "But you wouldn't have done a very good job. Emotional people rarely do, you know."

"I can't help but be emotional," she said. "My father died in one of his labor camps." Then she said, "How could you tell about me, just by walking past me there?"

"It takes one to know one," Smith said, sitting very much alone in a dark corner of the seat. "I had seven years of their best, myself. Had the luck to live through it, though it didn't seem good luck at the time."

"And now you're with the American State Department." The girl did not want to believe in his hardship.

"Only for today," Smith said. "I made a very good appearance as an emergency chauffeur. The Secret Service chap, the real one, was quite impressed."

She said, her tone suddenly different, "Did you—"

"Of course not," Smith said. "That accommodating police fellow will find the car, with my erstwhile employer knocking about in the trunk. Hardly hurt a bit."

They were back in the center of the city now. At a stoplight, Smith knocked on the glass and told the driver to stop. He got out and said, "Take the young lady wherever she wishes to go."

"Wait," the girl said. "If you did what you said, why did you stop me? Why did you let them go?"

"Mustn't embarrass our friends," Smith said. "No international incidents, no emotional assassinations, no uproar. No nothing. Forgive me for sounding critical, but one does not plan such a thing in a few days. Nor," he said, "a few years."

"But—"

"The dispatch case they insisted on taking along," Smith said. "So characteristic of them, so brutally characteristic to seize even so trivial an opportunity for demonstrating their superiority."

The girl looked at him, bewilderment still remaining on her face.

Smith said, "So they had to demonstrate what they are, and take my case. And now, out over the middle of the ocean, there will be no international incidents, no emotional assassinations, no nothing. Nothing."

She said, almost in a whisper, "But what if they had not taken the case?"

Smith's smile was very gentle.

"Then they wouldn't have been the people we know they are, would they?" he said, and closed the taxi door.

No question at all in my mind that Homer's urge to do his sister in was justified. For one thing, her name was Samantha.

A LITTLE SORORICIDE
BY RICHARD DEMING

Samantha Withers wasn't reticent about showing her feelings. "Can't you remember anything, you idiot?"

Homer Withers was a small, round, mild-appearing man, and he seemed to shrink even smaller under the blast from his spinster sister. Though she routinely treated him as though he were a mental incompetent, it never occurred to him to fight back. For too many years he'd been conditioned to her domineering manner.

Samantha Withers was a head taller than Homer, thirty pounds heavier, and as muscular as a man. Though she'd never actually offered him physical violence, she often seemed on the verge of striking him, and the thought made Homer cringe. He was quite certain he'd be defenseless against her in a physical battle.

"The policy won't lapse," he said in a placating tone. "The agent sends in the premium money when it's due, you see, and I simply repay him. I'll mail the check right after dinner."

"You'll mail it right now, if you expect any dinner," Samantha snapped. "And don't forget it's the mailbox you're heading for."

"I'm entirely capable of mailing a letter without detailed instructions," Homer said with unaccustomed asperity.

125

Then he wilted under the glitter of his older sister's eyes.

He rarely rebelled enough to give her a tart reply, and invariably wished he hadn't on the infrequent occasions he drummed up enough courage to do it. For usually she made his life miserable for days afterward.

He scooted out before she could open up her heavy artillery, but she managed to get in a parting shot. As he went down the porch steps, she shouted through the screen door, "Look both ways when you cross the street, stupid. Coming back I don't care. Once the premium's mailed, you can . . ."

Homer had heard it before—*you can drop dead, for all I care.* Those were the words, he knew, which he didn't wait to hear.

Homer sighed. She probably *would* be glad if he were dead. Why did he put up with her constant carping? Discouragedly he answered the mental question as soon as he asked it. He put up with it because of unbreakable habit.

As long as he could remember his sister had dominated him, even while their parents still lived. Since their death fifteen years earlier, the domination had gradually increased until at middle age her grip on his whole life was an enveloping, suffocating thing which had squeezed from him the last ounce of resistance and the last drops of individuality.

"It's not right for a person who's so carefully avoided marriage to be the most henpecked man in town," he thought, automatically following Samantha's instructions to look both ways before crossing the street.

He reached the other side and walked vaguely past the mailbox in the direction of the drug store; he wondered what it would be like to die and be free of Samantha. He almost hoped that her repeated suggestion would come true when suddenly a new thought occurred to him. Wouldn't it be nice if Samantha died?

This thought was so pleasant, he lost himself in it and

nearly passed the drug store. He halted to consider what Samantha had sent him for, found his mind a blank and finally grew conscious of the envelope in his hand. Shamefacedly he retraced his way to the mailbox, dropped the letter and recrossed the street.

The dream persisted, however. As he strolled back up the street, he envisioned how pleasant it would be to return from work each evening to an empty and silent house, one where he could smoke in the front room, sit around without a necktie, or even in his undershirt if he chose. He could even have beer in the refrigerator.

He completely lost himself in the reverie. He had mentally gone through the ordeal of Samantha's funeral, had completed the necessary period of mourning, and was busily converting her bedroom into a masculine den when he opened the front door. The daydream was so real, he let out a gasp when he saw Samantha standing there.

Samantha snapped at him, "What's the matter with you? You look like you're going to throw up."

"I . . . I don't feel too well," he said.

He went upstairs to wash, jolted from his dream world into full awareness of reality. As he examined his pale face in the bathroom mirror, he realized how intolerable that reality was as long as Samantha was alive.

The idea of killing his sister came to him effortlessly and with no sense of shock. His sole emotional reaction was surprise that he'd never thought of it before.

Unfortunately Homer Withers discovered there was a vast gap between reaching a decision to kill and carrying out the decision. He didn't discover this at once, however. That evening, as he prepared the hot chocolate he made for his sister each night, his plans took shape with remarkable ease.

Any plan as violent as strangulation was out of the question for the simple reason that Samantha was larger and

127

stronger than he. Shooting or stabbing were ruled out because he had no desire to hang for Samantha's murder. He toyed with the idea of staging a fatal accident but discarded it for the same reason he had discarded strangulation. He wasn't at all sure that if he attempted to push Samantha out of a window or down a flight of stairs, he wouldn't end up being the victim.

By the process of elimination he arrived at poison as the most practical means. A few minutes after he had carried Samantha's hot chocolate into the front room, he knew how to administer the poison. He watched as she took a sip to test the temperature, then set the saucer on the floor and poured some of the chocolate into it from the cup.

Roger, Samantha's cat, dropped from the window ledge, stalked majestically over to the saucer and sniffed at it. Roger licked tentatively, then sat down to wait for it to cool.

Homer decided that his sister took her chocolate so heavily sweetened it ought to disguise the taste of nearly any poison. It also occurred to him that her habit of sharing it with the cat presented a complication, but not a serious complication. Samantha liked her chocolate hot, while Roger preferred his cool; her cup always was empty before the cat lapped from the saucer.

He could simply wait until his sister had drunk the poison and died, then take the saucer away from Roger.

The next day Homer used his lunch hour for a visit to the public library, where he did some research on poisons. He decided on potassium cyanide for two reasons: it was quick and sure, and the death symptoms resembled those of a heart attack.

Up to this point his planning had proceeded without a hitch. He didn't run into a snag until he attempted to obtain the poison.

In a vague way Homer supposed that the law established certain restrictions against the indiscriminate sale of poi sons. He was quite prepared to be questioned about its intended use when he bought his cyanide, and he expected to be asked to sign a poison register of some kind. For this reason he went to a downtown drug store where he was unknown, intending to give a fictitious name.

However, he wasn't prepared to encounter a blank wall.

The druggist, an affable middle-aged man, chuckled indulgently when Homer told him in a diffident voice that he would like some potassium cyanide to use as a rat poison.

"You can't buy cyanide without a doctor's prescription, mister," he said. "You can't buy any poison without a prescription. It's a federal law. Here's what you want for rats."

He produced a small, round tin labelled: *Rat Poison*.

Homer looked at it doubtfully. "Do I need a prescription for this too?"

The druggist shook his head with a smile. "You only need a prescription for poisonous drugs which might be taken internally by a human."

"Mightn't this be taken by a human?"

The druggist shrugged. "Sure. Might even kill him. But chances are he'd throw it up. Rat poison contains white phosphorus, which is a deadly poison, but difficult to keep down. It works on rats because they don't know how to vomit. Anyway, the main reason for the federal law is to prevent murders. I guess they figure a suicide would find some way to kill himself even if he couldn't get poison. You might commit suicide with this, if you managed to keep it down, but you'd have a hard time poisoning anybody on the sly. The first sip would burn so bad, they'd spit it out without swallowing."

"I see," Homer said. "How much?"

As he left the store with the small tin in his pocket, he felt thankful that the druggist had been so informative. The thought of Samantha tasting her hot chocolate, spit-

129

ting it out and realizing he had meant to kill her, sent him into a cold sweat. She would be quite capable of forcing *him* to drink it.

A block from the drug store he took the tin from his pocket, looked at it ruefully and rolled it into a sewer opening.

Not being a very resourceful person, this incident brought Homer's murder plan to a dead stop. Aside from purchasing it in a drug store, he hadn't the faintest idea of how to obtain poison. Murder remained in his mind, but it ceased to be an active plan. He relapsed into his dream world, and except that he had a new fantasy to entertain him, his life went on much as it had before he ever thought of murder.

For twenty-five years Homer had held the title of "chief clerk" at the law firm of Marrow and Fanner, a designation which implied more prestige than the job actually involved. He was chief clerk because he was the only clerk; his real status was that of an exalted office boy.

Five days a week he did routine office work for the law partners, each Friday faithfully brought home his pay and handed over half of it to Samantha. What was left barely covered his expenses, including carfare and personal needs and the monthly insurance premium.

On the surface this routine continued, but secretly Homer began to live an entirely different life. By a sort of schizophrenic process he succeeded in imagining, whenever he was away from home, that the murder was an accomplished fact and that he now lived in carefree isolation. Riding the streetcar to and from work, he would plan how he meant to convert Samantha's old room into a den, would mentally frame newspaper ads for a cleaning woman to "come in" once a week, and would wrestle with the problem of what he ought to prepare for dinner that night.

However, he carefully avoided losing himself in the fantasy as completely as he had the evening Samantha's murder first occurred to him, for he had no desire to repeat the experience of being frightened into a near faint by seeing his sister's ghost. Each evening, just as he reached the porch steps, he automatically returned to reality in time to greet his sister without surprise. The fantasy would then take a slight twist; instead of the murder being *fait accompli*, it would become a deed planned for the next day.

But, of course, the next day never arrived.

It was within Homer's capacity to live in reasonable contentment with this fluctuating dream for years without taking any positive action and he probably would have if Samantha herself hadn't unsuspectingly furnished the impetus necessary to jar him into action.

Samantha developed a cold accompanied by a hacking cough which required the services of the family doctor. By the time Samantha let him go, it was past ten P.M. The local drug store was closed when Homer arrived with the prescriptions. The other two drug stores also were closed.

Homer didn't work on Saturday and he went out again with the prescriptions immediately after breakfast. Idly he looked them over.

The doctor had written both before tearing them from the prescription pad, then had ripped them off together so that they were still attached to each other by the glued top edge. Apparently he had flipped one sheet too many after writing the first, for there was a blank prescription sheet between them.

The top one was a prescription for some kind of nose drops. The bottom read:

> Tab. codeine $\overline{\overline{\text{XXX}}}$ TT ½ gr.
> Sig. one tab. Q 3 H.

Though he was unacquainted with pharmaceutical shorthand, Homer recognized the word "codeine" from his research on poisons. He couldn't recall whether or not it was a dangerous drug, but he did remember that it was some kind of opiate. Simultaneously it dawned on him that he had a blank prescription sheet, and with the original as a model, it would be a simple matter to forge a duplicate.

Instead of stopping at the drug store, he walked on two blocks to a branch public library, drew out a textbook of *materia medica* and retired with it to the reading room.

He discovered that one of the primary uses of codeine was to lessen coughing, which explained why the prescription had been written. He also learned that it was a compound of morphine and was one of the active alkaloids of opium. It was listed as a safer drug than morphine, and he searched every indexed reference to the drug without finding an indication of how much constituted a fatal dose, or even any indication that it was a dangerous poison.

However, he was certain it would be fatal in a large enough dose, for it was included under the general heading of "Brain and Spinal Cord Depressants," along with opium, morphine and the illegal drug, heroin. Rechecking the prescription, he deduced that the figure "XXX" probably meant thirty tablets. At a half grain each, this came to fifteen grains, certainly enough of any opiate to kill a person.

Satisfied that he had a poison which would work, he took out his fountain pen and carefully duplicated the prescription on the blank sheet. He forged a reasonable facsimile of the doctor's signature, not taking too great pains with it because he knew it would not be subjected to the same scrutiny a bank might give a check. The office heading and the fact that the terminology was authentic were enough to make it acceptable to the average druggist.

He walked six blocks to another drug store where he was unknown to get the forged prescription filled. Then he returned to his own neighborhood drug store to have the two filled which the doctor had written.

When he finally got home, he received a sound tongue lashing from his sister for taking so long, but he accepted it stoically. For consolation he fingered the extra bottle in his pocket.

For the first time in weeks Homer didn't retreat into his world of fantasy. For now he had the reality of definitely planned action to replace his dreams. He was in such a state of anticipation all week end he could hardly wait to get home Monday evening.

If there had been any lingering qualms in Homer Withers' mind about committing sororicide, they were extinguished by Samantha's reception. Her normal unpleasantness had been aggravated by her cold until she was impossible.

She greeted him with an ominous, "I suppose you forgot to mail the insurance premium again."

Time had on more than one occasion flitted by Homer unnoticed—it was a genuine surprise to him that a full month had passed since he had belatedly mailed the last premium.

Samantha launched into such a blistering attack on his mental shortcomings, he retreated headlong up the stairs in the middle of her tirade. His hands shook as he wrote the check. He was downstairs again and on his way to the mailbox before his sister could get her second wind.

The incident spoiled all chance of their last evening together being a pleasant one. Dinner was accompanied by a monologue by Samantha on her favorite subject: why didn't Homer do her the favor of dropping dead? Afterward, as they sat in the front room, she froze him with a silence so forbidding, he was afraid to open his mouth.

It was a relief when she finally indicated it was near bedtime by saying, "I'll have my chocolate now, if you think you have sense enough to put it together properly."

Homer had the hot chocolate all made and poured into a cup before he realized his oversight. It would have been better to have crushed the thirty codeine tablets into a powder so that they would dissolve more easily. He swore mildly at his chronic forgetfulness.

133

Pouring some of the tablets into his hand, he stared at them blankly for a moment. Then he got down an empty cup and began crushing them one at a time with a spoon.

It was a slow process; he was but two-thirds finished when Samantha's impatient voice called from the front room, "What are you doing, dreamer? Staring off into space?"

His heart hammering in fear she would enter the kitchen, he called back, "It's almost ready, Samantha. Just one more minute."

As rapidly as possible he crushed the remaining tablets, scraped the powder into the chocolate and stirred it vigorously. When it was completely dissolved, he touched his tongue to the solution and was panic stricken to find it faintly bitter. He shoveled in two extra teaspoonsful of sugar, stirred it and tasted it again. It now tasted normal.

He carried the cup and saucer out to Samantha who, after accepting it with a grunt, went through her usual ritual of pouring some into the saucer for Roger.

Immediately the cat dropped from his favorite spot on the window ledge, padded to the saucer and tentatively explored the chocolate's temperature. Then, instead of sitting back to wait for it to cool, he lapped the dish clean.

Homer stared in horror, realizing that the time consumed in crushing the codeine tablets had allowed the chocolate to cool sufficiently to please the cat. Homer watched, fascinated, as the animal licked its whiskers, stretched and rubbed itself against Samantha's calf.

Samantha took a sip from the cup, and exploded.

"You idiot!" she screamed at Homer. "Can't you do anything right? This chocolate is merely luke-warm!"

Homer gulped, his eyes on Roger. Roger looked up at him.

"Take it back to the kitchen." Samantha ordered. "Heat it up. You know I want *hot* chocolate."

Homer took the cup and carried it to the kitchen. Dumping the contents into a sauce pan, he turned the gas on full. Just before it boiled he removed the pan from the flame, poured the chocolate back in the cup. He got back to Samantha just as fast as he could.

For once Homer did an efficient job. Too efficient. The chocolate was too hot to drink. After sampling it by taking the barest sip, Samantha set the cup aside to let it cool.

As Homer watched the cat in an agony of apprehension, precious minutes dragged by. He knew he could never get Samantha to pick up the cup.

Roger was back on the ledge, purring, begging, Homer felt sure, for more chocolate. If Roger would just die quietly there, Samantha would never know.

Homer took a deep breath as Samantha finally raised the cup to her lips. She paused, said in an impatient voice, "Oh, all right, Roger, you may have a drop more."

The cat sprung off the window ledge, wobbled on his feet, looked up once more at Homer. The animal took a step toward the saucer, and suddenly his front legs collapsed.

Samantha stared at Roger in puzzlement, and Homer watched in terror, as the cat struggled to his feet, took another aimless step and fell over on his side. His eyes rolled and his breathing began to grow heavy.

Samantha glanced from the cat to her brother. Her eyes narrowed, and she said, "You drink my chocolate this evening, Homer."

Homer gibbered an unintelligible refusal. Roger's heavy breathing stopped.

"You actually meant to kill me, didn't you?" she said in a tone of soft satisfaction.

Homer gazed at her without immediate understanding. She added gently, "My dear brother, two can play at that game."

He understood her sudden air of satisfaction then. His act had given her the moral excuse she needed to turn her

135

often-expressed hope into reality, and Homer knew he was lost. He had no idea of where to obtain more poison, and no murder plan aside from poison.

But Samantha was different. She was efficient. She would be able to devise any number of alternate plans.

Any of which would work.

The whole matter of a criminal returning to the scene of his crime defies analysis. Be that as it may, the transportation companies will continue to be pleased by restless criminals. In our tale, it is plain that the return to the scene was made in that spirit of arrogance which truly distinguishes man from the lower forms of life.

THE MAN WHO GOT AWAY WITH IT
BY LAWRENCE TREAT

When he riffled through the batch of insurance claims that his secretary had left on his desk, he stopped at the big one—$100,000. He stared at the figures for maybe half a minute, thinking that with that amount somebody was rich. Then, still musing, he glanced at the name of the beneficiary, and he started. Mrs. Marvin Seeley.

Fran.

He swung around in his chair and stared at his reflection in the glass door of the bookcase. He saw a big, graying man, heavy in the face, with a short, broad nose and a neat mustache. There was no link between this individual—Hugh Bannerman, head of the claims department—and a bank teller wanted for embezzlement and murder. After twenty-five years, how could there be? And yet—

To see her again, to take the gamble and face her. Did he dare? His spine tingled, and his blood hummed through his veins with excitement.

She'd been a slender flame of a girl, young and lovely, with a dowry that made her even more desirable. But you need money to get money, and so he wooed her on bank funds. In their secret, lovers' world, he was Blinky and she

137

was Winky, and she was as good as hooked. He figured that after they were married, after he confessed what he'd done for love of her, she'd replace every cent.

The scheme was fool-proof, for banks don't prosecute when you make restitution, and he had a whole year before the auditors could catch up with him. And his plans would have worked, too, if her brother, Mike, hadn't stuck his nose in. Mike was assistant cashier, and Mike had always had it in for him.

Bannerman scowled, remembering the evening Mike had accused him. Pretending a forthright honesty, when he was really out for blood.

"Twenty thousand dollars," Mike said. "I thought I'd better tell you here, in front of Fran, before I report it to the bank. In case you have an explanation."

Bannerman felt the gun in his pocket. He carried it in those days, just in case, and it gave him the courage to brazen this out.

"What's twenty thousand to you and Fran? You have it. You can get me out of this. For friendship, for love—"

Fran let out a little cry. "How can you!" she exclaimed. And Mike said contemptuously, "Why, you cheap fraud!"

That was when he took out the gun and leveled it at Mike. "Say that again," he remarked quietly. "If you have the nerve."

Fran screamed, "No—don't!" She tried to grab the gun, and that gave him an added excuse to fire. What right did Mike have to go on living, when he'd pulled a trick like that?

The bank teller disappeared immediately after the shooting, and he left no trace. With a little luck and a little police bungling, a smart man doesn't get caught. Plastic surgery, a careful change of voice and gesture, and the personality of Hugh Bannerman had emerged.

Smiling, he divided the stack of papers in front of him into two piles, one on each side of the desk. He was still uncertain as he left the Seeley file in the center. Then he rang for his secretary.

"You can give these to Perkins," he said, pointing. "The rest are for Davis."

"And that one?"

He stared at the Seeley claim, and his words seemed to come from other lips. "A hundred thousand is a lot of money," he said. "I think I'll handle that one myself."

He nodded casually, reached for the phone and called her. Just one more claim to close out, just one more routine appointment, in which to persuade a beneficiary to leave her money with the company, at interest.

He heard the buzz of the phone, and her answering voice. He recognized it at once, the queer little lilt of excitement in it, as if she expected something wonderful to happen at any moment. No, her voice hadn't changed. But his had with much practice, of course.

He made the appointment for the next morning, ten o'clock at her house.

He had no fears. In the past five years, since he had had this job, he'd occasionally run into former friends. They hadn't recognized him; they suspected nothing when he brought the conversation around to Fran. They told him her married name, and they discussed the long-ago story of the bank teller who had shot and killed her brother, and was probably dead.

Bannerman's work brought him in contact with the police, too. He'd been in and out of precinct houses and had even sat down with a police inspector. So he knew his identity was safe.

He thought about her on and off, all day. When he saw her, he'd say, "We have friends in common. They've told me a lot about you. I feel as if I knew you."

He'd be polite. He'd say, "You're a brave woman, Mrs. Seeley, to have built up a new life after that early tragedy." Then he'd smile and add thoughtfully, "Because you must

139

always wonder whether, if you hadn't been foolish enough to grab the gun, your brother would have been shot."

That would be a nice touch, to plant the doubt in her conscience again, to make *her* feel guilty. And it would be added protection for himself, too. He began looking forward to the appointment. It was destiny; it was adventure. He was only forty-seven, with good years ahead of him. Anything could happen.

He slept well that night. He didn't dream, and he awoke sound and fit. He had his usual drugstore breakfast, drove to the office and parked in the company lot. He went over his mail, sorted it and dictated a few routine letters. Then he went downstairs and drove to the suburbs for his first appointment. With Mrs. Marvin Seeley.

He judged the house to be worth about fifty thousand dollars. It was in good taste, as Fran's was bound to be. The doors of the three-car garage were open, and he could see a convertible in it. Wealthy, he told himself, but not flaunting it. Probably one servant, and maybe a part-time maid. Fran might open the door herself. But he was prepared for that, too.

He'd see a plump, middle-aged widow, and she'd see a stranger, Hugh Bannerman, from the insurance company.

He rang the bell, and waited eagerly. He heard a quick, light step, and the door swung open. As if in a dream, he saw that she was young and lovely and unchanged. Her blue eyes still sparkled with the marvel of the world, her blonde hair still shone and she had the same young, slim litheness. For a fleeting moment he was stunned, unable to believe in the miracle of her youth.

"Winky!" he exclaimed.

She looked at him in astonishment. Then, mocking him, enjoying the joke, she glanced behind her and said in that familiar voice, "Mother, there's somebody here who wants Winky. Who would that be?"

With a gasp, he lurched back. His foot missed the step and his ankle twisted and folded up underneath him. He felt a stab of pain as he went sprawling headlong.

He was unconscious for only a few seconds, but he kept his eyes closed, thinking hard, telling himself the blunder wasn't fatal, he'd get out of it somehow.

He heard footsteps come from the house, and someone stooped down beside him, but he didn't look at Fran Seeley yet. In an inspired flash, he decided to claim the girl had misunderstood him. Then he'd leave, and let Perkins come tomorrow and settle the insurance.

Winky—Seeley—the sounds were close enough. And he could certainly handle a couple of women who were upset and flustered over an accident. He'd done it often enough, in the course of his work.

Confidently, proud of his quick wits and supremely sure of himself, he opened his eyes.

Fran was older. She was a bit heavier and her face, soft and still beautiful in maturity, was compassionate, as if she had suffered deeply. Her eyes glowed with the tenderness of her sympathy, and she was evidently concerned with nothing but his pain. Which, as far as he was concerned, was all to the good. The mishap was working out in his favor.

"I'm afraid I gave my ankle a bad wrench," he said shakily.

"I'm terribly sorry. Do you think you could stand up? If you lean on us, Ethel and I can help you inside."

"I'll try," he said.

He raised himself awkwardly and rested his weight on the shoulders of the two women. Panting with the effort, he hobbled into the house and sank heavily into the deep cushions of a couch near the fireplace, where the light was subdued. His ankle gave him another twinge, and the warm, sumptuous room seemed to waver in front of his eyes.

"I hate to bother you," he said. "But if you'll call a doctor, he'll strap up my ankle and I'll be able to take care of myself."

"What you need right now," Fran said energetically, "is a drink of whisky. You're white as a sheet." She turned, showing her clear, molded profile. "Would you get the decanter, Ethel? And a glass from the kitchen?"

"Of course, Mother."

The girl left, and Fran leaned forward. She appeared to be undergoing a struggle, and she studied him in rapt concentration.

He jerked away, sharply aware that this was the first time anyone had had a reason to study him so closely. Never before had his disguise been put to the test.

"I hope," he said lightly, pretending amusement, "that your daughter doesn't get mixed up on the drinks the way she did on the name."

Fran didn't answer. If only he could get up, run, push her out of the way, escape. Anything except sit here and wait, exposed to her intense scrutiny.

He put his hand to his face, to screen it. He massaged his cheek briskly, and dropped his hand flat. He shouldn't have done it that way. Not with his old gesture, so familiar to her.

"That drink," he said, with growing panic. "I need it. What's taking so long?"

Then, finally, she spoke. "Blinky," she said, slowly and with distaste.

By way of introduction, may I present this bit of folklore. Among a small tribe of peace-loving cannibals, there was one more ingenious than all the rest. Not satisfied to merely eat the white man, he learned his ways. And so during one bountiful harvest season, he reduced his village's food supply to ashes, and placed the ashes in small jars labelled Instant People.

SECRET RECIPE

BY CHARLES MERGENDAHL

"You're sure?" Simon said into the phone. "Nothing you want me to pick up on the way home?"

"No, everything's fine, dear. Polly's gone off with little Susie Steele, and I've planned a very exotic dinner—just like you suggested."

"Well, it is important," Simon said.

"Of course it is, dear." Sheila's voice sounded calm, almost too calm, and for a moment he felt serious doubts.

He shook them off. "Well," he said, "we'll be there in a few minutes."

"I'll be waiting."

"And Mr. Brevoort likes his martinis very dry."

"I'll place the vermouth bottle quite near the gin, then snatch it right away again." She laughed, almost gaily.

He said good-bye and hung up, then sat there a moment, still hearing the gay laughter. "Not tonight," he prayed. "Please, God, *not tonight.*"

His secretary appeared in the office doorway. Her liquid eyes looked at his nervous hands, his teeth biting down on a lower lip. "It's five o'clock, Simon."

"Oh . . . Thanks, Ida."

"Mrs. Brevoort arrived just a minute ago. I told Mr. Brevoort you'd pick them both up on your way out."

"Yes, that's fine."

Ida hesitated, then moved into the office and closed the door behind her. "Simon?"

"Yes?"

"You think it's wise?"

"What else can I *do?*" He waved his hands helplessly. "The promotion comes up next Tuesday, and you know Brevoort—he likes to visit a man's home before making any real decision about him. So I've *got* to have them to dinner, and there's just no way out at all."

"Poor Simon." Ida sat on the edge of the desk and caressed the little brown hairs at the back of his neck. "I keep remembering," she said softly, "those six months when your wife was away."

"Yeah." He laughed ironically. "Away."

"She *might* go away again," said Ida.

"She *will,*" he said.

Silence for a moment, while Ida's fingers stroked his neck. Then suddenly she bent and kissed him, her familiar lips moving roughly against his own. "Poor Simon," and then matter-of-factly, "well, it's five after five." She slipped off the desk and straightened her blouse. She said, "Don't worry, it'll work out," and left the office.

"It'll work out," Simon said. He rose, wiped off Ida's lipstick, and began clearing his desk. Beyond the door one of the stenographers giggled, and he sat again and put his hands over his ears. "*Not tonight.* Please, Sheila, don't do anything wrong *tonight.*" He pulled upright and straightened his tie. He took a deep breath, put on his hat, smiled reassuringly at Ida as he passed her, and strode down the hallway toward the office of Mr. Walter Brevoort, President.

The October leaves fell like huge brown snowflakes as he drove through the early evening streets toward his home in Brentwood. Behind him in the rear seat, the Brevoorts sat apart from each other, staring out opposite windows. Mr. Brevoort was squat and bald with a fringe of white hair above his ears. His wife was plump and jolly.

Mrs. Brevoort said, "You have a daughter, don't you, Simon?"

"Yes. Polly, twelve, and she's quite a beautiful child." He laughed, apologizing for his own pride. But Polly was beautiful all the same. Blonde and slender and he loved her terribly. In a domineering way, perhaps; possessively, perhaps. "She's beautiful," he said again.

"Must get it from her mother." Mr. Brevoort chuckled at his own joke, and Simon said that yes, Sheila was attractive, too, and remembered that he had actually thought so once—before she'd been sent away to the sanitarium and returned with her "odd" ways that he'd tried to tolerate and now despised. "She *might* go away," Ida had said, and "She *will*," he had said. And she *would*, too, because that was the way he had planned it. Push her and push her. Exaggerate her idiosyncrasies to Doctor Birnam. Turn Polly against her. Drive her to the breaking point. Make her into a blabbering idiot. But not tonight. "Not tonight," he said aloud.

"What's that, Simon?" Mr. Brevoort asked.

"Nothing. Nothing." And he drove on through the dropping leaves, to the neat white house on the corner beneath the trees.

"Lovely," said Mrs. Brevoort as he helped her out.

He said, "We love our little house," and practically held his breath all the way up the walk, and did not breathe easily again until Sheila opened the door to greet them, and he saw that everything was going to be all right. She was dressed smartly in black, her dark brown hair done up neatly, her words slow and gracious, so that nothing gave her away at all—except perhaps the unusual brightness in her dark eyes, the twisted little smile on her lips when she raised them for his greeting kiss.

145

Mrs. Brevoort said, "What a liveable room!" and Mr. Brevoort slumped his squat body into an upholstered chair and said, "Tell a lot about a man from his home life. A man's life gets upset at home, it's bound to show up in his work."

"Yes, sir," Simon said.

"Bound to."

"Yes, sir."

"Like to meet your daughter, Simon."

"Later," Simon said. "She's off with some friends just now." He looked at Sheila, who was serving the cocktails. "Where'd Polly go, dear?"

"The early movie," Sheila said. "She'll be back by seven."

"Then we *can* meet her," said Mrs. Brevoort.

"She's her father's daughter," said Sheila, and went into the kitchen.

Simon looked after her, frowning.

"Charming," said Mrs. Brevoort.

"Lovely wife," said her husband. "Don't know how you lived without her all those months she was visiting her family."

Simon mumbled something about its having been a difficult time for everyone, downed his own martini, murmured an apology, and went into the kitchen, letting the door swing shut behind him.

Sheila was bent over the stove, stirring the casserole before slipping it into the oven. "Everything all right?" he asked carefully.

"Perfect. Except you're planning to send me back to the sanitarium and take Polly away from me and keep carrying on with that Ida girl."

"Sheila . . ."

"Otherwise everything's fine."

"*Not tonight*, Sheila."

"Last night and last week and last month. But not tonight."

146

"If you'd try to understand—"

"Oh, I do, Simon. I understand perfectly. I'm to play a little game that will help you get a promotion at the office. After that you'll get rid of me and keep Polly for yourself."

"Look, Sheila—"

"And maybe you will get rid of me, but you *won't* get Polly."

"All right," he said. "Not now. Not *now!*"

She turned and smiled a little. Her eyes had become very bright, he thought, like that night months ago, just before the men had come in their white coats. He felt suddenly cold and said, "Anything I can do?"

"Take out the garbage if you like."

"After dinner."

"Now, before it smells up the kitchen."

He stepped on the pedal and drew the pail from the white container. The disposal bag was full, sealed tight.

"Don't open it," she said. "It'll make you sick."

He shrugged, carried the pail out the back door, dumped the bag into the garbage can, then returned to the kitchen.

"Anything else?" he said.

"Just remember what I told you."

"I'm *warning* you, Sheila—" But he stopped then. He could not threaten her now. He should not have threatened her last night either. She was insanely jealous, and he had to handle her very delicately until after the Brevoorts had gone.

He went back to the living room and poured everyone a second martini. The phone rang. It was Mrs. Steele. She wanted to know if Susie were visiting Polly, and if so, to send her right home to dinner. He told her that Polly and Susie had gone to the five o'clock movie, and Mrs. Steele said that was funny because Susie hadn't come home to ask her permission.

"Just a minute." He put down the receiver and called to Sheila. "You're sure Polly went to the movies?"

"Of course I'm sure." Sheila came out of the kitchen and stood there watching him.

"But Mrs. Steele said that was funny—"

"It isn't funny. I don't see what's funny about it." Her eyes were peculiarly bright again. He mumbled something to Mrs. Steele, then hung up and rejoined the Brevoorts. They were talking about a new television series that was a perfect howl, and he agreed, but could not seem to concentrate. He looked out the window and saw that dark had come rather suddenly tonight. He thought that Polly should not be out in the dark. He looked at Sheila, who was talking animatedly to Mrs. Brevoort. He thought her eyes should not be quite so bright, her lips not quite so moist and red. She should not be laughing quite so much.

"Simon."

He started.

"Phil Silvers—"

"Yes, a riot."

"You're not paying attention," Sheila chided.

"I'm sorry. I was thinking about what Mrs. Steele said. I was wondering where Polly's really gone."

"I told you, Simon, I *know* where she's gone."

Her laughter again, as from another room, another world, before she rose and announced that dinner was ready.

Simon sat at the head of the rectangular table with Mrs. Brevoort on his left and Mr. Brevoort on his right. Sheila lit the candles, then went into the kitchen and brought out the casserole in a large copper chafing dish. She lit the little burner in the wrought-iron frame and set the chafing dish over it. "It won't really cook this way," she explained, "but it looks nice, and it does keep it hot."

Simon looked out the window again. Dry leaves brushed against the glass. He clenched his hand under the table. He thought Sheila was talking too much. It was deep dark outside. He heard Mrs. Brevoort give a little exclamation of delight as her plate was served. He heard Mr. Brevoort

say, "Curry . . . Anything curried . . . Love it, love it
. . ." Then his own plate was set before him and he looked
down at it, steaming there in the candlelight.

Mrs. Brevoort had taken a tentative taste. She said,
"Mmm," and "Delicious, but what in the world is it?"

"A secret recipe," Sheila said, "though I have to admit
I've never tried it before."

"A triumph," said Mr. Brevoort.

"Simon?" Sheila said.

"Oh, yes . . . Yes." He tasted the casserole. It was
heavily seasoned, disguising another odd flavor he could
not distinguish. "Not bad," he said. He glanced up and
noticed that Sheila's plate was empty. "Aren't you having
any?"

"I'm not hungry."

"But you *never* miss dinner."

"I know. But tonight I'm just not hungry."

That laughter again, the red moist lips, the bright
gleaming eyes. Outside a slight wind began rustling the
trees, and a child shrieked something in the darkness. He
felt cold again. He wished Polly were home. He wished
tonight were over and the promotion were all set so that
he did not have to pretend with Sheila any longer. He
could get her committed—for good—and he could sell this
house he hated and take Polly with him and go to Ida.

"You're not eating, Simon."

"Yes, it's good. Very good." But he was not hungry. He
had never liked strange foods, and had only insisted on this
exotic dish because of the Brevoorts. He took another tentative mouthful, noticed a long blonde hair on his fork, and
drew it off surreptitiously, thinking idly that it was one of
Polly's of course, because Sheila's hair was a darkish
brown. He was vaguely aware of the trees shaking in the
rising wind. Mr. Brevoort said, "Yes, I will have seconds,
please," and Mrs. Brevoort said, "You've simply *got* to give
me the recipe. Onions and mushrooms and peppers and
curry . . . And I presume the meat was sautéed, but what

is it?" Sheila laughed secretly and he took another bite, and it was then that he found the fingernail. It was small and sharp and curved. It had caught between his teeth, and when he first examined it under the flickering light of the candle, he was not quite sure what it was. Then, when he did understand, it was only with a strange sense of detachment, until he looked up again and found Sheila smiling at him.

"Something the matter, dear?"

"No. Just something I—"

"Don't worry, dear. I *know* where Polly is."

"I know . . . I know." He placed the fingernail carefully on the side of his plate. He stared at it vacantly. "You will *not* get Polly," Sheila had said. "I *know* where she is . . . It's a secret recipe . . . And take out the garbage, but don't open the bag or you'll be sick . . ." Her eyes were too bright. She laughed too much, and deep down she'd always disliked his affection for Polly, and she'd never refused to eat dinner before. She had brown hair and her fingernails were long and red, and had not been cut for days. The wind sighed through the trees. And it was funny, Mrs. Steele had said. And why didn't Polly come home, and why had he been so terribly cold all evening, and why was he dizzy now, his hand trembling beyond control, his body beginning to shake, too, in a horrible spasm that would not stop?

"Chicken?" said Mrs. Brevoort.

"No, not chicken."

"Veal?" said Mr. Brevoort.

"No."

"Lamb?"

"No."

"Pork?"

"No." Sheila was still smiling. "Do you want to guess, Simon? Or did you peek? I bet you peeked when you were taking out the garbage. Simon . . . Simon?"

Simon screamed. He rose and screamed again and then

again. He rushed to the door and screamed into the windy night. "Polly! . . . Polly!" He ran back through the house and out the kitchen door, down the steps to the garbage can. He raised the lid, put out a hand, then snatched it back again and let the lid drop with a clatter. He was violently ill, leaning shuddering against the porch while the leaves whirled up around him. "Oh, God," he sobbed, "Oh, my God, my God!" He staggered back up the steps and into the living room. The Brevoorts were leaving, hurriedly, talking of getting a taxi. He hardly saw them. He was still screaming. The door closed and Sheila turned to him and said, "Now see what you've done, Simon? They don't think we have a happy home at all."

He kept on screaming. "You're *crazy* . . . *Really crazy* . . . And this time you're going away for *good*," and "Oh, my God, oh, my God," as he stumbled to the phone and dialed Doctor Birnam with trembling hands. His words were nearly incoherent. "I never *realized* . . . Something terrible . . . Bring the ambulance . . . Bring a strait jacket . . . Oh, my God!" while he laid his head against the receiver and shuddered and sobbed hysterically and could not stop.

"Terrible," Doctor Birnam said, after the white-coated men had taken the protesting figure through the doorway. "Simply terrible."

"But *why?*" sobbing uncontrollably. "*Why . . . Why?*"

The doctor shrugged. "These things are hard to explain. If you'd only seen it coming—but you couldn't possibly have guessed."

"And tonight, too—of all times—of all times when tonight was so *important*."

"I just don't—know." The doctor put out a reassuring hand, then moved slowly toward the door. "Of course, we'll do everything we can. A strait jacket for a while, and then treatment—I just don't know." He opened the front door and said, "Well now, how's my favorite little girl?"

"I'm fine," Polly said as she stepped inside. The doctor left and Polly said, "Susie's going to get the dickens for going to the movies without telling her mother." She looked around and said, "Where's Daddy?"

"Gone away."

"For a long time?"

"I'm afraid so."

"He said *you* were going away. But I'm glad it's him instead of you."

"Are you, darling?" She dried her tears. "Are you?"

Polly nodded, and said, "I'm famished."

"So am I."

They sat at the table and she served them both a large portion of the casserole, still hot over the little burner.

"It's good," Polly said. "What is it?"

"Guess."

"Chicken?"

"No, not chicken."

"Veal?"

"No."

"Then what?"

"A secret recipe," she said, and smiled fondly, faintly at her daughter.

*It is generally agreed that it takes all kinds to make a world
—an imperfect world, that is. This tale of mounting un-
comfortableness contributes a singularly unattractive vil-
lain, a Mr. Heavenridge. Anent Mr. Heavenridge, it is my
humane feeling that they also serve who smell quite badly.*

DADDY-O
BY DAVID ALEXANDER

Marcia had run away again. That was the
short, sad history of her younger sister's life, Helen
thought bitterly. Marcia always ran away. She could never
face up to unpleasantness, to any reality. When something
like this occurred, Marcia ran. She had many means of escape. The sleeping pill Marcia had just taken was one;
alcohol, another. But mostly Marcia escaped through
some queer mental process of her own, into a world of fantasy where everything was exactly as she wanted it to be.
She could never accept things as they were.

Helen had warned her, of course, about Paul Carter.
Paul was the latest of many young men in Marcia's life.
Helen had warned her sister about most of them, but
Marcia would never listen. Never listening was another
method that Marcia employed to run away from the reali-
ties of existence. Paul was a nice enough young man in his
weak-chinned way, Helen supposed. He was pleasant of
manner, vacuously good-looking, well-dressed, financially
secure. But he was married and he was the father of two
children. What was worse, he was married to the daughter of Mr. Enright, who owned the firm where Marcia
had been employed as a secretary. As Paul Carter's secre-

tary, in fact. Paul's father-in-law had made him vice-president of the Enright Advertising Agency.

Helen felt sure that the affair had been none of Paul's doing. Marcia had probably thrown herself at young Carter. When Marcia had quit her job, a well-paying job, because her relations with Paul had become too noticeable, she had been sure that Carter would divorce his wife, sacrifice his career and marry her. Of course, that hadn't worked out any more than Marcia's other fantasies had. Tonight Paul had come to the apartment to tell Marcia he couldn't see her any more, that stories had got back to his wife and his father-in-law. It must have required an unusual amount of courage on his part to do that. Paul, like Marcia, had a way of running away from issues instead of facing them.

Helen shivered and hugged the dressing robe tight around her slim body as she thought of the horrible scene that had ensued. She had been working on an illustration for a fashion magazine in her bedroom, which also served as her studio. Through the closed door, she had heard Marcia screaming hysterical imprecations at Paul. She had thought of the living room window that opened on an areaway, the possibility of the neighbors hearing what was going on, and had rushed to close it. That was when Marcia had smashed the vase over Paul's head. It was a heavy vase, but the blow was so hard that it had been broken into a dozen pieces. The fragments of pottery still made an unsightly litter on the floor. Paul had slumped from his chair and had lain there on the floor, terribly motionless, his face drained of color, blood seeping slowly and insidiously from the cut on his head. For an awful moment, Helen had thought he was dead. Of course, Marcia had run away, had run to her own bedroom and locked the door. Helen had bathed and dressed Paul's wound and then he left the apartment, still very unsteady on his feet. Helen glanced at the clock. That was more than half an hour ago, she thought. I hope he's all right. I hope he had sense enough to find a doctor. I hope he has some believable explanation for his split scalp when he gets home.

Helen noticed that the living room window was still open, that the shade had not been lowered. The thing had happened with such sickening suddenness, that she had forgotten her reason for having come into the living room. Oh well, she thought, the apartment across the areaway is dark. The apartment was usually dark. It was occupied by a grossly fat old man who apparently lived alone. Helen had encountered him in the hall a time or two.

It was a large apartment for an old man to live in alone, Helen thought, trying consciously to keep her mind from the violent incident that had just occurred. The layout, she knew, was the same as that of the flat she and Marcia occupied. The building was a huge old graystone New York apartment house, off upper Broadway, once a good neighborhood that was going into dry rot from neglect. The streets were filled with brown-faced youths who wore leather jackets. Their eyes were hard beyond their years. Helen was frightened by them. She did not like coming home alone, late at night. She was frightened for Marcia, too. Marcia often stayed out very late. But their apartment was large and the rent was reasonable. There were two bedrooms. When Marcia had come to New York she had demanded a bedroom of her own, saying she was nervous and slept poorly at best. Helen's own bedroom had a north light and was therefore also able to serve as a studio. Helen made her living as an illustrator, for fashion magazines, and she worked at home.

Helen glanced at the clock again. It was after midnight now. I must go to bed, she thought, even if I can't sleep. She began to switch off lamps in the living room. She caught a glimpse of herself in a wall mirror. She thought she could see the beginning of little crow's tracks around her eyes and mouth. I'm twenty-eight, she thought. That makes me a spinster, I guess. She had devoted the best of her youth to taking care of her younger sister.

She was about to turn off the last of the lamps, when there was a sudden, loud knocking at the door to the apartment.

She stood frozen for a moment, paralyzed with fear. It's the police, she thought. Paul must have collapsed from loss of blood and somehow they've found out what happened here.

There was a little peephole in the door, covered by a hinged metal lid. Helen raised the little lid. The fat old man who lived in the front apartment was standing at the door, thudding down repeatedly with the small brass knocker.

Helen said through the small peephole, "Please stop that knocking! My sister's asleep. What is it?"

It was the first time she had ever heard the old man speak. His voice was deep and unctuous, though he made an attempt to keep it low.

"Open up, my dear," he said. "It's most important. A matter of life and death, in fact. I can't speak through this little hole."

Helen hesitated. Finally she opened the door, attempting to block the entrance with her body, but the bulk of the old man pushed her aside and he walked into the room.

"Really!" Helen exclaimed. "Please tell me what this is all about. It's after midnight!"

"I apologize for the intrusion, my dear," the old man said calmly. "Allow me to introduce myself. My name is Heavenridge. George M. Heavenridge. Past seventy, retired, and quite harmless, I assure you, my child. And there you have my history. Now, as to my business." His thick lips smiled at Helen. The room was filled with the odor of his unclean clothes and of stale cigar smoke. He rubbed his gray-stubbed chin, the flabby jowls, with a pudgy hand. The fingers were brown with nicotine and tipped by black half-moons.

"What business?" Helen asked, realizing her voice was far too shrill.

The old man seated himself, without an invitation.

"It's about the room, my dear," he said. "The room you advertised for rent in the evening paper."

Helen regarded the old man in blank astonishment, for a moment. Then she said, "I advertised no room for rent! There's some mistake. Even if I had, this is an odd time of night to inquire about it."

The old man waggled a stained and stubby finger at Helen. His thick, moist lips smiled over dentures that were ghastly white.

"Ah, yes, my dear. You advertised a room for rent. We'll agree on that, I think. And we'll agree at once that I become your boarder. Immediately. Tonight, you understand? I live in the front apartment. I will bring only the things I need tonight. Tomorrow and in the days to come I can move in my other possessions. I have the right to sublease my own flat. There's no hurry. I'll wait to find a proper tenant who will pay a proper price. But your own need is great. Yours and your sister's. You must have my protection immediately. That is vital, my dear. We'll agree on that, too."

Helen regarded the smiling old man, dumbfounded. She shook her head slowly.

"This is quite mad!" she said. "Why on earth should my sister and I require your 'protection,' as you call it?"

The fat old man was still smiling as he said, "Because they found the body, my dear. The police, I mean. They found the body just outside the house a little while ago. Such a young man. So tragic to be struck down in the prime of life."

Suddenly, Helen was conscious of only one sensation. She was very cold. Then she realized she could not focus her eyes properly. She saw the old man and the familiar furniture of the room, but everything was distorted, as if she were observing objects through the tumbling stream of a waterfall. She clutched the back of a chair and forced herself to speak.

"I'll ask you to explain yourself as briefly as possible, Mr. Heavenridge. Then you will please leave this apartment, or I will be forced to call the superintendent."

Mr. Heavenridge was lighting a foul cigar. He blew smoke, said, "I hope you don't mind cigars. I smoke a great many of them. An old man's only vice, my dear. I prefer very strong tobacco, but I'm sure you'll become used to it."

He regarded the glowing tip of the cigar, nodded with satisfaction. Then he said, "You and your sister are most careless about your window shades, my child. Perhaps it is because you live in the rear of the building, on the first floor, and fancy you aren't observed. But I have watched you often. I sit in darkness, you see. The dark is kinder to an old man than the light. The darkness is filled with memories. In the darkness my own two daughters come back to me from the grave. I see them plainly in their summery frocks and their broad-brimmed hats, with the sweet flush of youth upon their cheeks. Then one day, soon after you and your sister moved into this apartment across the areaway, I realized that those dim figures of the darkness had become real, alive! You are so like my eldest, Alice. Sweet and calm, always obedient. And your little sister, she is like my younger daughter, Dora. Willful, but lovely. I see now I was not stern enough with her. But it is not too late to rectify my mistake. You and your sister will become my daughters, my dear. And I will become your loving father, always near to protect you, from this night until the dear Lord calls me to his bosom. Oh, we will be so happy, the three of us!"

The old man expelled cigar smoke. "I killed my daughters, you know," he said. "I killed them more than twenty years ago."

The waterfall veiled Helen's eyes and thundered in her ears. She could no longer control her voice.

"You—you *killed* your daughters?" she fairly shrieked.

The old man nodded calmly. "It wasn't exactly murder, my dear," he replied. "Not like the terrible thing that happened here tonight. I indulged my daughters too much. Their mother died when they were very young. When they became young ladies, they wanted a car. I bought one, but I was a poor driver and so one day I smashed the car. Now you don't think I did that on purpose, do you? At any rate, Alice and Dora were both killed. I alone was spared to exist in lonely solitude. But that is ended now. You and your sister will become my daughters. I will be firm with you, but always understanding."

Helen's teeth were chattering from the strange, numb cold that had crept over her. "No!" she cried. "No! No!"

The old man shrugged his heavy shoulders. "It is your choice, entirely," he said. "I doubt they would electrocute your sister; she is so young and lovely. But she will spend her life behind gray prison walls, that is certain. I saw it all. I saw her strike him down. When he left, I saw how he staggered. I know something of these head injuries. It takes a little while to die after one is inflicted. I watched him through my front window as he reeled out into the deserted street. He fell. I went out and examined him. His heart had stopped. I called the police, but I did not tell them my name. They rang the superintendent's apartment and talked to him. I listened through the crack of my door. But the superintendent knew nothing. If I move in here and I am questioned, I will swear I was with you all evening. Any father would do that much for his daughters."

The old man paused, sighed, waggled his bald head. "But if you refuse—then I must tell what I know, of course, as any good citizen doing his duty would."

Someone cried out. Marcia was standing in the room supporting herself against the bedroom door. Her eyes were wild and glazed.

"Don't call the police!" she begged. "Oh, please, Helen, don't let him!"

159

The old man rose from the chair. He was remarkably agile for a fat old man. He crossed the room rapidly and gave Marcia a resounding slap in the face.

"Go to your room, Dora!" he thundered. "Your sister and I will arrange matters."

And matters were arranged, because there was nothing else to do. At least, the dazed and terrified Helen could think of nothing else to do. And Marcia had fled to her bed. The covers were pulled up around her head and the bed shook with her sobbing.

Mr. Heavenridge moved in that night. He took the room which had served as Helen's bedroom-studio. Helen had to move into the small room with Marcia.

Mr. Heavenridge said that loud sounds disturbed him. He could not abide street noises and he disliked sunlight. He kept all the windows shut, and the blinds lowered. He called the business office of the telephone company at once and had the phone service discontinued. He removed the tubes from the television and radio receivers.

The apartment became insufferably stuffy; it no longer had its pleasant girl-smell of perfume and powder and scented soap and fresh flowers. It took on the overwhelming, heavy odor that clung to the old man. The two girls had only one closet between them for all their clothes, for he claimed the others. This problem was alleviated, in a sense, by a dictatorial step that the old man took. He made an inventory of their wardrobes and if he considered a garment immodest, he ripped it to pieces and suggested the fragments of cloth be used for dust rags.

On the very first morning, Helen found him examining her bank book and account books and personal correspondence. When she protested, he simply waved her away, and chided her for rising at so late an hour.

"From now on," he said, "you and your sister will rise at six-thirty. That is my accustomed hour. I will expect to have my breakfast on the table by seven sharp."

He demanded that they retire at ten-thirty. One evening

he found a light showing beneath the girls' bedroom door after the hour he had set. He stormed in and detached all the light bulbs. From then on, he removed the light bulbs every night at the bedtime he had ordered.

He called the sisters "Alice" and "Dora." He brought a heavy family Bible from his apartment and required one of them to read to him every evening, as his daughters had done, for an hour or more. He was especially fond of passages from the Book of Revelations.

He was an enormous eater. He preferred food heavily seasoned with garlic and went into a towering rage if a window of the kitchen was opened while a meal was being cooked. He was inordinately fond of strong cheeses that he kept ripening on kitchen shelves. Often he would sit and listen to Marcia or Helen reading the Bible, while he nodded his egg-bald head and licked Limburger or Liederkrantz from his soiled fingers.

Sometimes Helen thought that he was senile, completely out of his mind. He would charge them with pranks and misdeeds that his two daughters had apparently committed when they were children. He did not hesitate to slap them and rain blows on them when he was displeased.

He was a messy old man. He spewed ashes over the carpets. He burnt the polished wood of tables with his smouldering cigar butts. He said that he was afraid of slipping in the bathtub. So, when he bathed at all, he took sponge baths at the bathroom sink. He would splash a pool of soapy water over the tile floor, for the girls to clean away.

They were not only his daughters, his servants, his cooks, his companions. They also served as his nurses. He took several different kinds of medicine. There was a liquid for his dyspepsia which they had to give him at mealtimes. There were his vitamins first thing in the morning. He had a weak heart and high blood pressure. For these ills, he kept white pills in a little vial on the bathroom shelf. He warned them to give him a pill promptly if he had a seizure. One of the girls had to rub his flabby old back with alcohol every night.

He demanded that the sisters address each other by the names of "Alice" and "Dora." If they forgot, he made a scene.

Each day he left the house for an hour or so. He would force Helen to write a check made out to "Cash" and endorse it. With this he would buy food, medicine, cigars. During his brief absences they at least could air out the fetid apartment. And they talked ineffectually of escape. He had possessed himself of all the keys. When he went out, he locked them in. The apartment was on the street level and all the windows were barred. Helen had often complained that the bars made the apartment seem like a prison, never realizing the prophecy of the remark. The idea she had of sawing through them with a nailfile, she dismissed as hopeless melodrama.

Mr. Heavenridge would not allow Helen to deliver her art work to magazines. He forced her to write letters to all the art editors she knew, stating that her telephone had been disconnected because its ringing distracted her and that from now on, she would accept commissions only by mail. Commissions arrived and the old man was a grim taskmaster in seeing that she fulfilled them. When she wrote to the magazines, he read her letters carefully. He even read the instructions to the engravers that she pencilled on her drawings, to see if she had inserted some sly appeal for help. When checks came from publishers, Mr. Heavenridge forced Helen to endorse them. He would fold the checks and place them in his wallet. Helen never saw the money. Often the checks were for large sums.

On the first day of his occupancy, the old man had appropriated Marcia's diary. From that he had learned that the man he had seen in the apartment was Paul Carter.

He always brought a newspaper back with him from his shopping tours. During the first week after he moved in, the first or second page of the paper would have an item torn from it. Mr. Heavenridge said the missing items were stories of Carter's murder. He thought it would distress the girls to read too much of it. After the first week, there were apparently no further stories about Carter, for no items were torn from the papers he brought home.

Apparently, the old man had forgotten his intention of renting his own apartment down the hall. From time to time he would visit his old quarters and bring back shoddy pieces of furniture that would crowd the overcrowded apartment even more.

Only at night, when they slept together on a narrow single bed, in a pitch-dark room, did Helen and Marcia have any semblance of privacy. And even then they were afraid to whisper. The fat old man was a hovering presence in their lives. They always fancied he was listening at the crack of their bedroom door.

To Helen, the most abhorrent thing of all was calling him "Daddy." His own daughters had called him that, he said, and he insisted Helen and Marcia do the same. The taste of the word was sour bile in Helen's mouth.

Marcia tried desperately to retreat into the world of fantasy that had always been her haven in the past, but for once it failed her. The presence of the old man bulked too large. When Marcia sought refuge in this peculiar world of her own, Mr. Heavenridge always noticed immediately. He would loom over her threateningly and say, "You're daydreaming, Dora! Don't make Daddy angry! You know what happens when you make Daddy angry, child!"

He supervised their dress and their toilettes. He threw out their wave sets, demanded that they let their hair grow and fix it in a knot at the back of their necks. He would not permit them to use rouge or perfume or nail polish.

It wasn't surprising that Helen's hand was shaky when she held a pen or brush or crayon. Drawings were returned more and more frequently by editors who found them un-

163

satisfactory. She lost several of her best accounts, and the old man raged at her.

As for Marcia, she hardly ate or slept at all. The old man had found her sleeping pills and had thrown them in the garbage, calling her a dope addict.

Marcia grew ill and feverish with flu. Helen begged the old man to call a doctor, but he refused. He forced Marcia to dose herself with salts and aspirin. As she lay helpless and burning with fever, he sat beside her bed by the hour, reading aloud from the Bible.

Marcia recovered. Despite her weakness, the old man drove her to perform her share of household tasks. Helen, he said, must have the time to make a living for all of them with her art work.

In time, Helen found herself moving mechanically, like a puppet manipulated by the fat man's pudgy fingers. She had lost all sense of time, all ambition, all hope. They would never escape, and she resigned herself to that fact. She thought wildly of screaming at passing policemen from the window; then she realized what that would mean for Marcia. She thought, too, of murdering the old man, and when that occurred to her, she realized she had retreated into her younger sister's impossible world of fantasy.

She told herself that she had died the night the old man knocked upon the door. She and her sister had been parties to the awful act of murder and now they were in hell. She seldom spoke to her sister any more. There was no use in recalling the past—if there had ever really been a past. Nothing was real except the old man and his whims and his power over them, which was now complete.

He had been with them more than a month the night that Marcia came into the living room, her face flushed, her eyes unnaturally bright, a queer little smile playing on her pale lips. The old man was sitting in a big chair, munching Limburger and crackers. A cigar was burning on the scarred edge of a maple end-table at his side. Ashes and cracker crumbs littered the floor around him.

Helen roused from her usual lethargy enough to look curiously at her sister. Marcia was carrying a newspaper the old man had brought home from his shopping tour.

"I want to read you something, Daddy-O," Marcia said.

The old fat man almost choked. Cracker crumbs drooled over his beard-spiked chin.

"What did you call me, Dora?" he demanded.

"I called you Daddy-O," Marcia answered. "It's kind of a pet name for a fat old man."

The old man rose from the chair, still spluttering crackers from his mouth. He advanced toward Marcia, his log-like arm raised threateningly.

Marcia laughed at him. "You shouldn't hit me until after I've read you something, Daddy-O," she said. "I might scream for the police and tell them what a dirty old man you are."

The old man stood stock-still and lowered his arm. There was a look of alarm on his face. It was followed by a look of cunning. He backed to his chair and dropped heavily into it.

"You are right, daughter," he said. "It is almost time for the Bible. Read to me."

"Not the Bible, Daddy-O. I want to read you something from the newspaper."

"I've read the paper, child," the old man replied. "I have little interest in worldly news. You and your dear sister and I have a warm little world of our own here. We must keep it to ourselves, sacred to our happy little family."

"I don't think we can any longer, Daddy-O," said Marcia. She unfolded the paper.

She looked at the old man. There was mockery in her smile now.

"This is from the society page, Daddy-O," Marcia said. "I doubt you ever read the society page."

She paused, teasing the old man. He sat perfectly still, staring at her. His cigar dropped from the table and began to scorch the rug. Helen saw it but did not move to pick it up.

Marcia began to read.

> Mr. and Mrs. Paul Carter of Rye, N.Y. were among the passengers on the S.S. Constitution which sailed for Europe today. They will make an extended tour of England and the Continent. Mrs. Carter is the former Sylvia Enright. Mr. Carter is vice-president of the Enright Advertising Agency.

Marcia put the paper down and laughed aloud at the old man.

"Paul Carter is the man you claim I killed, Daddy-O," she said.

The old man's face went suddenly ashen. He began to breathe heavily, noisily.

"Mistake," he gasped. "I told you, police—"

Suddenly, his face was contorted with pain and his body bent forward. His hands clutched at his chest.

"Attack," he said. "Get tablets. Quick. Bathroom."

Marcia continued to snicker. "Why, sure, Daddy-O. Dear little Dora will get you your tablets."

She walked toward the bathroom. Helen sat, her body stiff, staring fixedly at the old man.

I really believe he's dying, she thought. *I didn't think he could ever die. I never saw anyone die before. Mother and Dad died when we were both so little. I never saw anyone die before, and I don't feel a thing.*

Marcia returned from the bathroom, the little smile still on her face.

"I'm sorry, Daddy-O," she said. "But you must have taken all the tablets. There's not one left. Not a single one left. It's too bad we haven't got a phone. I might call a doctor if we had."

The old man was making snorting sounds. He slumped forward until half his body was on the floor.

He gasped, "Please . . . please . . ."

He might have been pleading with Marcia. He might have been pleading with his God.

He said "Please," again, and then he stopped breathing.

Marcia, still smiling, reached down and began to twine a single wisp of hair on his bald head between her fingers.

"Poor Daddy-O," she said. "I think poor Daddy-O is dead, Helen."

There was a long silence.

Finally, Helen said, "Oh, my God, Marcia, what will we do? They mustn't find him here!"

For once Marcia didn't run away.

"It won't be easy because he's so fat," she said. "We'll wait until it's late at night. He's kept his apartment. The key is in his pocket. We can't carry him, but we'll drag him down the hall. Then we'll put all his stuff back in his apartment. They'll find him there, dead of a heart attack. That'll be the end of it."

Marcia reached into the pocket of her housecoat and held up a vial of white tablets.

"We'll put these alongside his body," she said. "That'll be a nice touch, don't you think?"

Suddenly Marcia and Helen began to giggle foolishly.

They'd giggled something like that when they were children, and had been up to mischief.

*Wanting something for nothing has been man's dream,
since he first saw the advantages of being intolerably
greedy. It has been dreams such as these that have made
man what he is. Flaw-wise, man is tops.*

THE CRIME MACHINE
BY JACK RITCHIE

"I was present the last time you committed
murder," Henry said.

I lit my cigar. "Really?"

"Of course you couldn't see me."

I smiled. "You were in your time machine?"

Henry nodded.

Naturally I didn't believe a word of it. About the time
machine. He *could* actually have been present however,
but not in that fantastic manner.

Murder is my business and the fact that there had been
a witness when I disposed of James Brady was naturally
disconcerting. And now, for the sake of security, I would
have to devise some means of getting rid of Henry. I had
no intention of being blackmailed by him. Not for any
length of time, at least.

"I must warn you that I have taken pains to let people
know that I have come here, Mr. Reeves," Henry said.
"They do not know why I am here, but they do know that
I am here. You understand, don't you?"

I smiled again. "I do not murder people in my own
apartment. It is the height of inhospitality. And so there
will be no necessity for you to switch our drinks. I assure

168

you your glass contains nothing stronger than brandy."

The situation was basically unpleasant, but nevertheless I found myself rather enjoying Henry's bizarre story. "This machine of yours, Henry, is it a bit like a barber's chair?"

"To some degree," he admitted.

Evidently we had both seen the same motion picture. "With a round reflector-like device behind you? And levers in front which you pull to propel you into the past? Or the future?"

"Just the past. I'm still working on the mechanism for the future." Henry sipped his brandy. "My machine is also mobile. That is, it not only projects me into the past, but also to any point on the earth I desire."

Excellent, I thought. Quite an improvement over the old model time machines. "And you are invisible?"

"Correct. I cannot participate in any manner in the past. I can only observe."

This madman did at least think with some degree of logic. To so much as injure the wing of a butterfly ten thousand years ago could conceivably re-shuffle the course of history.

Henry had come to my apartment at three in the afternoon. He had not given me his last name, which was entirely natural since he intended to blackmail me. He was fairly tall and thin, with glasses that gave him an owlish appearance and hair that tended toward anarchy.

He leaned forward. "I read in yesterday's newspaper that a James Brady was shot to death in a warehouse on Blenheim Street at approximately eleven in the evening of July the twenty-seventh."

I thought I could supply the rest. "And so you hopped into your time machine, set the dials back to July the twenty-seventh and to Blenheim Street and were there at ten-thirty for a ringside seat, waiting for me to re-commit the crime?"

"Precisely."

169

I would have to discuss this particular form of insanity with Dr. Powers. He is a quite mature and—since I disposed of his wife—wealthy psychiatrist.

Henry smiled thinly. "You shot James Brady at exactly ten-fifty-one. As you stooped over him to make certain that he was dead, you dropped your car keys. You said, 'Oh, damn!' and picked them up. At the door of the warehouse, you looked back and lifted your hand in a mock salute to the corpse. Then you departed."

Unquestionably he had been there. Not in that fabulous time machine, but probably hiding among the thousands of boxes and bales inside the warehouse—an accidental witness to the murder. It was one of those unfortunate coincidences that occur occasionally to mar an otherwise perfect killing. But why did he bother to resort to this fantastic story?

Henry put down his glass. "I think that five thousand dollars would be sufficient for me to forget what I saw."

For how long, I wondered. A month? Two? I took a puff of my cigar. "If you went to the police, it would be your word against mine."

"Could you bear an investigation?"

I really didn't know. I am a very careful practitioner of my craft, but it was still possible that here and there I might have made some slight revealing error. I certainly would not welcome the interest of the authorities. Of that much I was positive.

I replenished my glass. "You seem to have fallen into an interesting and profitable business. Have you approached many other murderers?" I looked at his suit. It had undoubtedly been sold with two pairs of trousers.

Perhaps he read my mind. "I have just started, Mr. Reeves. You are the first murderer I have approached."

He smiled primly. "I have done considerable other research on you, Mr. Reeves. On June the 10th, at eleven-twelve in the evening, an automobile which you had stolen for the purpose ran down a Mrs. Irvin Perry."

He could have read about Mrs. Perry's death in the newspapers. But how did he know that I had been the driver? A wild guess?

"You parked approximately one hundred yards from the intersection. You kept your motor running while you waited for Mrs. Perry to make her appearance. Ten minutes before she arrived, a collie ran across the street. Seven minutes before she arrived, a fire engine sped past. Three minutes before she arrived, a model A Ford filled with teenagers raced by. The automobile's muffler was faulty. It was quite noisy."

I frowned. How could he possibly have known those things?

Henry was enjoying himself. "On September 28th, last April at two-fifteen of a chilly afternoon, a Gerald Mitchell 'fell' off an escarpment near his home while he was taking a stroll. You had a bit of trouble with him. Though he was a small man, he showed remarkable strength. He managed to tear the left pocket of your coat before you could throw him into space."

I caught myself staring at him and quickly took a sip of brandy.

"Five thousand dollars," Henry said. "Small bills, of course. Nothing larger than a five hundred. Naturally I didn't expect you to have that much cash lying about. I shall return tomorrow evening at eight."

I pulled myself together. For a moment I had almost entertained the thought that Henry actually might have a time machine. But there was some other explanation and I would have to think it out.

At the door to the hallway, I smiled. "Henry, would you hop into your time machine and find out who Jack the Ripper really was? I'm frightfully curious."

Henry nodded. "I'll do that tonight."

I closed the door and went into my living room.

My wife Diana put aside her fashion magazine. "Who was that strange creature?"

171

"He claims to be an inventor."

"Really? He certainly looks mad enough for the part. I imagine he wanted to sell you an invention?"

"Not exactly."

Diana is green-eyed and cool and she is perhaps no more predatory or unfaithful than any other woman who marries a man with money who is thirty years her senior. I am fully aware of the nature of our relationship, but I realize that one must pay by various means for the enjoyment of a work of art. And Diana is a work of art—a triumph of physical nature. I value her quite as highly as I do my Modiglianis and my Van Goghs.

"What is he supposed to have invented?"

"A time machine."

She smiled. "I am partial to perpetual motion machines."

I was faintly irritated. "Perhaps it works."

She studied me. "I hope you have no intention of letting that queer man talk you out of money."

"No, my dear. I still retain my mental faculties."

Her solicitude for my money would have been touching, except that I realized that she preferred to spend it on herself. Henry's chances of acquiring any of it were nil as far as she was concerned.

She picked up the magazine. "Has he asked you to see it?"

"No. And even if he does, I have no intention of doing so."

And yet I wondered how Henry could possibly have managed to know the details of those three murders. His presence at one of them could be an acceptable coincidence. But three?

There was no such a thing as a time machine. There had to be some other explanation—something that an intelligent man could believe.

I glanced at my watch and turned my mind to another

matter. "I have something to attend to, Diana. I'll be back in an hour or two."

I drove to the main post office downtown and opened my box with a key. The letter I had been expecting was inside.

I conduct most of my business by mail and box number. My clients do not know my name, even on those occasions when personal contact is necessary.

The letter was from Jason Spender. We had exchanged some correspondence and Spender had been negotiating for the elimination of a Charles Atwood. Spender did not give his reasons for that desire and for my purposes they were not necessary. In this case, however, I could hazard a guess. Spender and Atwood were partners in a building concern and evidently sharing the profits no longer appealed to Spender.

The letter accepted my terms—fifteen thousand dollars —and provided the information that Atwood had a dinner engagement tomorrow evening and would return to his home at approximately eleven. Spender would have an alibi for that particular time in the event that the police might make embarrassing inquiries.

I drove on to the Shippler Detective Agency and went directly to Andrew Shippler.

I cannot, of course, employ his agency continuously to follow my wife. But several times a year I made a precautionary use of his services for a week or two. It is usually sufficient.

In 1958, for instance, Shippler discovered a Terence Reilly. He was extremely personable—fair, athletic, and the type to which Diana seems to be drawn—and I cannot blame Diana too much.

However Terence Reilly soon departed this world. I was not paid for the demise. It was a labor of love.

Shippler was a plump man in his fifties with the air of an accountant. He took a typewritten page from a folder

173

and adjusted his rimless glasses. "Your wife left your apartment twice yesterday. In the morning at ten-thirty she went to a small hat shop for an hour. She finally purchased a blue and white hat with . . ."

"Never mind the details."

He was slightly aggrieved. "But details can be important, Mr. Reeves. We try to be absolutely thorough." He glanced at the page again. "Then she had a strawberry soda at a drugstore and went on to . . ."

I interrupted again. "Did she see anyone? Talk to anyone?"

"Well, the owner of the hat shop and the clerk at the drugstore counter."

"Besides that," I snapped.

He shook his head. "No. But she left the apartment again at two-thirty in the afternoon. She went to a small cocktail bar on Farwell. There she met two women her age, apparently by prearrangement. It appears that they had been college classmates and hadn't seen each other for years. My man overheard most of their conversation. They discussed their former classmates and what they were doing now." Shippler cleared his throat. "It seems that they were most impressed that your wife had . . . ah . . . caught such a man of means."

"What did Diana say?"

"She was extremely noncommittal." Shippler folded his hands. "Your wife consumed one Pink Lady and one Manhattan during the course of two hours."

"I am not interested in my wife's liquor preferences. Did she see anyone else? A man?"

Shippler shook his head. "No. At four-ten she left the two women and returned to your apartment."

The human mind is a peculiar thing. I was relieved, of course—and yet, a trifle disappointed.

"Shall we keep watching her?" Shippler asked hopefully.

This time I had had Diana under a surveillance for

about a week. I mulled over Shippler's question. Shippler charged one hundred dollars a day and that was rather expensive. I smiled slightly. Now if I had Henry's time machine, I could save a great deal of money. "Watch her a few days more," I said. "And I have something else for you."

"Yes?"

"At eight tomorrow evening, I am expecting a caller. He will be with me ten to twenty minutes. When he leaves, I want him followed. I want to know who he is and where he lives." I gave Shippler a description of Henry. "Phone me as soon as you find out."

I went to the bank and withdrew five thousand dollars.

At seven the next evening Diana left to see a motion picture. Or at least so she informed me. I would find out about that later.

Henry arrived punctually at eight o'clock and I took him into my study.

He took a chair. "He was a clerk with an importing concern."

"Who was?" I asked.

"Jack the Ripper. A timid-looking man—in his early forties, I'd estimate. He was apparently a bachelor and he lived with his mother."

I smiled. "How interesting. What was his name?"

"I haven't gotten that yet. You see people don't go about with signs hanging from their necks and it can be difficult to find out who they actually are."

He could easily have invented some name for this Jack the Ripper, but this was really more clever—and logical.

Henry said, "Do you have the five thousand dollars?"

"Yes." I got the package and handed it to him.

He rose. "Tonight I think I'll go back to Custer's massacre. I find history fascinating."

I had only one consolation. When the time came to kill him, I would enjoy every moment of it.

When he was gone, I sat beside the phone and waited

175

impatiently. At nine-thirty it rang and I quickly lifted the receiver.

"This is Shippler."

"Well, where does he live?"

Shippler's voice was apologetic. "I'm afraid my man lost him."

"What?"

"He transferred from bus to bus and finally disappeared. I think he suspected he was being followed."

"You blundering idiot!" I roared.

"Really, Mr. Reeves," Shippler said stiffly. "It is my man who is the blundering idiot."

I hung up and poured myself some bourbon. This time Henry had eluded me, but there would be other times. He would be back. Blackmailers are never satisfied.

I became aware of the time and realized that I still had work to do that night. I got into my coat and hat and went downstairs to the apartment garage.

Charles Atwood's home was a large one embedded in several acres of wooded property. It was a situation I fancied, since it offered the maximum of concealment.

The dwelling was dark, except for lights on the third floor where I imagined the servants were quartered.

Atwood's three car garage was detached from the house. I took a stand behind a clump of trees near it and waited.

At eleven-fifteen a car swung into the driveway and made its way to the garage. It stopped momentarily while the automatic doors rose, and then it disappeared into the garage.

Thirty seconds later, a side door opened and a tall man stepped into the moonlight. He began walking toward the house.

I had my revolver and silencer ready and I waited until he came within fifteen feet of me before I left my concealment.

Atwood stopped with an exclamation of startled surprise as he saw me.

I pulled the trigger and Atwood dropped to the ground without a sound. I made certain that he was dead—I do not like to leave things half done—and then made my way back through the woods and to the street where I had parked my car.

The assignment had been entirely successful and, for the first time in thirty-six hours, I felt a certain peace with the world.

I returned to my apartment a little before midnight and I was relaxing when the phone shrilled.

It was Henry. "I see that you killed someone else to-night," he announced pleasantly.

My hands were moist.

"When I arrived home," Henry said, "I got into my time machine and turned it back to the time when I left your apartment. I wanted to see if you had attempted to follow me. I have to be cautious, you know. After all, I am dealing with a murderer."

I said nothing.

"You didn't follow me, but you did leave your apartment and I followed in my machine as a matter of curiosity."

That infernal time machine! Was it possible?

"I'm just wondering," Henry said. "Was that the man you were supposed to kill—the one you killed?"

What was he getting at?

"Because there were two men in the car," Henry said.

I spoke involuntarily. "Two?"

"Yes. You shot the first man as he came out of the garage. The second man left it about forty-five seconds later."

I closed my eyes. "Did he see me?"

"No. You were gone by that time. He just bent over the man you'd shot and called, 'Fred! Fred!'"

I was definitely perspiring. "Henry, I'd like to see you."

"Why?"

"I can't discuss it over the phone. But I've got to see you."

His voice was dubious. "I don't know."

"It means money. A lot of money."

He thought it over. "All right," he said finally. "Tomorrow? Around eight?"

I couldn't wait that long. "No. Right now. As soon as you can get here."

Henry required more seconds to think. "No tricks now, Mr. Reeves," he said. "I'll be prepared for anything."

"No tricks, Henry. I swear it. Get here as soon as you can."

He arrived forty-five minutes later. "What is it, Mr. Reeves?"

I had been drinking—not to excess, but I simply found that accepting such an idea—and I was on the verge of accepting it—was painful to my intelligence. "Henry, I'd like to buy your machine. If it really works."

"It works." He shook his head. "But I won't sell it."

"One hundred thousand dollars, Henry."

"Out of the question."

"A hundred and fifty thousand."

"It's my invention," Henry said peevishly. "I wouldn't dream of parting with it."

"You could make another, couldn't you?"

"Well . . . yes." He eyed me suspiciously.

"Henry, do you expect me to mass produce time machines once I get yours? To sell them to others?"

His face indicated that evidently he did.

"Henry," I said patiently. "Having anyone else in the world get hold of that machine is the last thing I want. After all, I am a murderer. I wouldn't welcome other people delving into the past, especially my past—now would I?"

"No," he admitted. "Somebody else might want to turn you over to the police. There are people like that."

"Two hundred thousand dollars, Henry," I said. "My last offer." Actually money was no object to me now. With Henry's machine—if it worked—I could make millions.

A crafty light crept into his eyes. "Two hundred and fifty thousand. Take it or leave it."

"Henry, you drive a hard bargain. But I'll meet your price. However I've got to be satisfied that the machine works. When can I see it?"

"I'll get in touch with you," he said cagily. "Tomorrow, the next day, maybe in a week."

"Why not right now?"

He shook his head. "No. You're very clever, Mr. Reeves. Perhaps you've devised a trap for this moment. I prefer to set the time and terms myself."

I was unable to shake him out of his determination and he left five minutes later.

I rose at seven in the morning and went downstairs to purchase a newspaper. I had indeed killed the wrong man. A Fred Turley. I had never even heard of him before.

Atwood and Turley had returned from the dinner and an evening of cards together and driven into the garage. Turley had gone out of the side door, but Atwood remained behind to lock his car. Then he had seen his briefcase still on the rear seat. After he had recovered it, relocked the car, and left the garage, he had found Turley dead on the path leading to the house. At first he had thought Turley had suffered a stroke of some kind. When he finally discovered the truth, he had raised an alarm. The police had no clues either to the identity of the murderer or the motive for the killing.

I found myself fretting about the apartment all morning waiting for Henry to phone me. I skimmed through the paper a half a dozen times before an item in the local section caught my eye.

It seemed that once again some fool had bought a "money machine."

This form of swindle was probably as old as currency itself. The victim was approached by a stranger claiming to have a money machine. One simply inserted a dollar, turned the handle, and a twenty dollar bill emerged from the opposite end. In this case, the victim had purchased the machine for five hundred dollars—the stranger claiming that he was forced to sell because he needed cash.

People are incredible idiots!

Couldn't the victim have the basic intelligence and imagination to realize that if the machine were actually genuine, all that the stranger had to do to get five hundred dollars himself was to turn the handle twenty-five times and transform twenty-five dollars into five hundred?

Yes, people are monumental . . .

I found myself reading the article again. Then I went to the liquor cabinet.

After two bourbons, I allowed myself to bask in the returning sun of sanity.

I had almost fallen into Henry's trap. I had, I reluctantly admitted, been just a bit stupid.

I smiled. Still . . . it might be a rather amusing adventure to see Henry's time machine—to see in what manner he hoped to convince me that it actually worked.

Henry came to my apartment at one o'clock in the afternoon. He appeared shaken. "Horrible," he muttered. "Horrible."

"What's horrible?"

"Custer's massacre." He wiped his forehead with handkerchief. "I'll have to avoid things like that in the future."

I almost laughed. Rather a neat touch. Henry knew how to act. "And now we see your machine?"

Henry nodded. "I suppose so. We'll take your car. Mine's in the garage for repairs."

I had driven him about a mile, when he told me to pull over to the curb. I glanced about. "Is this where you live?"

"No. But from here on I drive your car. You will be blindfolded and you will lie on the back seat."

"Oh, come now, Henry!"

"It's absolutely necessary if you want me to take you

the machine," Henry said stubbornly. "And I've got to search you to see that you aren't carrying a weapon."

I was not carrying a weapon and Henry's idea of a blindfold consisted of a black hood that fitted over my entire head and was fastened by strings at the back of the neck.

"I'll be keeping an eye on you through the rear view mirror," Henry cautioned. "If I see you touch that blindfold the whole thing is off."

Automatically I found myself trying to remember the turns Henry made as he drove and attempting to identify sounds which might tell me where he was taking me. However, the task proved too complicated and I finally relaxed as much as I could and waited for the drive to end.

After an hour, the car finally slowed to a stop. Henry left the wheel and I heard what I believed to be the sound of garage doors being opened. Henry returned to the car; we moved forward fifteen feet or so, and stopped again.

The doors were closed and I heard a light switch flicked on.

"We're here," Henry said. "I'll take off that blindfold now."

As I had surmised, we were in a garage—but plywood sheets had been nailed over all the windows and a single electric light burned overhead. A stout oak door was in the cement building-block wall to the left.

Henry produced a revolver.

A horrendous thought gripped me. What a fool I had been! I had blindly—literally and figuratively—allowed myself to be lured here. And now, for reasons unknown to me, Henry was about to kill me!

"Henry," I began, "I'm sure we can talk this over and come to some . . ."

He waved the gun. "This is just a precaution. In case you have any ideas."

I was too uneasy to have any ideas.

Henry produced a key and went to the oak door. "This used to be a two-car garage, but I divided it in half. The time machine is in here." He unlocked the door and switched on an overhead light.

Henry's time machine was just about as I had anticipated—a metallic chair with some scant leather upholstering, a large mirror-bright aluminum shield or reflector behind it, and a series of levers, dials, and buttons on a control board attached to the platform on which the chair stood.

The room was windowless and all four walls—with the exception of three grated ventilators approximately shoulder high—were solid cement block. The floor was concrete and the ceiling was plastered.

I smiled. "Henry, your machine looks almost like an electric chair."

"Yes," he said musingly, "it does look rather like that, doesn't it?"

I stared at him. Could he have been so insidious as to actually . . . I studied the machine again. "Naturally I want a demonstration. How does it work?"

"Get into the chair and I'll show you which levers to pull."

The device *did* look a great deal like an electric chair. I cleared my throat. "I have a better idea, Henry. Suppose *you* take a trip in the chair. I'll just wait right here until you return."

Henry gave it a thought. "All right. But you'll have to leave the room."

Ah ha, I thought.

"You see when I start the machine," Henry said, "it creates quite a disturbance around me. That's why I had to make this room so solid. I've installed ventilators to take care of some of the turbulence, but I'm not too sure how well they work. I have no idea what might happen to you if you remained."

I smiled. "I might possibly be injured? Or killed?"

"Exactly. So if you'll leave and close the door I'll get on with it. And another precaution. When I return, you've got to be out of the room, too."

I chuckled to myself as I left and closed the door behind me. I lit a cigar and waited, amused.

What happened next was most impressive. First there was a low whine, as though a generator were starting. It rose gradually in pitch and then came a rumbling sound mixed with the undulating keen of a fierce wind. It increased in volume and lasted for approximately a minute.

Then it stopped abruptly and there was absolute silence.

Yes, I thought. Altogether a good show. But then it would have to be if Henry expected to extract two hundred and fifty thousand dollars from me.

I went to the door and opened it.

The room was empty!

I stood there gaping. It couldn't be! The only way out of the room was the door I had just entered and even that was certainly too small to pull the chair through. And the only other openings were the three grated ventilators and they were less than two feet square!

The whining suddenly rose again. Strong air currents swirled around the room and I found myself gasping as I ded the room and slammed the door behind me.

The noise became deafening and then, just as abruptly as before, it stopped.

The door clicked open and Henry stepped out of the room. Behind him I could see the time machine back in ts place.

Henry appeared thoughtful. Finally he shook his head. "Cleopatra wasn't even good-looking."

My heart was still pounding. "You were gone only a minute or two."

He waved a hand. "In one time sense. Actually I spent n hour on her barge." He came back to the present. "You an raise two hundred and fifty thousand dollars?"

I nodded weakly. "It will take a week or two." I wiped

my forehead. "Henry, I've got to take a trip on that chair."

Henry frowned. "I've been thinking that over, Mr. Reeves. No. You could steal my invention."

"But how? Wouldn't I have to come back here?"

"No. You could go into the past and then return to any place in the world. Perhaps a thousand miles from here."

He pulled a small wrench from his pocket and began disconnecting a section of the control panel.

"What are you doing?"

"I'm taking out some key transistors. I think I'll keep them on my person. That way if someone should steal my time machine he would find it useless."

Henry drove me back to my apartment, taking the same precautions as before, and then he left me.

In America we seem to have a feeling of guilt about discarding old license plates and Henry had been no exception. There had been four old sets of them nailed to the garage wall and I had memorized two of them.

I got Shippler on the phone. "Can you trace license numbers?"

"Yes, Mr. Reeves. I have connection at the state capitol."

I gave him the numbers. "The first is a 1958 license number and the second is 1959. I want the name and address of the owner as soon as possible. Phone me the moment you get the information."

I was about to hang up.

"Oh, Mr. Reeves. We have the report on your wife for yesterday. Would you like me to give it over the phone?"

I had forgotten about that. "Well?"

"She left the apartment yesterday morning at ten-thirty. She bought some orange sticks and nail polish at the drug store."

"What shade of nail polish?" I asked dryly.

"Summer Rose," he said proudly. "Then she went to—"

"Never mind all that. Did she meet anyone?"

"No, sir. Just the drugstore clerk. A woman. But in th

evening she again left your apartment at three minutes after seven. She met a woman named Doris. My man overheard Doris say that she has twins."

I sighed.

"They went to a show and left at eleven-thirty."

I was not going to ask him the name of the picture. "Is that all?"

"Yes, sir. She returned to your apartment at eleven-fifty-six. The name of the picture . . ."

I hung up and made myself a whiskey and soda.

The idea of a time machine was fantastic. But was it really? We are all aware that there is a fourth dimension. And future travelers in space will eventually have to use space warp in order to reach planets that are physically inaccessible in the present time sense.

Diana came into the room with a manicure kit. "You look thoughtful."

"I have a lot to think about."

"Does it have anything to do with that man who was here? The inventor?"

I sipped my whiskey. "Suppose I told you that his time machine works?"

She began working on her nails. "I hope you haven't been taken in?"

I noticed that one of the bottles beside her was named Summer Rose. "And why should a time machine be impossible?"

"Don't tell me he's convinced you?"

I felt a bit defensive. "Perhaps."

She smiled. "Has he asked you for money?"

I watched her use nail polish remover. "How much do you think a time machine would be worth?"

She raised an eyebrow.

I held up a hand. "Let us just *suppose* that there is such a thing? How much would *you* be willing to pay for it?"

She examined her nails. "Perhaps a thousand or two. It might be an amusing toy."

"A *toy?*" I laughed. "My dear, don't you realize the tremendous import of such a thing? You could go into the past and ferret out any secret at all."

She glanced up. "Perhaps try simple blackmail?"

"My dear Diana, not *simple* blackmail, but blackmail extended, double, quadrupled. No nation's secrets would be safe from discovery. You could sell your services to the government . . . any government . . . for millions. You could be present at the most important council chambers, the most isolated laboratories . . ."

She looked up again. "Is that what you'd do if you had such a machine, use it for blackmail?"

I had let myself get carried away. I smiled. "Just indulging in fantasy, dear."

Her eyes seemed to calculate me. "Don't do anything foolish."

"My dear, I am the most cautious man in the world."

I decided that I would not hear from Shippler within the next half an hour and so I went to the post office.

I had a letter from Spender. He expressed keen disappointment that I had killed Turley instead of Atwood. He had played golf with Turley a number of times and would miss him. He also suggested that I return the fifteen thousand dollars or complete my assignment.

Shippler phoned at three-thirty.

"Both of the license numbers belong to the same person," he said. "A Henry Pruitt. He lives at 2349 West Headley. This city."

I waited until ten that evening and then got my flashlight, a tape measure, and my ring of special keys from the wall safe and went down to my car.

Henry's house was in a sparsely populated section of the city—there were empty lots on either side of his home. It was a two story building, but still relatively small. A garage stood next to the alley.

I parked my car a hundred feet down the street and lit a cigar. At eleven the lights in the living room went out and a few moments later they reappeared in what was evidently an upstairs bedroom.

After ten minutes, they too went out.

I waited another half an hour and then made my way through the littered lots to the garage. It had originally been a common two-car structure, but now the left-hand doors had been replaced by a solid cement block wall. I couldn't peer into the right-hand unit, because, as I'd noticed before, the windows had been covered by plywood. Henry clearly believed in absolute secrecy for his invention.

I measured the outside of the garage, the height, width, and length. Then I took the ring of keys out of my pocket and, after a few tries, succeeded in opening the door. I stepped inside, closed the door behind me, and turned on my flashlight.

Yes, this was the place I had been in earlier in the day —the four pairs of license plates nailed to the wall, the workbench at the far end, and the door leading to the time machine on the left.

I switched on the overhead light.

The door to the next room was also locked, but it presented no problem to me. I turned on the light, somewhat apprehensively.

Yes, there it was. The time machine!

For a moment, the idea of stealing it crossed my mind. But then I remembered that Henry had a section of the controls. And besides, how would I get it out of the room? The doorway was obviously too small.

For that matter, how had Henry gotten the machine *into* the room?

I pondered on that and decided he must have brought it in piece-meal and then assembled it.

What really concerned me was how he had managed, earlier in the day, to get the time machine *out* of the room.

That was what I was there to find out.

I began by examining the walls. They were cement block on all four sides and absolutely solid. I took measurements of the room and the entire inside of the garage. My computations showed that there were no secret compartments, no false chambers. I examined the ventilator grates thoroughly. I tried to shake them loose, but they were securely screwed into place. They could not be removed without some time and effort. I examined the floor. It was compact and unbroken cement.

There was one more possibility. The ceiling. Perhaps Henry had some device—some series of hoists—that would whisk the machine into a ceiling crevice.

I got a step ladder from the other room and went over the ceiling with minute thoroughness. The plaster was old and a bit grimy, but there was not even one crack that might indicate access to some secret compartment above.

I got off the ladder and found myself trembling.

There was no possible way out of this room. None at all.

Except by the time machine!

It was ten minutes before the weakness left me. I turned out the lights and locked both doors behind me.

The next morning I began converting my capital into cash.

Shippler called in the afternoon with his daily report: "Mrs. Reeves attended a card party at the home of this Doris at two yesterday afternoon. I found out her last name. It's Weaver. The names of the twins are . . ."

"Confound it, I don't care what the names of the blasted twins are."

"Sorry. Your wife left there at four-thirty-six. She stopped at a supermarket and bought four lamb chops, two pounds of . . ."

"She went shopping for the cook," I stormed. "Now do you have anything *important?*"

"Nothing really important, I guess."

"Then send me your bill. I won't be needing you any more."

"Well, if you do," Shippler said brightly, "you know where we are. And congratulations."

"Congratulations? On what?"

"Well . . . on your wife's . . . ah . . . faithfulness . . . this time."

I hung up.

No. I wouldn't be needing Shippler any more. If I wanted to find out anything at all about Diana, I would soon be able to do so myself.

My thoughts went to Henry. He could undoubtedly build another time machine, but I couldn't allow that. In order for my plans to be effective I had to have a monopoly. Henry would have to go and I would see to that after I possessed the machine.

At the end of the week, I had the two hundred and fifty thousand dollars in cash. I was tempted to phone Henry, but I was afraid he might shy away entirely if he knew that I had discovered his identity.

Three excruciatingly long days more went by before Henry rang the door bell of my apartment.

I drew him quickly inside. "I have the money. All of it."

Henry rubbed an ear. "I really don't know whether I should sell the machine."

I glared at him. "Two hundred and fifty thousand dollars. It's all the money I have in the world. I won't pay another cent."

"It isn't the money. I just don't know if I ought to go through with it."

I opened the suitcase. "Look at it, Henry. Two hundred and fifty thousand dollars. Do you know what that much money can buy? You can make yourself dozens of time machines. You can gold-plate them. You can set jewels in them."

He still held back.

"Henry," I said severely. "We made a bargain, didn't we? You can't go back on that."

Henry finally sighed. "I suppose not. But I still think I'm making a mistake."

I rubbed my hands. "Now let's get down to my car. You

may blindfold me and drive me to your place."

"Blindfolding won't be necessary now," Henry said morosely. "As long as you're getting the time machine you'll be able to find out who I am and where I live anyway."

How true. Henry was doomed.

"But I will search you," Henry said.

The ride to Henry's garage seemed interminable, but at last we were inside. Henry fumbled with the keys to the next room and I almost yielded to the urge to snatch them from him and do the job myself.

Finally he had the door open and switched on the overhead light.

The machine was there. Beautiful. Shining. And now it was mine.

Henry took the vital control unit out of his pocket and threaded it into place. He took a sheet of paper from his breast pocket. "These are the directions. Don't lose this paper or you might become stranded somewhere in time. Better yet, memorize them."

I took the sheet out of his hands.

"You may not get the exact date you want at the first try," Henry said. "Because calendars have been changed and besides, once you get back more than five hundred years, you'll find all sorts of errors in history. But you can approximate the time and then use this fine tuner over here in order to pinpoint . . ."

"Stop your babbling and get out of here!" I snapped. "I can read directions as well as anyone."

Henry was a bit miffed, but he left the room and closed the door.

I got into the chair and read the typewritten directions. They were absurdly simple. But I read them again and then put the paper in my pocket.

Now, where would I go?

I studied the controls.

Yes. I had it. The New Year's Eve party at the Lowells.

Diana had disappeared at ten-thirty and I hadn't seen her again until two A.M. of 1960. She had never given me a satisfactory explanation for her absence.

I adjusted the time control and the direction knob. I did not know the exact distance to the Lowells from this point, but I would use the fine tuner directly under the mileage dial once I got underway.

I hesitated a moment, took a deep breath, and then pressed the red button.

I waited.

Nothing happened.

I frowned and pressed the button again.

Nothing.

I took the slip out of my pocket and feverishly reviewed the directions. I had committed no errors.

And then I knew! The entire thing had been a hoax!

I leaped out of the chair and rushed to the door.

It was locked.

I pounded with my fists and called Henry's name. I cursed and shrieked until my voice was hoarse.

The door remained closed.

I managed to get some control over myself and darted to the time machine. I wrenched loose a section of the chair piping and returned to the door.

The piece of pipe was aluminum and fiendishly light and malleable. It took me more than forty-five minutes before I managed to force the pins out of the door hinges and get out of the room.

I found an envelope under the windshield wiper of my car and tore it open.

The typewritten pages were, of course, intended for me.

My dear Mr. Reeves:

Yes, you have been thoroughly hoaxed. There is no such a thing as a time machine.

I suppose I could leave it at that and allow you to go mad attempting to arrive at some reasonable explanation, but I shall not. I am quite proud of my little project and would like the attention of a truly appreciative audience.

I think you will do nicely.

How did I manage to know those interesting details of your last four murders?

I was there.

Not in the time machine, of course.

You are undoubtedly aware that it was not your urbanity, your charm, which attracted Diana to your hearth. She married you for your money—of which you gave indications of having a lot.

But you were extremely reticent about the extent and source of your wealth—an evasion which unquestionably can drive a woman to desperate curiosity. Especially a woman like Diana.

She had you followed and for the purpose employed a detective agency. Shippler, I believe the name was. They are quite thorough and I recommend them highly.

It was indeed fortunate for you—and certainly now for Diana and me—that you did not choose that particular time to commit one of your murders. But it was during one of your periods of unemployment and you were not followed for long. A week.

The reports concerning your activities were mundane, but Diana did fasten on one particular repeated detail they contained. And details are so important.

Every day you went to a rented box at the main post office.

Now why would you want a private box? Diana wondered. After all, you do have a home address and that should be sufficient for ordinary mail. Ordinary mail. That was it. This wasn't for ordinary mail.

It was child's play for Diana to get an impression of your box key while you slept and to have a duplicate made, for her use.

She made it a practice to go to your post office box each morning—you go there in the afternoon. Whenever she found a letter, she removed it, steamed it open, read the contents, and returned it to the box in plenty of time for you to pick it up the same day.

And so you see it was possible for her to know the details of your negotiations to murder, when the murders were scheduled to be committed and the places where they were to occur. And *that* made it possible for me to be there early, conceal myself, and *watch* you work.

Yes, we've known each other for some time—meeting discreetly—very discreetly. Diana remembers a Terence Reilly and his sudden disappearance. And as an added precaution—since we were on the verge of acquiring a quarter of a million dollars and wanted nothing to prevent that—we have not seen each other for almost a month.

Our original plan had been only blackmail. But again the question of danger arose. How long could I blackmail you and get away with it?

And so we determined to strike once and get *all* of your money.

At the moment you are reading this, Diana and I are increasing the distance between you and us. The world is a large place, Mr. Reeves, and I do not think you will find us. Not without a time machine.

And how did I manage that time machine?

It was an elaborate hoax, Mr. Reeves, but with two hundred and fifty thousand dollars at stake, one can afford to be elaborate.

When you left me alone with my time machine ten days ago, Mr. Reeves, I turned on two devices concealed above the room. One created noise and the other created wind.

And then I quickly *folded* the time machine.

You have no doubt by now noticed that it is extremely light. And if you will look again, you will discover that there are a number of concealed hinges which allow one to fold it into a compact shape.

Then I removed the grate of one of the "ventilators," pushed the collapsed machine through into the small cubicle behind the wall, followed into the cubicle myself, and pulled the grating back into place behind me.

I watched as you re-entered the room, Mr. Reeves, and I allowed you only thirty seconds of astonishment before I turned on the noise and wind machines again. I did not want you to collect your wits and examine the room.

When you left, I simply crawled out of my hiding place and unfolded my machine.

I think that was rather ingenious, don't you?

But you say that is impossible? There *is* no hiding place for the time machine—even folded—and for me?

The room is absolutely solid? You have examined it yourself and you would stake your life on it?

You are right, Mr. Reeves. There is no hiding place here. The room *is* solid.

But you see, Mr. Reeves, there are *two* garages.

The first one, to which I took you blindfolded, is in reality located several miles from here. It is the same type of building—a standard brand erected by the thousands in this area—and I took great pains to make it an exact duplicate of the one you are in now —even to the position of the tools lying on the bench, the ladder against the wall.

The two garages are identical—with some exceptions. The time machine room in one of them is slightly smaller—to allow for the hiding place—and the noise and wind machines are installed under the eaves. As for the ventilators, with the exception of the one I used to enter my hiding place, they are actually blowers.

After I drove you back to your apartment, I returned, packed my time machine, took the license plates off the wall, and brought them here.

Those license plates?

You are a clever man, Mr. Reeves. I grant that and I have taken advantage of that cleverness. I nailed them to a conspicuous place on the wall with the express hope that you would utilize them to track me down—but to *this* place.

I wanted you to examine *this* garage. I wanted you to be absolutely satisfied that the time machine had to be genuine. I was in a neighboring lot watching you after I had turned out the house lights.

I am, of course, not Henry Pruitt. The license plates belonged to the former tenant of the house.

Nevertheless, for the purposes of this letter, I remain, most gratefully,

Your servant,
Henry Pruitt.

I tore the letter to bits and snatched a peen hammer from the workbench.

As I smashed the time machine to smithereens, I couldn't help the horrible thought that perhaps someone, in a *real* time machine, might at that very moment be in the room watching me.

And laughing.

Unquestionably, gentlemen have a place in the mystery stories of my fine publication. For one thing, their correct behavior can be something of an irritant. And sometimes —ever mindful to do the right thing—they turn to murder.

HOMICIDE AND GENTLEMEN
BY FLETCHER FLORA

Lieutenant Joseph Marcus walked past the ninth hole, par-four, with a fine official disregard of the green. It wasn't quite disregard, however, for there was in his performance a degree of deliberate malice that expressed itself by a digging-in of the heels and a scuffing of the toes. Lieutenant Marcus, who had been a poor boy and was still a poor man, felt an unreasonable animus for the game of golf and a modest contempt, in spite of certain famous devotees, for the folk who played it. He was by nature gentle and tolerant, though, and he was faintly ashamed of his feeling and its expression of petty vandalism.

With Sergeant Bobo Fuller at his side, although a half step to the rear, he descended from the green on a gentle slope and moved rapidly across clipped grass toward a place where the ground dipped suddenly to form a rather steep bank. Sergeant Fuller, whose name was really something besides Bobo that almost everyone had forgotten, did not lag the half step because he found it impossible to stay abreast. Neither did he lag as a pretty deference to rank. Sergeant Fuller did not give a damn about rank, to tell the truth. He didn't give a damn about Lieutenant Marcus either, and that was why he maintained the half step interval. He considered Marcus a self-made snob who read books and put on airs, and the interval was subtle evidence of a dislike of which the sergeant was rather proud and the lieutenant was vaguely aware.

Going over the lip of the bank, Marcus dug in his heels again, this time with the perfectly valid purpose of retarding his descent. At the bottom he was on level ground that again tilted, after a bit, into a gentle slope. Fifty yards ahead was a small lake glittering in the morning sunlight. Between Marcus and the lake, somewhat nearer to him and almost in the shade of a distinguished and gnarled oak, was a group composed of four men and a boy. The boy was holding, in one hand, a fishing rod with a spinning reel attached; in the other, a small green tackle box. Two of the four men were uniformed policemen who had been dispatched from police headquarters to maintain the status quo for Marcus, who had not been on hand at the time, and a third was, as it turned out, a caretaker who had walked into a diversion on his way to work across the course. The fourth man was lying on his face on the grass, his head pointed in the direction of the bank behind Marcus and Fuller, and he was, Marcus had been assured, dead. That was, in fact, why Marcus and Fuller were there. They were there because the man on the grass was dead in a manner and place considered suspicious by public authorities hired to consider such things, which included Marcus, who also secretly considered the whole development something of an imposition.

Speaking to the pair of policemen, with the air of abstraction that had contributed to his reputation for snobbishness, he knelt beside the body to make an examination that he felt certain would yield nothing of any particular significance. This pessimistic approach was natural to him, and he was always surprised when things turned out better than he had hoped or expected. Well, the man was dead, of course. He had been shot, apparently in the heart,

197

by what appeared to have been a small caliber gun. From the condition of the body, he judged that the shooting had occurred not many hours earlier, for rigor mortis was not advanced. These things were always hedged about by qualifications, however, and it was doubtful that the so-called estimate of the coroner, who was presumably on the way, would be much closer to the truth than Marcus's guess. Sometime between was the way Marcus expressed it somewhat bitterly to himself. Between midnight, say, and dawn.

Still with the irrational feeling of being imposed upon, Marcus made other observations and guesses. Age, thirty to thirty-five. Height, about five-eleven. Weight, give or take ten pounds on either side of one-seventy. Hair, light brown and crew cut. Eyes, open and blind and blue. White shirt, blood stained. Narrow tie, striped with two shades of brown, and summer worsted trousers, also brown. Brown socks, brown shoes. Lying on the grass, about five paces away, a jacket to match the pants. In the right side pocket of the pants, coins amounting to the sum of one dollar and twenty-three cents. Also a tiny gold pen knife. In the left hip pocket, buttoned in, a wallet. In the wallet, besides eighteen dollars in bills, several identifying items, including a driver's license and a membership card in Blue Cross-Blue Shield. *Well,* Marcus thought, *they won't have to pay off on this one.* According to both the license and the membership card, the dead man was someone named Alexander Gray. With all items officially appropriated and in his own jacket pocket, Marcus walked over to the brown jacket on the grass and found nothing in it. Nothing at all.

"Who found the body?" he asked of whoever wanted to answer.

"The kid found him," one of the policemen said.

Marcus turned to the boy, about twelve from the looks of him, who still held the rod and reel and tackle box as if he feared that they, too, might be appropriated. Marcus had no such intention, of course, but he wished he could bor

198

row them and spend the day using them instead of doing what he had to do. Marcus liked kids, but he seldom showed it. It was his misfortune that he seldom showed anything, and much of the little he did show was a kind of characteristic distortion of what he actually thought and felt.

"What's your name, sonny?" he said.

"William Peyton Hausler," the boy said.

It was obvious that he was stating his name fully in an attempt to secure a status, however limited by his minority, that would establish his innocence and insure the respectful treatment to which he was entitled.

"You live around here?"

"On the street over there, the other side of the golf course." He gestured with the hand holding the rod and reel to indicate the direction.

"Looks like you're going fishing."

"Yes, sir. In the lake."

"You fish here often?"

"Pretty often. The manager of the club said it was all right."

"It doesn't look like much of a lake. Any fish in it?"

"It's stocked. Crappie and bass, mostly. Club members fish in it. I'm not a member—my dad isn't—but the manager said it was all right for me to fish."

"What time was it when you found the body?"

"I don't know exactly. It hadn't been light long. About six-thirty, I guess. I wanted to get to the lake early because the fish bite better then."

"That's what I hear. Early morning and late evening. What'd you do when you found the body?"

"Nothing much. I walked up close to it, and I spoke a couple of times to see if there'd be any answer, but there wasn't, and I was pretty scared because I could tell something was wrong, and just then Mr. Tompkins came along."

"You touch anything at all?"

"No, sir. Not a thing."

"Who's Mr. Tompkins?"

"This is him. He's one of the caretakers."

"Okay. Thanks, sonny. You better go and see if you can still catch some fish."

The boy went on down the gentle slope to the little lake, and Marcus turned to Tompkins, who was a leathery-looking man who appeared to be in his sixties. He was dressed in faded twill pants and a blue work shirt of heavy material like the ones that Marcus had worn with roomy bib overalls as a kid.

"Is that right?" Marcus said. "What the kid told me?"

"I guess so. Far as I know. When I got here, he was just standing and staring at the body. He looked scared."

"No wonder. Kids don't find a body every day. What'd you do?"

"I looked at the body, not touching it, and I could see a little blood where it had seeped out in the grass. I told the kid to stay and watch things while I hustled up to the Club House to call the police."

"The Club House open that early in the morning?"

"No. There's a phone booth on the back terrace. I happened to have a dime."

"Lucky you did. I usually don't. After you called the police, did you come back here and wait?"

"That's right. Just came back and waited with the kid and didn't bother anything."

"Good. You did just right. I don't suppose you know this guy?"

"The dead man, you mean? I never saw him before."

"All right. You might as well go on to work." Marcus turned away to a uniform. "You go up to the Club House and bring the manager down here. You can tell him what's happened if he's curious."

The caretaker and the policeman went off in different directions, one toward the Club House and the other, presumably, toward whatever building sheltered the equipment for taking care, and Marcus began to prowl slowly the area around the body. He wasn't looking for anything in particular, just anything he could find, and he found nothing. No significant marks in the clipped grass growing from hard earth. No small item conveniently dropped that might later point to a place or person. Not even, he thought bitterly, a lousy cigarette butt.

The brown jacket bothered him. Why the hell had the dead man taken it off? Before he was dead, of course. And why had he left it lying on the ground five yards or so from where he had walked to be killed? Unless he had been moved *after* being killed, which didn't seem probable. And why, for that matter, had he been here on the golf course at all? A golf course did not seem to Marcus to be a likely place to be in the hours between midnight and dawn, sometime between, but then a golf course did not seem to Marcus a likely place to be at any time whatever, unless you came, like the kid, to fish in a lake or to lie on the grass under a tree and wish that you were something besides what you had become.

Fuller, watching Marcus, was tempted to ask him what he was looking for, but he resisted the temptation. Anyhow, quite correctly, he guessed that Marcus didn't know himself, and he was determined to avoid giving, in front of the uniform, the impression of a dumb cop appealing to his superior for enlightenment. Marcus was already, in Fuller's opinion, sufficiently overrated at headquarters. As it turned out, after a few minutes, the appeal went the other way, but it was no triumph for Fuller, after all, for it only forced him to admit what he had hoped to conceal.

"Any ideas, Fuller?" Marcus said.

"Not yet," Fuller said. "I've been trying to figure it."

"So have I, but I haven't had any luck, and I doubt if I ever do. As I see it, a guy who got himself shot on a golf course must have been crazy, and crazy people make the worst kind of murder victims from a cop's point of view because it's almost impossible to figure logically why they did what they did that got them killed."

Sure, Fuller thought. *Read me a lecture about it, you topnotch snob. The Psychology of Nuts by Dr. Joseph Marcus.*

He was saved from making a reply by the return of the other uniform and a small man in Bermuda shorts and heavy ribbed stockings that reached almost to his knees. Marcus approved of the shorts, for he was always one for keeping comfortable, but he was damned if he could understand why anyone would deliberately qualify the effect of the shorts by wearing the stockings. Which was, however, he conceded, none of his business.

"You the manager of this club?" Marcus said.

"Yes," the small man said. "Paul Iverson."

"I'm Lieutenant Joseph Marcus, Mr. Iverson. We've got a body here."

"Yes, yes. I know. The officer told me."

"He was shot."

"It's incredible. I can hardly believe it."

"It looks like someone took advantage of the privacy of your golf course to commit a murder."

Iverson's expression, although indicating shock and a shade of nausea, was primarily one of resentment. Among the activities of the club, he palpably felt, one expected and accepted certain indiscretions and transgressions of the peccadillo type, but murder was neither expected nor acceptable and ought to cause someone to lose his membership.

"Are you certain that it's murder?" he said. "Perhaps he killed himself."

"With his finger, maybe?"

"Oh, I see. There's no gun."

"Right. No gun. Besides, there's no powder marks on his shirt. He was shot from a distance."

"Do you think it could have been an accident of some sort?"

"It could have been, but I don't think so."

"Well, it's a terrible thing. Simply terrible. I can't understand it at all."

"You're luckier than me. You don't have to understand it. All you have to do is see if you recognize the body."

Iverson hesitated, then walked over to the body and looked intently for a moment into blind blue eyes. When he straightened and turned back to Marcus, the shade of nausea in his face had deepened, but there was also a new element of relief, as if the worst, which had been anticipated, had not developed.

"I don't know him," he said. "I can assure you that he was not a member of this club."

"Well, that's all right," Marcus said with an unworthy feeling of spite. "Maybe the murderer is."

"I believe you'll find that he is not. I find it inconceivable that a member of this club should be involved in anything like this. It will create a dreadful fuss, I'm afraid, as it is. We may have some withdrawals."

"Are you positive this man was not a member? His name was Alexander Gray."

"I'm quite positive. Our membership is limited, rather exclusive, and I'm acquainted with all members. That's why I'm convinced that none of them could be involved."

"Even exclusive people can commit murder, Mr. Iverson. Possibly even exclusive people you happen to be acquainted with. Never mind, though. Thanks for coming down."

Marcus turned away abruptly, and there was in his movement an implication of disdain that made Iverson flush and Sergeant Fuller curse softly under his breath. Aware that he had been dismissed, the manager went back across the course toward the Club House, only the roof of which was visible beyond the rise. Marcus went over and

203

picked up the brown worsted jacket from the grass where he had dropped it after exploring the pockets.

"I wonder where the coroner is," he said.

"He'll be along," Fuller said.

"Well, I won't wait for him. You stay here and find out what he's got to say. Nothing much, I suspect. Because he never does."

Sergeant Fuller was curious about Marcus's plans, but he was damned if he would give him the satisfaction of knowing it. He watched Marcus go off toward the Club House, where they'd left their car in the parking lot, and he cursed again under his breath, Marcus for what he was, and the coroner for not coming.

In the car, unaware that he had been cursed, or even that he had given cause for cursing, Marcus checked Alexander Gray's driver's license for an address. The street and number rang a faint bell, and he sat quietly for a minute, concentrating, trying to fit the location properly into a kind of mental map of the city. If his mental cartography was correct, which it was, Gray had lived not more than a mile from the entrance to this club. Probably somewhat less. Marcus looked at his watch and saw that it was two minutes after nine o'clock. Starting the car, he drove down a macadam drive and slipped into the traffic of a busy suburban street. He swung off after a while and was soon parked at the curb in front of a buff brick apartment building which displayed in large chrome numbers above the double front doors the address on the license.

Inside on the ground floor, he found the apartment of the building superintendent, who turned out to be, when he had opened his door in response to Marcus's ring, a wispy little man with wispy gray hair and pince-nez clipped to the bridge of a surprisingly bold nose. Marcus introduced himself and received an introduction. The superintendent's name was Mr. Everett Price.

"Is there an Alexander Gray living in the building?" Marcus asked.

"Yes." Mr. Price removed the pince-nez, which were, of course attached to a black ribbon, and held them by the spring clip in his right hand. "He's in three-o-six. He shares the apartment with Mr. Rufus Fleming."

"Oh? Have Mr. Gray and Mr. Fleming shared the apartment long?"

"About two years, I think. Yes, two years this summer. Perfect gentlemen, both of them. Quiet and good-mannered. There is, in fact, something old-fashioned in their manners. Rather courtly, you know. It isn't often, nowadays, that you find that quality in younger men."

"I agree. It's rare. Do you know if Mr. Fleming is in at the moment?"

"No, I don't. It's possible, however, this being Saturday. Mr. Fleming doesn't work on Saturday."

"I wish I didn't. I believe I'll just go up and speak with Mr. Fleming, if you don't mind."

Mr. Price looked confused. He scrubbed the lenses of the pince-nez with a clean white handkerchief and clipped them to his big nose again, peering at Marcus as if he had decided that some revision of his first judgment of him had become necessary.

"Excuse me," he said. "I thought you wanted to see Mr. Gray."

"I didn't say that," Marcus said. "I only asked if Mr. Gray lived here."

"Yes. So you did. I made an assumption, I suppose. In any event, it's quite likely that both gentlemen are in this morning."

"I wonder if you would come up with me. Just in case neither of them is."

Now Mr. Price looked startled. Possibly he had suddenly gathered from Marcus's tone that Marcus was certainly going up in spite of anything, although willing to make a nice pretense of asking permission, and that the superintendent was damn well coming up with him, whether he was agreeable or not.

"What on earth for?" Mr. Price said.

"So that you can let me into the apartment, if that is necessary."

"Oh, I couldn't do that without authorization from the tenants. It's unthinkable."

"Is it? I don't believe so. You can try thinking about it on the way up. You may change your mind."

"I'm reasonably certain that either Mr. Fleming or Mr. Gray will be in on a Saturday morning."

"Mr. Fleming, maybe. Not Mr. Gray. Mr. Gray will never be in again. He's dead. He has, it seems, been murdered."

The pince-nez popped off Mr. Price's nose and jerked and swung at the end of their ribbon. Marcus had a bleak vision of a trap sprung, a body hanging.

"What did you say?"

Marcus didn't bother to repeat himself. He merely waited for the information to soak in and become tenable.

"This is dreadful," Mr. Price said.

"So it is."

"Why would anyone murder Mr. Gray? He was such a pleasant man."

"Pleasant people are sometimes murdered. Usually by unpleasant people."

"When did it happen? Where?"

"Never mind that now. You'll know soon enough. Everyone will. Now I would like to go upstairs and see Mr. Fleming if he's in, or look through the apartment if he's not."

"Yes," said Mr. Price. "Yes, of course."

They went up three floors and rang the bell of three-o-six. Mr. Fleming was either not in or not answering. The former was true, as Marcus learned immediately after Mr. Price had opened the door for him. The apartment consisted of a living room, a large bedroom with two beds, a bath and a small kitchen. No one was there. The beds were made and the kitchen was clean and the living room was orderly. Mr. Gray and Mr. Fleming had been tidy housekeepers. Mr. Fleming, so far as Marcus knew, still was.

"Did Fleming spend the night here?" he asked.

"I don't know. He was here early, as Mr. Gray was, but he may have gone out again and not returned."

"All right. Thanks. I won't need you any longer. And don't worry about the apartment. I'll leave it in good order."

Mr. Price didn't look convinced, but he left. Marcus went into the bedroom and began to prowl. He opened drawers and looked into closets, but all he achieved was confirmation of the judgment he had already made—that Mr. Gray and Mr. Fleming were clean and orderly enough to please the most fastidious woman. In the living room, after poking into places and scanning the titles of books that struck him as being intolerably dull on the whole, he stopped before the mantel of a dummy fireplace to look at a picture. A photograph of a young woman. Inscribed. He took it down and read the inscription: *For Rufe and Alex with all my love, Sandy.* The double inscription implied a Platonic meaning at variance, it seemed to Marcus, with the totality of love. He scratched his head and examined Sandy's face.

It was a lovely face. A wistful face. Shaped like a small, lean heart. Big eyes with sadness in them. Tenderness in them. Passion in them? Passion, at least, in the soft lips set in the merest of smiles. In spite of the suggested passion, however, there was—Marcus groped for the word—a kind of mysticism. He was falling, in an instant, half in love.

Putting the photograph back on the mantel, he turned away. Then he turned back. On the mantel, placed squarely below a reproduction of Daumier's *Don Quixote and Sancho Panza* that hung on the wall above, was a sizable leather case. He removed the case and opened it. Inside, nested in plush, was a matched pair of .22 caliber target pistols. Both clean. Both lately oiled. Beautifully cared for. *The purloined letter still makes its point,* he thought. In his attention to drawers and closets, he had nearly overlooked the case in plain sight. Not, so far as he could see at the moment, that it would have made any particular difference if he had. Nevertheless, he appropriated the case and took it with him when he left. That was after he had returned once more to the bathroom and stood for a few minutes with an abstracted air before the open medicine cabinet above the lavatory.

Downstairs, he rang the superintendent's bell again. Mr. Price, clearly relieved to see him on his way out, made a polite effort not to show it.

"Are you finished, Lieutenant?" he said.

"Yes. For the present, at least. I'm taking this with me. It's a pair of matched target pistols. Was either Mr. Gray or Mr. Fleming an enthusiast for target shooting, do you know?"

"Both were, as a matter of fact. Sunday mornings, fair days, they have gone off regularly for matches. I believe they made small wagers. I do hope you will take good care of the pistols."

"The best. I'll give you a receipt for them if you want me to."

"I'm sure that won't be necessary."

"Thanks. By the way, there's a photograph on the mantel upstairs. A young lady. Blonde hair cut quite short. Very pretty face. It's signed Sandy. Do you know her by any chance?"

"I've met her. Miss Sandra Shore. She was introduced to me in the hall one evening when I happened to encounter her with Mr. Gray and Mr. Fleming. Afterward, on several occasions, I exchanged a few words with her when she came to call."

"Has she come here often?"

"Frequently. Many times, I suppose, when I didn't see her. I'm sure that it was all quite proper. She was equally the friend of both gentlemen. They had been friends, she told me once, since childhood. It was quite a charming relationship."

"I'm sure it was. Tell me, do you know Miss Shore's address?"

"No, but it's probably in the directory."

"Would you mind checking it for me?"

"Not at all."

Marcus was invited in, but he preferred to wait in the hall. After a few minutes Mr. Price returned with the address written down on a sheet from a memo pad. Engaging again in mental cartography, Marcus located the address in relation to where he was.

"One more question, if you don't mind," he said, "and I'll run along. I assume both Mr. Gray and Mr. Fleming own automobiles?"

"Only one between them, which they both used. One might think that such an arrangement would lead to difficulties, but they apparently worked it out very well."

"Mr. Gray and Mr. Fleming seem to have been extremely compatible. Share apartment. Share car. Share girl. Most commendable. Where is the car kept?"

"There's a garage at the rear, just off the alley. Stall number five. The automobile, if you wish to know, is a Ford. I'm not sure of the model. Recent, however."

"Thanks again. You've been most helpful."

Marcus turned with his sometimes offensive abruptness and went out of the building and around to the garage. Stall number five was occupied by a 1960 Ford. Mr. Fleming, wherever he was, was obviously moving either by Hank's mare or in some other vehicle than his own. Marcus, in the one furnished by the department, drove to the address on the memo sheet, and this time it was unnecessary to disturb the superintendent, for there was a di-

rectory of tenants in the entrance hall that told him where
to go, and he went.

The photographer who had taken Sandra Shore's picture, he learned, was an artist. He had caught on paper
precisely the elfin and haunting quality of her face. The
sadness and tenderness and passion assembled in the lean
heart. Now, in person, there was more, of course. A small
and slender body exquisitely formed, suggesting its delight
in a boyish white blouse and a narrow skirt. Marcus, in the
hall, held his hat and offered up a short and silent paean.

"Yes?" Sandra Shore said.

"My name is Marcus," Marcus said. "Lieutenant Joseph
Marcus. Of the police. I wonder if I may speak with you
for a few minutes?"

She surveyed him gravely, her head cocked a little to
one side.

"Whatever for?"

"It will take only a few minutes. I'd appreciate it very
much."

"Well, if you are actually a policeman, you will certainly
speak with me whether I am willing or not, so there isn't
really much use in asking my permission, is there?"

"It distresses me, but I must admit that you're right.
Thank you for clarifying the situation so nicely. May I
come in?"

She nodded and closed the door after him, when he was
across the threshold. Following her into the living room
to a chair in which he sat, he admired her neat ankles and
lovely legs. When she was in another chair across from him,
the narrow skirt tucked primly beneath her knees, which
showed, he continued to admire the legs for a moment
discreetly, but soon went back to her face, which was the
best of her, after all, in spite of distractions.

"You don't look like a policeman," she said.

"Don't I? I wouldn't know. What is a policeman supposed to look like?"

"I'm not sure. Not like you, however. What do you wish to speak with me about?"

"Not what, really. Who. A young man named Alexander Gray."

"Alex?" She managed to appear slightly incredulous without, somehow, disturbing the serenity of her expression. "What possible interest could the police have in Alex?"

"He's dead. Murdered, apparently. Someone shot him sometime early this morning on the course of the Greenbrier Golf Club."

She sat quite still, her only movement the folding of her hands in her lap. In her great, grave eyes there was a slight darkening, as if a light had been turned down.

"That's ridiculous."

"The truth is often ridiculous. Things don't seem to make sense."

"Alex isn't even a member of the Greenbrier Golf Club."

"Apparently you don't have to be a member to be killed on the course."

"I simply refuse to believe you. It's cruel of you to come here and tell me such a lie."

"It would be cruel if I did. And pointless."

"I see what you mean. You would have no reason. Unless there's a reason that I can't understand. Is there?"

"No. None whatever. Surely you realize that."

"I suppose I do. I suppose I must believe you after all." She stood up suddenly and walked over to a window and stood there for a minute looking out, slim and erect against the glass, her pale hair catching afire from the slanting light. Then she returned, sitting again, tucking the skirt and folding her hands. "Poor Alex," she said. "Poor little Alex."

He hadn't been so little. Average height, at least, but Marcus skipped it. Miss Sandra Shore was striking him as a remarkable young woman. There was genuine grief in her

211

voice, in her darkened eyes, but her face was in repose, fixed as serenely in shock and grief as it had been in the photograph.

"You are very composed under the circumstances," he said. "I'm relieved and thankful."

"Perhaps I can't quite accept it yet, in spite of knowing that it must be true."

"Sometimes it takes a while for things to hit us hard. Do you feel like talking with me now?"

"What do you want to know?"

"You were a good friend of Alexander Gray's. Is that true?"

"Yes, it's true, but I can't imagine how you know. Unless you've talked with Rufe. Have you?"

"Rufus Fleming? No. I'd like to talk with him, however. I don't know where he is."

"Have you been to the apartment? Alex and Rufe lived together, you know."

"Yes, I know. I've been there. Do you have any idea where Fleming could be?"

"Just out somewhere, I imagine. He'll show up soon."

"His car was in the garage."

"Rufe often walks places. Quite long distances sometimes. He enjoys it."

"There was a photograph of you in their apartment. A very good one. I noticed that it was inscribed to both Gray and Fleming. All your love. Were you an equally good friend to both?"

"Equally? That's so hard to judge, isn't it? I loved them both. I still love them both, even though Alex must be dead, since you say so."

"Did they both love you?"

"Oh, yes. We all loved each other."

"Isn't that a rather unusual relationship to exist among two men and a woman?"

"I don't think so. Perhaps it is. It has been that way for so long that it seems perfectly natural to me."

212

"Didn't it ever get complicated?"

"Well, it was difficult in certain ways. They both loved
ne and wanted to marry me, and I loved both of them,
which was all right, and wanted to marry both of them,
which was not, and that's where the difficulty was."

"I understand. Bigamy is no solution. Besides being
legal."

"Yes. Anyhow, I couldn't bear to marry one of them and
ot the other, for that would surely have meant giving up
ntirely the one I didn't marry. If only I could have mar-
ed one of them and kept the other one around as always,
would have been all right, but it wouldn't have worked,
m sure, for a husband is different from a friend, no mat-
r how good and tolerant he may be, and will become
ossessive and insistent upon his rights and resentful of the
tentions to his wife of another man."

Marcus didn't quite believe her. Not her words. He be-
eved *them,* all right. He didn't quite believe *her.* That she
isted. That she was sitting this instant in the chair across
om him with her knees together and her skirt tucked in.
e was, in fact, more than a little confused by what seemed
once perfectly logical and utterly insane. That was it,
decided. It was logical, but nuts. There was not neces-
rily any contradiction in that.

"You said this relationship had existed for a long time,"
said. "How long?"

"Oh, years and years. Ages. Since we were very young."

"You all knew each other then?"

"Isn't that what I said? Went through school together
d have remained close to each other since."

"It's strange, to say the least, that two men should re-
ain such friends in such circumstances."

"Well, they were very sweet and tolerant and under-
nding, and they kept thinking something could be
rked out, but, as I said, there was no way to work it sat-
actorily."

'Now, however, the problem has resolved itself."

"You mean, because Alex is dead, that there is nothin
to keep me from marrying Rufe? That may be true, bu
I'll have to think about it. It doesn't seem quite fair t
Alex. A kind of unfair advantage for Rufe, you know.
may be compelled by fairness to give him up also."

Marcus slapped a knee sharply and stood up and walke
around his chair and sat down again. He closed his ey
and opened them, and she was still there.

"There was a pair of target pistols in the apartment," h
said. "The superintendent told me they were bugs abou
target shooting. Is that so?"

"Oh, yes, and so am I. I have a pistol like the ones yc
saw. It all started when we were quite young. In the b
ginning, we used bb pistols. We lived in a small town, on
a short walk into the country, and we used to go out t
gether frequently, the three of us, and have matche
Would you like to see my pistol?"

"It would be kind of you to show it to me."

"Not at all."

She got up and went to a desk and returned in a minu
with the pistol, which was, as she had said, apparen
identical with the two he had appropriated. Clean, recer
ly oiled. He took it and examined it and handed it back
her. She sat in her chair again, the pistol lying in her l
beneath her hands.

"Do you happen to have a photograph of Mr. Fleming
he asked.

"Of Rufe? No. I'm sorry."

"Not even a snapshot?"

"Not even that. It's rather strange, isn't it, when y
come to think about it? Neither Alex nor Rufe were mu
for having their pictures taken."

"Perhaps you could describe him to me."

"Why?"

"Oh, just in case I happen to see him or something.
might save me some time and trouble."

"Well, he's quite tall. About six-three, I'd say. Rat

thin, but quite strong. He has a long face with thick eyebrows that grow across the bridge of his nose and black hair that's wiry and doesn't stay brushed very well. His shoulders are somewhat stooped, and I keep telling him to pull them back, but it doesn't do any good. I think he stoops deliberately to avoid appearing as tall as he is, especially when he's with me. As you can see, I'm rather small."

"Yes. I see." Marcus stood up, holding his hat, and looked around the room. An open entrance to a small kitchen. A door closed upon what must be a bedroom. Off the bedroom, certainly, a bath. No different, basically, from the place shared by Gray and Fleming. "Tell me," he said. "Can you think of anyone at all who might have wanted to kill Alexander Gray?"

"No. No one. Surely it must have been some kind of accident."

"He was in no trouble that you knew of?"

"None. If Alex had any trouble, it must have been minor."

"I see. Well, thank you very much, Miss Shore. If you see Mr. Fleming, please have him contact me at police headquarters."

She followed him to the door and showed him out; the last thing he saw was her grave face and darkened eyes as the door closed between them. It was now well past time for lunch, and so he went on and had a steak sandwich at a small restaurant and went on from there to headquarters, where he read a brief report from the coroner as to the estimated time of Alexander Gray's death, which estimate was, as Marcus had predicted, not much different from Marcus's guess. The coroner thought that Gray had been killed by a .22 caliber bullet, but there had been no time as yet to recover it from the body, due to an accumulation of work, and an autopsy was promised as soon as possible.

Marcus carried the pair of matched pistols to ballistics

and left them with instructions for tests, and then returned to his desk and began to clear up some paper work, including his own report of the Gray case. He tried three times without success, during the rest of the afternoon, to reach Fleming at his apartment, and he kept thinking that Fleming might call in, but he didn't. Late in the afternoon, Fuller came in and reported on what had happened at the golf course after Marcus had left, but it didn't amount to much.

Alone, Marcus rocked back in his chair and closed his eyes and tried to think. He thought mostly about Sandra Shore. He still had difficulty in convincing himself that she was real, and he wondered if she was truly so remarkably self-contained as she had appeared, or if she had only found it impossible to express more effectively her shock and surprise at news that was really no news at all. Had she in fact known that Alexander Gray was dead before Marcus had arrived to tell her so? Marcus wondered, but he didn't know.

He sat there thinking for a long time, not really getting anywhere, and then he tried Fleming's apartment again without any luck. He decided to go out and eat and go home, and that's what he did. In his bachelor's apartment, he read for a while and had three highballs, bourbon and branch, and listened, the last thing before going to bed, to a Toscanini recording of Beethoven's Sixth. The next morning, which was the morning of Sunday, he got up early and drank two cups of coffee and went back to headquarters, and he was at his desk there when Fuller, reluctantly on duty, brought in a young man to see him. The young man, according to Fuller, had something to say about the Gray case, now public knowledge, that might or might not be significant. The young man's name, said Fuller, was Herbert Richards.

"Sit down and tell me what you know," Marcus said.

"Well," said Herbert Richards, sitting, "I was driving out there yesterday morning on the street just east of the

216

Golf Club where this guy was killed, and my old clunker quit running all of a sudden. I've been working on a construction job, and I was on my way to meet some of the crew at a place in town. We were going on together in one of the trucks, you see. Anyhow, my clunker quit, and I had to hurry terribly to make it on time, walking, and so I cut across the corner of the golf course, walking in a kind of gully that runs diagonally across the corner, and all of a sudden I heard shots."

"Wait a minute," Marcus said. "Did you say *shots?*"

"Yes, sir. Two of them. I read about the murder in the paper last night, and it said this guy was only shot once, so I wondered if I could have been mistaken, but I've thought about it, and I'm sure I'm not. They came so close together that they did sound almost like one shot, but I'm sure there were two."

"What did you do when you heard the shots?"

"Nothing. Just kept on going down the gully."

"Didn't it occur to you that something might be wrong?"

"Why should it? I've heard lots of shots in my life, or sounds like shots. This is the first time it ever turned out to be someone getting murdered."

Marcus conceded the validity of the point. Honest folk going about their business just didn't jump to the conclusion of murder at every unusual sight or sound, even the sound of shots.

"What time was this?" he said.

"That's mostly what I wanted to tell you. It was just daylight. Just after dawn. I know it's important to know the time something like this happens, and that's why I came down here."

"I'm glad you did."

"You think it may help?"

"I think so. Thanks. If you don't have anything else to tell me, you can go now."

Herbert Richards left, visibly pleased, and Marcus closed his eyes and thought for a moment about the scene of Alexander Gray's murder. Opening them again, he looked for Fuller, who was waiting.

"Fuller," he said, "you remember that high bank we went down about twenty yards or so from where Gray was lying? You take a couple of men and go out there and dig around in it and see if you can find a bullet."

Fuller, who resented the assignment, betrayed his feelings. Marcus, who marked the resentment, did not.

"Who cares if one bullet missed?" Fuller said. "We got the one in Gray, soon as the coroner digs it out this morning, and that's all we need. Besides, from the position of his body, Gray was facing the bank; the killer wasn't. Any bullet that missed him would have gone in the opposite direction."

"Go dig around anyhow," Marcus said. "It doesn't do any harm to be thorough."

Fuller gone, Marcus assumed his favorite position for thinking, chair rocked back, eyes closed, fingers laced above his belly. He thought this time about several things in a rather fantastic pattern. He thought about Alexander Gray and Rufus Fleming and Sandra Shore in an emotional triangle so crazy that it could certainly have been sustained only by a trio who were themselves a little crazy. He thought about Alexander Gray lying on a golf course. He thought about a brown worsted jacket lying on the grass about five paces from Gray's body. He thought about Herbert Richards, a construction worker in the act of trespassing, hearing two shots fired so closely together that they were barely distinguishable from one. He thought about a matched pair of target pistols placed in accidental symbolism below a reproduction of Daumier's *Don Quixote*. He thought about a cabinet above a lavatory in which there was only one razor and one toothbrush.

I don't believe it, he thought. *By God, I simply don't believe it.*

After a while, he went to ballistics and got a report, but still lacked the specific comparison he needed, which waited upon the coroner. In his car, he drove slowly, with an odd feeling of reluctance, to Sandra Shore's apartment building. He rang her bell and waited and was about to ring it again when she opened the door. Her eyes widened a little in the faintest expression of surprise, recovering almost immediately their grave, characteristic composure.

"Good morning," he said.

"Good morning," she said. "Do you want to come in again?"

"If you don't mind."

"I do mind, rather, to tell the truth, but I suppose I must let you."

"Thank you. I'll try to be brief."

They sat as they had yesterday, in the same chairs, and he was silent for a while, looking down at the hat in his hands and wondering how to begin. Then he looked up at Sandra Shore, at the grave eyes in the serene heart, and let his own eyes slip away and fix themselves deliberately on the door closed upon her bedroom.

"May I go into your bedroom, Miss Shore?" he said.

"No. Certainly not." She sat very still, watching him until his eyes returned to her, and then her small breasts rose and fell slowly on a drawn breath and a sigh. "Well," she said, "I see you have been as clever as I was afraid you would be, but I'm glad, really, quite glad, because he seems to be getting worse instead of better, and I have been afraid he would die in spite of everything I could do. It was impossible to get a doctor, you see, and so I took out the bullet myself, but he seems to be getting worse, as I said, and I've been wondering what I should do."

"Did you also return the pistols to the apartment and pick up a razor and toothbrush while you were there?"

"Yes. How *very* clever you are! Alex and Rufe simply decided between them what they must finally do, the way to settle matters for good and all, and so they walked out there to the golf course together, which was the handiest place where it could be done, and it might have turned

219

out all right for Rufe, although not for Alex, except that he got hit, too, in the shoulder, and that made everything much more difficult. He had to go somewhere, of course, and so he came here, and I helped him. He had the pistols, and I thought the best thing to do was to clean them and oil them and take them back to the apartment, and that's what I did."

"It was a mistake. Surely you know we can match the bullet in Alexander Gray with one of those pistols."

"That's true, isn't it? I suppose I didn't think of it at the time because I was upset and not thinking clearly about anything. It's odd, isn't it? I wanted so much to help Rufe, and I tried, but I guess I only did him harm instead."

"The fools! The crazy fools!" Marcus spoke with low-key intensity, slapping a knee. "Why the hell couldn't they have drawn high card for you or something?"

"Oh, no!" She stared at him with scorn, as if he had betrayed himself as a sordid sort of fellow with no discernible sense of honor. "Alex and Rufe would never have treated me so cheaply."

"Excuse me," he said bitterly. "I concede that you've done your best for Rufe, whom you love, but what about dear Alex, whom you loved equally and who is unfortunately dead as a rather irrational consequence?"

"If it had turned out the other way around," she said, "I'd have done as much for Alex."

"I see." He stood up, his bitterness a taste on his tongue that he wanted to spit out on the floor. "I'll call an ambulance, and then you and I can go downtown together."

He was at his desk, doing nothing, when Fuller came in that afternoon.

"We dug all over that bank," Fuller said, "and there's no bullet in it."

"That's all right," Marcus said. "I know where it is. Or, at least, was."

"The hell you do! Maybe you wouldn't mind telling me."

"Not at all. It was in the shoulder of a fellow named Rufus Fleming. He and Gray had a duel out there yesterday morning. That's how Gray got killed."

"A *duel!*" Fuller's eyes bulged, and he was so certain that Marcus had gone off the deep end that he felt safe in saying so. "You're always talking about someone being nuts," he said, "but in my opinion you're the biggest nut of all."

Marcus was not offended. He closed his eyes and smiled bleakly.

Well, he thought, *it takes one to catch one.*

Dear Readers:

By now, I hope, you have read each and every one of the stories in this Dell Book Anthology, and your appetite for crime-mystery-fiction has been whetted to a keen edge as a result. There is always the possibility, of course, that you are one of those who start reading a book from the back instead of from the front. Psychologists have a name for this habit, which I shall not define further, since I have no wish to invade any other field of research. I am kept quite busy laboring in my own vineyard, to mix a metaphor. Others enjoy the fringe benefits of my labors. For example, the postal employees of the Riviera Beach, Florida, branch Post Office have noted a heavy increase in their daily burdens since we moved the editorial offices of Alfred Hitchcock's fine publication to an enchanting location, at 2441 Beach Court, Palm Beach Shores, Riviera Beach, Florida, facing the blue Atlantic. If you are interested in learning further particulars about this excellent publication, please write to me at the above address. I look forward to hearing from you, one and all.

KURT VONNEGUT, JR.

"One of the best living American writers."

—Graham Greene

CAT'S CRADLE

A fantasy about the end of the world—replete with atomic scientists, ugly Americans, gorgeous Sex Queens, Caribbean dictators and God.

A Dell Book: $1.25
Also available as a Delta paperback: $1.95

GOD BLESS YOU, MR. ROSEWATER

A satirical and black-humored novel about Eliot Rosewater, president of the Rosewater Foundation, dedicated to bring love into the hearts of everyone.

A Dell Book: $1.25
Also available as a Delta paperback: $1.95

THE SIRENS OF TITAN

At the same time a deep and comic reflection on the human dilemma, this novel follows the richest man in America, Malachi Constant, as he gives up a life of unequaled indulgence to pursue the irresistible Sirens of Titan.

A Dell Book: $1.25
Also available as a Delta paperback: $2.25

SLAUGHTERHOUSE-5, or The Children's Crusade

A supremely unconventional war novel based on the experiences of the author as a prisoner of war during the catastrophic fire-bombing of Dreseden during World War II. The hero of his story also survives the fire-bombing and is to some extent reconciled to life as it is lived on Earth. But Vonnegut is not, and in this remarkable book he has expressed his terrible outrage.

A Dell Book: 95c
Also available as a Delta paperback: $1.95

WELCOME TO THE MONKEY HOUSE

The long-awaited volume which brings together the finest of Kurt Vonnegut, Jr.'s shorter works. It is a funny, sad, explosive, wildly gyrating gathering, a mind-boggling grab bag in which every selection is a winner.

A Dell Book: $1.25
Also available as a Delta paperback: $1.95

If you cannot obtain copies of these titles from your local bookseller, just send the price (plus 15c per copy for handling and postage) to Dell Books, Post Office Box 1000, Pinebrook, N. J. 07058.

HOW MANY OF THESE DELL BESTSELLERS HAVE YOU READ?

1. **LAST TANGO IN PARIS** by Robert Alley $1.75
2. **THE OSTERMAN WEEKEND** by Robert Ludlum $1.50
3. **THE TRUTH ABOUT WEIGHT CONTROL**
   by Dr. Neil Solomon $1.50
4. **THE BLUE KNIGHT** by Joseph Wambaugh $1.75
5. **THE MOON'S A BALLOON** by David Niven $1.75
6. **THE KINGMAKER** by Henry Denker $1.75
7. **SCORING** by Dan Greenburg $1.50
8. **THE ATHELSONS** by Jocelyn Kettle $1.50
9. **MILLIONAIRES** by Herbert Kastle $1.50
10. **KISSINGER: THE ADVENTURES OF**
    SUPER-KRAUT by Charles Ashman $1.50
11. **THE HAPPY HOOKER** by Xaviera Hollander $1.50
12. **WORD SEARCH PUZZLES** by Kathleen Rafferty .95
13. **70 SUTTON PLACE** by Joseph DiMona $1.50
14. **DELIVERANCE** by James Dickey $1.25
15. **THE POSEIDON ADVENTURE** by Paul Gallico $1.25

If you cannot obtain copies of these titles from your local bookseller, just send the price (plus 15c per copy for handling and postage) to Dell Books, Post Office Box 1000, Pinebrook, N. J. 07058.